Adventures With the Wife in Space

Neil Perryman fell in love with *Doctor Who* when he was three years old and, forty years later, he still can't stop thinking about it. Neil has also been responsible for a number of popular websites over the last ten years, including Tachyon TV and Behind the Sofa. He lives in County Durham with Sue and her daughter, Nicol.

Sue was raised in the north-east of England. When she's not rescuing feral cats, building houses or playing tennis, she teaches video production at the University of Sunderland. Thanks to her husband, she has now seen more episodes of *Doctor Who* than you have.

Further praise for *Adventures of the Wife in Space*:

'A warped but wonderful ménage à trois . . . Five stars.'
Sci Fi Now

'Neil and Sue Perryman's triumphant blog experiment has spawned a thoughtful, funny, honest companion book. You should read it.'
www.two minutetiny

'There's a ma   nuinely
being ab   acking
in . . . e   related

writing ever. It's not a good *Doctor Who* book; it's a good book period. One that happens to have a comprehensive set of ratings of *Doctor Who* episodes at the back.'
www.philipsandifer.com

'Neil and Sue have added something fascinatingly unique to the fandom and I'd love someday to have the chance to buy them a drink and thank them. In the meantime, I'll be over here, rereading this book a dozen times.'
www.neowhovian.com

ADVENTURES WITH THE WIFE IN SPACE

Living with *Doctor Who*

NEIL PERRYMAN

with constant interruptions from Sue Perryman

from an idea that seemed like a good one
at the time by Neil Perryman

ff

FABER & FABER

First published in Great Britain in 2013
by Faber and Faber Limited
Bloomsbury House
74–77 Great Russell Street
London WC1B 3DA
This paperback edition first published in 2014

Typeset by Faber and Faber Ltd
Printed in England by CPI Group (UK) Ltd, Croydon, CR0 4YY

A CIP record for this book
is available from the British Library

ISBN 978–0–571–29811–2

FSC
www.fsc.org
MIX
Paper from
responsible sources
FSC® C101712

2 4 6 8 10 9 7 5 3 1

I love my wife. I love *Doctor Who*. I believe my wife loves me. My wife does not love *Doctor Who*. I think I can make her change her mind about the latter without upsetting the delicate balance of the former. But do I have the right?

Contents

Introduction

This story begins in a static caravan that was not, I can promise you, bigger on the inside.

I lived in this caravan (a Lyndhurst 2000) with my wife Sue, my teenage stepdaughter Nicol, a golden Labrador named Buffy, and a ginger tomcat named Gallifrey *for three and a half years.* I would have got less for manslaughter, which I considered a few times, because it was Sue's fault that we ended up living in the middle of nowhere, with frozen toilets, no telephone line and hardly enough room to swing Gallifrey. At least in prison I would have got a good night's sleep, especially when it rained.

We moved into this caravan in July 2004, and for eight months I focused exclusively on moving into a real house. However, on Sunday 6 March 2005 I had something to take my mind off our not-temporary-enough living arrangements.

Yes, *Doctor Who* was coming back. After a hiatus of sixteen years, the BBC had finally seen sense and commissioned a brand-new series. It was going to be amazing: thirteen episodes; a decent budget; a traditional Saturday evening timeslot; a respected and influential writer at the helm; Christopher Eccleston, one of the greatest actors of his generation, cast in the lead role; and the pop star Billie Piper as his companion, Rose Tyler.

As a *Doctor Who* fan, this made me very happy. (Except for the part about Billie Piper: that bit really worried me.)

If there were a scale that measured how much of a Whovian you are, where 1 is a Trekkie and 10 is someone who names their firstborn Adric, I'd be a 7, maybe even a 7.5. If the term Whovian didn't make me prickle with embarrassment, I would probably be an 8. However, in all conscience, I cannot award myself a 9. I cannot reel off production codes like some of my more specialist friends; it's been known for me to confuse the 1976 serial 'The Seeds of Death' with 1969's 'The Seeds of Doom'. Or is it the other way round? And, aside from a school cricket match in 1982, I've never consciously dressed up like the Doctor, an activity which must be considered the summit – or trough – of Whovianity, unless you happen to be one of the actors who have played the part. And I do know they are actors. Even more importantly, I possess some social skills. So I won't ever be a perfect 10.

On the other hand, I have studied for a PhD in the subject of *Doctor Who*. I have had a short story, which I set in an Ann Summers lingerie store, published in an officially licensed *Doctor Who* anthology. For six years I ran a website called Behind the Sofa. In addition to this, I've interviewed several *Doctor Who* actors and writers for a series of podcasts, my best friend has appeared in an episode of *Doctor Who* and I have been the guest at a wedding where the happy couple walked down the aisle to the accompaniment of the *Doctor Who* theme music played on the church organ. I even named an innocent cat Gallifrey. So I am not what you would call a 'casual fan'. I really, really like *Doctor Who*.

When I awoke that Sunday morning in 2005, and I learned that a Canadian had leaked the first episode of the new series all over the internet, three weeks before it was due to turn up on BBC One, my celebratory dance set our caravan a-rocking. However, because – and this point bears repeating – we lived in a caravan without a broadband connection, I couldn't download it. In the end I had to beg a friend to send a copy over in a taxi. I made Sue and Nicol huddle around the laptop with me to watch it. Nicol made it as far as the scene with the belching wheelie bin before going outside to walk Buffy, but Sue stayed to the end.

That new episode of *Doctor Who* was great. No, actually it was *really* great – all the things *Doctor Who* can be when it's done right: scary, funny, exciting, thought-provoking, unique. When it was over, holding back tears of relief and joy, I asked my wife what she thought of it.

Sue: It was all right, I suppose.

And although neither of us realised it at the time, this was the beginning of a great idea.

*

In 2005 *Doctor Who* didn't just come back, it took over the world like one of its own villains. Suddenly everybody loved *Doctor Who*. Even my wife. Colleagues at work wanted to share their wild theories about the meaning of Bad Wolf – the story arc of that first season – and friends who had relentlessly taken the rise out of the programme when it wasn't on television were suddenly texting me to tell me how brilliant Billie Piper was. But of course she was. I always knew she would be. Ratings remained consistently high; Christmas Day became *Doctor Who* Day; even the most highbrow critics heaped praise on it. For the first time since the 1970s, life without *Doctor Who* became unimaginable.

And if that weren't fantastic enough, I got to live in a real house again.

Skip forward to a Monday evening in late January. The year is 2011 and Matt Smith is the Doctor. I'm sitting on the sofa with Sue – in our real house – and we are trying to get into *Downton Abbey*.

> **Sue:** Haven't you got a DVD we could watch instead? This is terrible.
>
> **Me:** We could watch *Doctor Who*.
>
> **Sue:** We've seen them all, haven't we?
>
> **Me:** Not the new series. I mean old *Doctor Who*, the stuff I like.
>
> **Sue:** Why would I want to do that?

I was talking about the original series of *Doctor Who*, which ran for twenty-six years and had been ignored by Sue for almost fifty. I had attempted to introduce her to it when we first met, but despite a positive reaction to 'Genesis of the Daleks', she hadn't paid much mind to vintage episodes of *Doctor Who* since then.

> **Me:** We could watch from the very beginning. It might be fun. If we paced ourselves and watched one or two a night, it would only take a few months.*
>
> **Sue:** I'll repeat the question: Why would I want to do that?

It was a very good question. But I had a very good answer:

---

* 'A few months' here = at least twenty-four.

Me: Look, fans embark on marathon viewings of *Doctor Who* all the time, but that's just the problem. *They're fans.*

Sue: I know. That's why they do it.

Me: Yes, but imagine if you could convince someone who hasn't seen the episodes to sit through them all? Someone who wouldn't know if a story was supposed to be good or bad before they'd even sat down to watch it; a person who didn't know what was coming next; a person who'd agree to watch the whole thing with an open mind and without prejudice. That's where you come in, Sue.

Sue: (*uncertainly*) Right . . .

But there was a catch:

Me: I want us to do it in public.

Sue: How many times, Neil? The answer to that will always be 'no'.

It was the twenty-first century, I told her. This was the age of the internet, where everyone shared everything, even if 90 per cent of it seemed to be related to cats. Why should we be any different? We could even include our own cats (we now had three: Captain Jack, Rose and Tegan; Gallifrey had died of old age). I also told her that *Doctor Who* fans loved the internet. If she could entertain them with her honesty, wit and swearing, she'd be performing a valuable public service by keeping them off the streets.

Me: Trust me, it will be brilliant.

I failed to mention that if we did this as a blog, and people actually read it, I could use that to pressure her into continuing when she inevitably begged me to stop.

> **Sue**: But it would just be me telling you that old *Doctor Who* is crap. Why would anybody be interested in that? Give your head a shake, Neil.
> **Me**: You might think it's not crap.

Sue: Oh. My. God.
Me: I'm guessing that 'ambitious' isn't the word you're looking for?
Sue: Oh dear. I know I'm not supposed to slag off the special effects, but come on! What were they thinking? Or taking?
Me: They were trying to push the envelope.
Sue: They're pushing their bloody luck.

> **Me**: Well, not all of it anyway.

Sue: This is great. It's just a shame that the picture is over-exposed. William Hartnell's face looks like it's melting off.
Me: This is a copy of the VHS tape that was released about ten years ago. The story is out on DVD soon. It will look better then.
Sue: We could watch it again.
Me: I beg your pardon?
Sue: I wouldn't mind watching this one again.

Me: Whatever happens, it would be nice for me to get a
   fresh perspective on *Doctor Who*. You never know, you
   might enjoy it.
Sue: Will I have to watch Jon Pertwee?
Me: Yes, but . . .
Sue: How long will Jon Pertwee take?
Me: About a month.*

Watching all of *Doctor Who* from the very beginning with
my wife had never been a life-long ambition of mine but,
as I gently reminded her, perhaps the thousand-plus days I
had spent living in a static caravan so she could pursue her
life-long ambition of building a house should be taken into
account.

Sue: Payback, you mean.
Me: It might bring us closer together.
Sue: So did the caravan, and you didn't like that very
   much.

But in the end she agreed. After all, it was only watching
TV. How hard could it be?
   When we launched the blog Adventures With the Wife
in Space, I called it an 'experiment', hoping to conjure up
images of the Ludovico technique from *A Clockwork Orange*
– leather restraints, bloodshot eyeballs, that sort of thing.
But then something surprising happened. I quickly felt
as though I was the one in the Ludovico chair. What was
supposed to be a bit of inconsequential fun was now being
scrutinised by a growing number of readers. Some of our

* 'About a month' = about five months.

audience thought we were engaged in an important ethno-
graphic study, others enjoyed the way Sue would say things a
fan wouldn't usually say, or notice things a fan wouldn't usually notice (invariably involving the quality of an episode's
carpentry). And in turn, as 'a few months' stretched to over
two years, Sue never thought about giving up and letting
our followers down. Not once. She never begged me to stop,
not even when Captain Jack had a life-threatening urinary
tract infection.* She was indomitable.

I, on the other hand, proved laughably domitable. In
the two years the experiment took to run, I thought about
giving up before, after or during nearly every episode. But
I couldn't – it was me who felt pressured into continuing
because it was all happening online. People were commenting, arguing and watching us. We were being monitored by
an enthusiastic panel of 8s, 9s and even some 10s who converted Sue's scores for each story into statistical data and bar
charts. And as we slogged our way through 157 different
stories and nearly 700 different episodes – including more
than a hundred that technically didn't exist any more –
something even more surprising happened.

Strapped to our sofa, eyes fixed forcibly on the TV, I
began seriously to rethink my love for *Doctor Who*, a love
that began forty years ago.

---

* The cat, not John Barrowman.

Part One

Doctor Who is watched on several levels in an average household. The smallest child terrified behind the sofa or under a cushion, and the next one up laughing at him, and the eldest one saying 'Ssh, I want to listen!' – and the parents saying, 'Isn't this enjoyable?'

TOM BAKER, THE FOURTH DOCTOR

A Carnival of Monsters

It's Saturday 3 February 1973. A silver-haired man and a young, pretty woman are hiking through a swamp when an unfamiliar sound stops them in their tracks. They hear it again: a plaintive, mournful cry. They scan the horizon for the source of this strange noise when suddenly, without warning, the landscape explodes with a blood-curdling scream. 'Look!' cries the woman, as a ferocious dog with an impossibly long neck rises out of the mud to tower above them, marsh water dripping from its razor-sharp fangs.

The woman stares in wide-eyed horror as an identical monster forces its way out of the ground to join its kin. But wait . . . That isn't its neck . . . That's its body. The head of a vicious dog on the body of a giant, hairy slug.

This isn't just my first memory of *Doctor Who*; it's my first memory of *anything*.

*

My name is Neil because I was born on Monday 6 October 1969. For a while, my parents Sandra (a nurse) and Michael (a welder) seriously considered naming me after the second man on the moon, which means you might now be reading a book by Aldrin Perryman. I would have preferred Buzz. Either way, it would probably be quite a different book from this one.

Me: What was I like as a baby, Mum?

Mum: You were very well behaved. I wish I could give
   you something more interesting for your book, but
   you were a very boring baby.

Me: Thanks.

Mum: Although there was this one time when we
   almost lost you. You were only a few months old and
   you probably don't remember it.

Me: What do you mean, you almost lost me?

Mum: A lesbian kidnapped you. She tried to smuggle
   you over the border into France. You were asleep in
   your pram on a train platform in Switzerland when
   she took you. I definitely remember you filling your
   nappy on the flight back to England. You stank the
   plane out. You can put that in your book if you like.

The details of my early childhood are frustratingly vague
because, perhaps fortunately, Mum seems to have forgotten nearly everything. We may never know what really
happened on the Swiss border that day in 1970. There's
no actual proof that the woman in question was a lesbian;
according to my mum, she just 'dressed like one'. And as
Mum correctly surmises, I don't remember any of it, since
I was only a few months old and full cognitive powers were
still some way off.

A few weeks shy of my second birthday Mum and Dad
gave me a baby sister. Her name was, and is, Joanne. I don't
recall her arrival *chez* Perryman, but there is a black-and-
white photograph taken the day she was brought home from
the hospital. I am wearing black leather lederhosen and

grizzling – I look like a resentful member of the Hitler Kindergarten – so we can assume I was unhappy about either (a) the lederhosen, (b) Joanne or (c) both. But who knows? It's pure guesswork.

So, the first three years of my life are mysterious to me. But this all changes on Saturday 3 February 1973 at 6.13 p.m.: the precise moment that my brain's inbuilt recording equipment finally whirrs into action, just in time to capture an image of a silver-haired man in a green velvet smoking jacket traipsing through a swamp.

My wife isn't convinced.

> **Sue**: You've seen it so many times, you just *think* you remember seeing it when you were three years old.

She does have a point. I've lost count of the number of times I have thrilled to the cliffhanger of 'Carnival of Monsters', episode 2. I definitely saw it again at the age of twelve, thanks to a BBC Two repeat; when it was released on video cassette; again in 2003 when it came out on DVD (I took the day off work especially to watch it). And because you can never own too many copies of 'Carnival of Monsters', I happily bought it again when the BBC re-released it as part of a box set, carefully remastered for optimum glove-puppet clarity. And that doesn't include all the times I've seen it in trailers, documentaries, YouTube mash-ups and, of course, my dreams.

As an adult – of sorts – I know practically everything there is to know about that scene. I know that it was filmed at Tillingham Marshes in Essex, for example, and that the monsters' name – Drashig – is an anagram of 'dishrag'. I am also fully aware that they are not real monsters, and that the effect employed a technique called CSO, or colour separation overlay, today known as blue screen, although in those days they used a yellow backdrop (in reality a curtain), which would often result in a fizzy Ready Brek line around the monster. I also know that this era-specific technical phenomenon has its own name – fringing.

> **Sue:** I rest my case. You know far too much about it. It must be a false memory.

But I don't remember only the fringed Drashigs. I also recall the colour of our carpet in Lavender Avenue (brown), its walls (dark pine), and its curtains (orange). I can see myself sitting bolt upright in an armchair (black-and-white stripes) clutching a beaker of squash in one fist and a half-eaten Farley's rusk in the other. But there's more: Auntie Angie is there. She might have been babysitting, or she might have come to say goodbye. It's my last memory of her for a very long time, because she emigrated to New Zealand the following week. When we finally visited her six years later, I was elated to discover that New Zealand TV showed daily vintage episodes of *Doctor Who*.

Aged three, I wasn't afraid of the Drashigs. *Doctor Who* didn't scare me – yet. The fear would come, but I was still too young to fully understand it. In another memory I can see a group of angry lizard men shouting at the Doctor. Nothing else. Just that. The image is in black and white, so I probably watched it on my nana's TV. I can also work out when I first saw a Dalek – Saturday 14 April 1973: 'Planet of the Daleks', episode 2. I still wasn't scared, but I remember feeling sick: my head resting on my mother's lap and her telling me not to worry – 'Your tummy ache will go away soon' – as she gently stroked my hair. When I watch 'Planet of the Daleks' now I still wish someone would stroke my hair and tell me that everything is going to be OK.

Me: I have a vivid memory of watching this particular scene when I was three years old. All I know is that I was definitely ill at the time. Stomach ache, I think. It's a very sketchy image, but I'm definitely lying on the settee with a hot water bottle on my tummy. I can remember it like it was yesterday.
Sue: Really? I've just seen it and I've forgotten it already.

No, fear arrived a few weeks later. Icy cold tendrils of pure terror first wrapped themselves around me during a story called 'The Green Death'.

You may have heard of this one. When people talk about old episodes of *Doctor Who* they often talk about 'The Green Death' – or 'the one with the giant maggots', as it is often referred to. And these maggots – created not with CSO but by inflating some condoms – are pretty scary. But for me, aged four, it was what those giant maggots were destined to become that traumatised me.

In 'The Green Death', ordinary maggots have grown huge after being irradiated by poisonous sludge, so when they emerge from the larval state they metamorphose into giant toxic flies. Like normal flies, they vomit to aid digestion. However, because they are giant, irradiated and toxic, their spew is green and noxious, and if just the tiniest amount of it touches your flesh, you've had it. Painfully. It's my first memory of watching *Doctor Who* that brings up feelings of genuine dread and terror: that giant fly, squatting malevolently on a coal slag in Wales, with its ruby red eyes and twitching antennae . . . Just thinking about it now makes me feel a little uneasy. When push comes to shove, you could easily outrun a giant maggot, or just step over one. The maggots crawled around aimlessly, hissing, and could probably be popped with a pin anyway. But I was convinced the fly had a personal grudge against Neil Perryman, and it was coming to spew its toxic, green vomit mercilessly over *me*.

That summer, the suburb of Coventry where we lived was invaded by a colony of flying ants. I was too scared to go outside for three days, convinced that I would die screaming if one of them landed on me. I had glimpsed mortal terror in a handful of glowing CSO vomit. My mother, not unreasonably, didn't let me watch *Doctor Who* for ages after that.

The next story I remember vividly was 'Planet of the Spiders', which was broadcast a year after 'The Green Death', but not much had changed. Once again I was reliably and predictably terrified of the spiders.

Is 'Planet of the Spiders' responsible for my acute arachnophobia? When I jump on tables to avoid them, or scream in public places like that woman in the swamp, is it *Doctor Who*'s fault? Or did *Doctor Who* unknowingly compound an already inbuilt fear of the eight-legged creatures? If it's the former, then this story has caused me more missed heartbeats, more embarrassment and more nightmares than I care to recall. But if it's the latter, I don't hold it against the writers and producers. They were only doing their job.

When I was four, I didn't just like *Doctor Who*. I liked playing in the park on the swings and roundabouts; I liked sticklebricks, Lego, Play-Doh, *Play School*, Andy Pandy and playing with the kids next door. I liked scoffing Curly Wurlys, bathing with toy frogmen and sleeping with stuffed Wombles. But the thing I loved more than anything else – and probably still do – was being scared by *Doctor Who*.

For me, though, what I remember most about 'Planet of the Spiders' is that the Doctor was scared.

This horrified me at the time. The Doctor was never scared. It didn't matter if he was faced with Daleks, Ice Warriors or savage dogs with impossibly long necks, the Doctor was always in control. Even when things looked really bad (usually towards the end of an episode), I was never *that* worried. The Doctor would sort it out in the end. Those were the rules.

But in this particular episode, the Doctor has that look on his face. The look that says: someone has poured me into a tight pair of leather lederhosen against my wishes. The Doctor looked like he was going to cry. And with good reason. At the end of the story, the Doctor died.

Cue Titles

When I was five years old, my record collection consisted of just one LP: *TV Favourites and Other Children's Songs*. I can still see the cover (I just Googled it): a painting of Rupert the Bear, the Pink Panther and Dougal from *The Magic Roundabout*. But I didn't care about them. Only one thing interested me about this record, and that was Side 1, Track 5: the *Doctor Who* theme.

Nothing sounded like the *Doctor Who* theme. The unmistakable throb of the dum-de-dum bass line, foreboding and thrilling at the same time, accompanied by that strange, undulating wail, which is then slowly consumed by a rumbling, whooshing crescendo which leads inexorably to a liberating scream of . . .

Me: OOOOH-EEEEEEE-OOOOOOOOH!

My record sounded nothing like that. It was a bad cover version, the *Doctor Who* theme arranged for parping Stylophone, piccolo and snare drum. I knew it was wrong (there were trumpets in the middle eight, for heaven's sake), but it was still marginally better than nothing, so I played it to death, at least until it was time for me to hear the real thing again, on a Saturday afternoon, from a mono speaker on our television set.

The *Doctor Who* title sequence was terrifying but compelling. The first title sequence I remember begins with a rippling sea of coloured lights, which twist and bend themselves into the face of a man with an enormous nose, silver hair, and a very thin smile. His face turns a bright shade of green, and then it melts into the background as the words DOCTOR WHO bleed magically onto the screen. The words fade and a spinning blob takes over, rotating backwards and forwards, hypnotising me, drawing me in . . .

However, just when I got used to this title sequence, the people who made *Doctor Who* decided to change it.

I can't wait to show Sue the title sequence for season 11. The diamond-shaped logo! The space-time vortex! Jon Pertwee's legs!

Sue: They've changed the titles . . . And they've missed a bit.
Me: What?
Sue: The bottom left-hand corner. They've missed a bit. There's a hole in the titles. I like the new theme music, though.
Me: They haven't changed the theme music!

The music was exactly the same but everything else was different. A tunnel of tiny stars merge to form a turquoise whirlpool (aka the space-time vortex) from which the Doctor's face appears once again, only this time he isn't smiling. The Doctor looks upset.

Jon Pertwee's Doctor scared me, and it wasn't just because his face loomed out of the space-time vortex like some elderly ghost. It was because the Doctor could be more frightening than the monsters. When he wasn't barking at the villains he was shouting at his assistants, especially the Brigadier, who always seemed to be in his bad books. But there was something reassuring about the Doctor, too. Yes, he was intimidating and strict, but he was also the only person in the room who could stop the monsters. So I trusted him, even though the only time he looked truly happy was when he was beaming from the wrapper of a Nestlé chocolate bar. The Doctor definitely didn't look very happy when he was being flung backwards into the space-time vortex in this new title sequence, his arms folded indignantly across his chest.

But if I couldn't identify with the Doctor, I could latch on to his assistants. The Doctor was never alone. There was Jo Grant, the girl from the swamp. When she left, Sarah Jane Smith replaced her, and she was both beautiful and brave. In fact the Doctor had loads of friends, far more than I did. Most of them were soldiers who liked to blow things up. They asked the questions I wanted to ask, they faced the monsters I dared not face, and they stuck by the Doctor through thick and thin, even though he was often really rude to them.

Back at the naval base, the Doctor does something horrid. Forget blowing up Gallifrey, this is much, much worse. The Doctor steals some sandwiches from a clearly famished Jo Grant.

Sue: What a c**t! He had a sandwich in the last episode! That's probably the worst thing I've ever seen the Doctor do.
Me: Calm down. It's just some harmless comedy.

Sue: There's nothing even remotely funny about it. Poor Jo. Why does she put up with it? She's like an abused wife who keeps coming back for more. It's terribly sad.

The Doctor's friends never appeared in the *Doctor Who* title sequence, which is a shame, but when the programme makers decided to modify that whirling vortex again a year later, they chose to incorporate his principal mode of transport.

The Doctor's TARDIS is a space-time machine that is bigger on the inside than it is on the outside. It also looks like a police telephone box. I got my head around the first concept remarkably quickly, but the significance of the Doctor's choice of a blue box puzzled me for ages. There weren't any police boxes in Coventry in the 1970s so I never got to pretend that the Doctor's TARDIS had suddenly materialised at the bottom of a suburban street, although I did feel a rush of excitement whenever I passed our local police station, mainly because of the signage and the fact that its doors were painted a similar shade of blue.

One day, I learned that the Doctor's time machine looked like a police telephone box because it didn't work properly. I can't remember who told me this – it might have been the Doctor, an episode of *Blue Peter*, or perhaps even my mum – but it made perfect sense. Stuff broke down all the time in the 1970s: the telly, the buses, even the electric went on the blink every now and again. The TARDIS was supposed to blend into its surroundings but it had got stuck in the shape of a police telephone box in the 1960s, back when police telephone boxes were still relatively commonplace. The Doctor seemed not to care that his TARDIS didn't work properly in much the same way that my dad seemed not to care that the central heating in Lavender Avenue didn't work properly. You had to grin and bear it in the 1970s.

The Doctor decides to fix his ship's chameleon circuit, and to do that he will need to survey a real police box on Earth.

Sue: So the Doctor is finally going to fix his TARDIS? After all this time, he's actually going to fix it?
Me: Yes.
Sue: I know why he's suddenly decided to do it now. He's jealous of the Master, isn't he? He wants a TARDIS like his. One that can sit down in a chair and fire laser beams from its eyes. And who can blame him?

The next thing to appear in this title sequence is the diamond-shaped logo. A logo that was notoriously difficult to draw on a pencil case without the aid of a compass and protractor. And then the title of the story appears in white, bold letters – a warning of what to expect: planets infested with spiders, invading dinosaurs, or a monster on Peladon. But every once in a while, the title would contain a word that I recognised. A word that would send me over the edge . . .

   Me: DALEKS!

The first time I encountered a Dalek was outside Coventry's indoor market. This Dalek – bright red with blue orbs – looked incongruous next to the double-decker buses, tractors and a choo-choo train, and I only sat in it when all the other vehicles on the motorised merry-go-round were occupied. The Dalek didn't scare me. I just didn't understand it yet.

This lasted until I saw the Daleks on television. It was the voice that did it. That grating, hysterical staccato, bubbling with anger and hate. The Doctor could be a grumpy sod sometimes, but the Daleks were angry *all the time*. Utterly unreasonable, malicious and cruel, they even had their own catchphrase, and while I knew you couldn't imitate a Dalek perfectly – that was the whole point, they didn't look even remotely human – if I stuck my arms out like one and talked like one, people seemed to fall for it. *EXTERMINATE!*

The next time my mum took me to the market, and we approached the merry-go-round, I felt a mixture of excitement and dread. But even though this strange pepper pot-shaped object had a sinister aura about it, I never wanted to sit in a tractor or a choo-choo train again.

Sue: The Daleks look rubbish. How could anybody be scared of them?

Me: What? It's the same design that still scares kids today. It's a design classic.

Sue: Oh, they work fine today. They are built very nicely today – very sturdy. This lot look like you could lift up their lids with a nail file.

*Later, our heroes disarm a Dalek and Ian clambers inside it.
Sue is, to put it mildly, incredulous.*

Sue: What the hell are they doing? They can't do that, can
they? That just makes it blatantly obvious that the Daleks are
being driven around by middle-aged men in cardigans.

The title sequence over, I am immersed in the world of
Doctor Who. It's Proustian, Pavlovian, even Freudian: the
unearthly sounds and hallucinatory visuals have primed
my brain to embrace the impossible. And for the next
twenty-five minutes, the real world no longer exists.

Regeneration – and not a moment too soon

There's one element of *Doctor Who* that I haven't mentioned yet: regeneration. In a way, it's the most important, because without it, the show wouldn't have lasted for five years, let alone fifty. If the lead actor becomes too ill, or too difficult, or too unpopular, he can simply be replaced.

It was *Doctor Who*'s then-producer, Innes Lloyd, who came up with this idea after the First Doctor, William Hartnell, had become increasingly erratic in his ability to play the part. Because the Doctor was an alien being, he thought, there was nothing stopping him from renewing himself into a younger, healthier person. The character of the Doctor could be defined by the person who played him. Suddenly, a programme that had a finite shelf life could now last for ever, continually reinventing both the lead character and the format of the show.

I learned that other Doctors existed on Saturday 8 June 1974, the day the Third Doctor became the Fourth. An hour before the episode was broadcast, my mother sat me down and told me, in no uncertain terms, that my childhood hero was going to die.

Mum didn't use the word regeneration. No, this would be a resurrection. Just like Jesus, she said. Or the time our goldfish threw itself out of its bowl, or when next-door's cat was run over by a milk float. And in much the same way that the next-door neighbours got themselves a new cat, and we might get another goldfish one day (we never did), today everybody would get a new Doctor Who.

The regeneration itself lasts all of five seconds. It's a simple visual effect – as simple as it gets. The camera is locked-off, the actors lie down in the same spot and then they mix the two images together. But it's still one of the best tricks *Doctor Who* ever managed to pull off.

When the Doctor dies, Sue doesn't say a word. And I can't say anything either because I'm too choked up, and if I look at her she might see just how choked up I am, so I honestly don't know how she's reacting right now. And then she breaks her silence . . .

Sue: That was a good scene. I can't say I'm disappointed to see Jon Pertwee go but, yeah, that was very nicely done.

And then the Doctor transforms into . . .

Sue: It's Tom Jones!

To date, the Doctor has regenerated eleven times. I imagine you could name the twelve actors who have played the part on television, but just in case you can't, they are: William Hartnell, Patrick Troughton, Jon Pertwee, Tom Baker, Peter Davison, Colin Baker, Sylvester McCoy, Paul McGann, John Hurt, Christopher Eccleston, David Tennant, and Matt Smith.*

* Quantity and names of actors who have played the Doctor correct at the time of going to press.

However, it could be argued that many more actors have taken on the role of the Doctor, even if the part they are playing is incorrectly referred to as Doctor Who. These Doctors exist in a non-canonical alternative Whoniverse of comedy sketches, feature films and stage plays outside of the main Whoniverse (don't bother looking in the dictionary, it's not there).

Discussions of what is and what isn't part of the *Doctor Who* 'canon' are to the programme's fans what angels dancing on the head of a pin were to medieval theologians. Friendships can be wrecked over whether, say, Tom Baker's appearance in his *Doctor Who* costume on *Disney Time* in 1975 means that it was actually the Doctor who materialised on Bank Holiday Monday to present *Disney Time* during the four-month break between 'Revenge of the Cybermen' and 'Terror of the Zygons' (for the record – of course he bloody didn't).

However, should you ever find yourself ensnared in a tricky pub-quiz situation, and you are asked to name more than twelve actors who have played the Doctor, here are some of the less well-known regenerates:

Trevor Martin. Trevor Martin is a fabulous actor with an impressive CV of film and stage roles. However, in 1974 he played Doctor Who in a West End stage production entitled *Doctor Who and the Daleks in the Seven Keys to Doomsday*. For one small segment of the population, this means the actor's numerous appearances in plays by William Shakespeare and the like pale into insignificance compared to the three weeks he spent hanging around the stage of the Adelphi Theatre, waiting for a Dalek to trundle onto its mark.

Richard Hurndall. For the twentieth-anniversary story, 'The Five Doctors', neither Tom Baker nor William Hartnell was available to take part, one because he was sulking and the other because he was dead. Hurndall stepped in, giving an uncanny impersonation of the irascible First Doctor, except for the fact that he managed to deliver all his lines without mucking them up.

David Banks. More usually concealed inside a Cyberman costume on television, David Banks was also Jon Pertwee's understudy for a 1989 musical stage play called *Doctor Who: The Ultimate Adventure*. When Pertwee fell ill one day, Banks grasped the nettle with both hands, and for the lucky people who saw that matinee performance, it is said, not least by David Banks, that he gave *the* definitive portrayal of the Doctor. Unfortunately, the number of people who claim to have seen David's Doctor far exceeds the seating capacity of Birmingham's Alexandra Theatre, so this hyperbole should be taken with a pinch of salt.

Richard E. Grant. Two for the price of one, here. Grant has played the part twice, once in 2004 in a computer-animated story called 'Scream of the Shalka', and previously in 1999 when he appeared alongside **Rowan Atkinson**, **Jim Broadbent**, **Hugh Grant** and **Joanna Lumley** in a sketch for Comic Relief. None of them inhabited the part with a tenth of the conviction of David Banks.

But the most famous non-canonical Doctor of them all is surely **Peter Cushing**. After the success of the Daleks on TV, producer Milton Subotsky was responsible for bringing them to the big screen in the movies *Dr Who and the Daleks* and *Daleks: Invasion Earth 2150 AD*. The veteran Hammer Horror star Cushing was cast in the mistitled lead role. Now, these movies have their admirers – current producer Steven Moffat, for example – but as a child, I knew these films weren't kosher and this guy playing 'Doctor Who' was emphatically not the Doctor; as well as having the wrong name, he was just too human. Besides, rather than laser beams, the movie Daleks fired lethal blasts of compressed air – in a big-budget film, for God's sake! Like Milton Subotsky could give a shit.

Sue: What the hell is this? This is in colour.

Me: Well spotted.

Sue: This is the movie, isn't it? This wasn't part of the deal.

This wasn't the reaction that I'd hoped for. I thought she would be grateful for a splash of colour.

Sue: WHAT THE F**K?

As far as Sue is concerned, everything is wrong. Not just different. Wrong. The TARDIS interior; the Doctor; his extended family; the music; the Daleks; even the film's aspect ratio gets under her skin.

Sue: They called him Dr Who. That means his daughter's name must be Barbara Who and that must be little Susie Who. This is stupid. Why are we watching this again?

I persuaded her to stick with it, and while there were a few isolated moments that met with Sue's approval (explosion-based, mainly), they still couldn't mitigate for the wrongness that permeated every frame.

Sue: The most interesting thing about the film is that they made it so close to the TV show. It's not as if we are watching a remake thirty years later, with loads of expensive CGI. And yet they appear to exist in two completely different timeframes. On the one hand, the film is clearly much more impressive – it's quicker, bigger and better made – but at the same time it's a lot less impressive than the original. And the original wasn't that impressive to begin with.

She refused to give the film a mark out of ten.

Sue: It doesn't count.

Tom

The boys I went to school with were football crazy, football mad. All they wanted to do was talk about Saturday's goals and swap Panini stickers. All I wanted to do was swap *Doctor Who* Weetabix cards and speculate about how the Doctor might escape last Saturday's cliffhanger. Even the boys who did watch *Doctor Who* didn't want to talk about it. But then again, what do boys talk about? Even as adults, most of our interactions tended to consist of: 'Got . . . Got . . . Need . . . Swap . . . Got' and 'Tag! You're it!'

So I defected to the girls, who were a much more chatty and imaginative bunch. When we played *Doctor Who* in the playground, I was *always* the Doctor and the girls were always Sarah Jane Smith or, better yet, one of the monsters. I am still warmed by the memory of Bethany McKenna and Beverly Sharpe crushing me to death between their chests as they pretended to be the robotic bear-hugging mummies from 'Pyramids of Mars'. Bethany and Beverly, if you are reading this, please be aware that I am hoping to restage this event in 2015 as part of this classic story's fortieth anniversary celebrations. Do get in touch.

*

Tom Baker was my Doctor. I forgot about Jon Pertwee within the first ten minutes of Tom's debut. With his wild staring eyes and insane toothy grin, he was some way from the suave dandy played by Jon Pertwee, but by the time the Fourth Doctor had donned his floppy hat and wrapped his inordinately long multicoloured scarf around his neck, I was hooked. Mum thought he was 'much too silly' but she was wrong.

The new Doctor discharges himself from the infirmary but the medical officer, Harry Sullivan, manages to intervene before he can escape in his TARDIS. The Doctor believes that his new nose is a definite improvement on the last one.

Sue: Your entire face is a definite improvement! Cheer up! You're not Jon Pertwee any more!

The Doctor bamboozles Harry during an exceedingly strange medical, but Sue seems to enjoy it.

Sue: He is certainly larger than life and very charismatic – you can't take your eyes off him. But he will tone it down eventually, won't he? He's a bit full on at the moment.

As the scene plays out, Sue laughs. A lot.

Sue: He's very funny, but I'm not sure that the kids would have felt the same way. I think the Doctor's eyes popping out of his head would have frightened half of them to death.

As much as I had loved the Third Doctor, he had silver hair, which meant I thought about him the same way I'd think about a grandfather or a kindly uncle. The Fourth Doctor was different; we didn't know anyone like him. He looked like a nutcase, behaved like a nutcase, and, I would later learn, was being played by a nutcase. But what a nutcase.

In his second story, 'The Ark in Space', the Doctor has a famous speech about the indomitable spirit of mankind as a species. Tom Baker plays it like he's onstage at the Globe Theatre, and when I watch it now, it makes me profoundly grateful that the BBC happened to cast an actor who saw no reason not to take the part of a time-travelling extraterrestrial extremely seriously. He had all the mischief and all the heroism and wisdom of previous Doctors, but he was, perhaps, the first actor who really believed he was the Doctor.

I remember two things about watching 'The Ark in Space' as a child. One, it scared the willies out of me, and two, I couldn't wait to reproduce the terror I felt in the school playground the following Monday.

The monsters in 'The Ark in Space' – the Wirrn – were giant insects, and as you will have realised by now, giant insects always gave me trouble. This lot were a swarm of intelligent wasp-like monstrosities who wanted to impregnate you with their babies, and you knew you were in trouble if your flesh started to break out in green weeping pustules, an effect the cash-strapped BBC special effects department achieved by wrapping the actor's hand and lower arm in painted bubble wrap.

Body horror translated well to the playground. *Everyone* knew how the dreaded lurgy worked. I remember Beverly Sharpe walking around with her hand stuffed in her pocket – a sure sign that she'd been infected by the Wirrn – and when she tried to strangle me with it later, I was impressed to find that she'd gone to the trouble of wrapping several layers of Sellotape around it. Beverly was the first girl I ever kissed, by the way. On the lips and everything.

The Doctor tries to reason with Noah, who is now acting very strangely indeed.

Sue: So this is basically *Alien*?

Me: There are certain similarities, yes.

Sue: How did they sneak this idea into an afternoon teatime slot? It's horrific.

Me: This story gave me nightmares when I was a kid.

Sue: Yes, and you've been terrified of bubble wrap ever since. So when was *Alien* released?

Me: 1979.

Sue: So Ridley Scott might have seen this before he made *Alien*?

Me: It's possible.

Sue: Maybe he showed it to his crew and said, 'I want it to look like this, but with decent lighting, sets, monsters and music.'

---

*

I never hid behind the sofa when I watched *Doctor Who*. For a start, we called it a settee, not a sofa, and it was pushed right up against our living-room wall. So I'd sit on the floor with a cushion in my lap, and if things got too frightening for me, I'd bury my face in its folds. And if the sound effects were too disturbing, I'd press the corners into my ears.

I did this a lot when Tom Baker was playing the Doctor,

especially during the end-of-episode cliffhangers. Like the time Sarah Jane Smith fell from some scaffolding at the end of 'Genesis of the Daleks', part 2. I was so convinced that she couldn't possibly survive this fall, I ran into the kitchen to find Mum.

> **Me:** Sarah Jane's dead! Sarah Jane's dead! Sarah Jane's dead!
>
> **Mum:** Calm down and stop crying. The Doctor's friends don't die. I'm sure he'll catch her in the next episode.

(I didn't feel cheated when part 3 began with Sarah Jane falling safely onto a gantry *that wasn't there the week before*. She was still alive. That's all that mattered.)

The playground games fizzled out by the end of 1976 and our last hurrah was a homage to 'The Hand of Fear', which was ideal for the girls because all they had to do was walk around in a trance, a palm face up in the air, repeating the phrase 'Eldrad must live! Eldrad must live!' over and over again. Even I could have done that.

'The Hand of Fear' was also Sarah Jane's last story.

I didn't see it coming. One minute the Doctor and his best friend are running rings around Eldrad on a planet made from ice, the next minute he's dropping her off in Croydon because he isn't allowed to take her to Gallifrey. It didn't seem fair, not after everything Sarah had been through.

Sarah Jane's departure hit me for six. I wasn't used to companions leaving, and while I could vaguely recall her predecessor, Jo Grant, I had been too young to form any meaningful attachment to her. Sarah Jane was my first proper companion. She was the big sister I never had, the one I wanted to baby-sit me.

I wanted the Doctor to change his mind and return for her the following week, but he didn't. It was at these moments that Tom Baker really made you believe he wasn't quite human because a human being would have gone back for her.

*

There was one thing more frightening than watching *Doctor Who*, and that was missing *Doctor Who*.

Take Saturday 6 December 1975, for example. It's 5.55 p.m. and I should have been settling down to watch 'The Android Invasion', part 3 at home, but instead I was playing pass-the-parcel at some kid's birthday party. Seriously, what kind of idiot throws a birthday party when *Doctor Who* is on?

And then there was 'The Ribos Operation', part 1. Dad had taken me to see a non-league football match. I remember that it rained the whole time, there were no decent seats, the roof was leaking, neither team scored a goal and I was bored to tears. The only thing that made this treat bearable was the knowledge that a brand-new series of *Doctor Who* was due to start when I got home.

The match finished at 4.45 p.m., which gave us a good hour to make it home in time. However, because Dad didn't drive, we had to wait for a lift from his friend, Bob. Bob couldn't have been a *Doctor Who* fan; he wanted to have a quick pint instead. I stood in the cold, draughty corridor with a packet of pork scratchings because I wasn't allowed into the bar. The quick pint wasn't quick enough.

I knew we wouldn't make it back in time when, after several more quick pints, Bob finally decided to leave. I sulked all the way home about missing *Doctor Who*, which at least took my mind off being driven home by someone who must have been over the legal limit. Maybe, his judgement clouded, Bob actually put his foot down because in the event I only missed the first quarter of an hour. However, in the age before repeats, videos or the internet, I would not actually get to watch those missing minutes of 'The Ribos Operation' for another seventeen years. Thanks, Dad.

*

And then I saw *Star Wars*.

> **Mum**: You were *Star Wars* mad. *Doctor Who* went out the window when *Star Wars* came along. You were obsessed with it. Especially the toys.

My mum is half-right here.

When *Star Wars* was released in 1978, I, like every other small boy in the entire country, thought it was the most mind-blowing film I had ever seen or was ever likely to see. By the end of the 1970s, my bedroom had become a shrine to Kenner's range of *Star Wars* action figures. It was a drop in the ocean compared with what was out there, but enough for me to stage some very impressive battles at the bottom of our stairs. My favourite action figure was Bossk the bounty hunter (a crocodile in a yellow jumpsuit), but I had a soft spot for Luke's Landspeeder too, until Joanne stepped on it and snapped its wheels off.

However, I still liked *Doctor Who* and Tom Baker – a lot. Although the programme couldn't compete with the lavish special effects of *Star Wars* – no noticeable bubble wrap in sight – its lead actor, four years in, was still unassailable. The programme had grown noticeably sillier in recent months, in an attempt to appease an old lady named Mary White-house, but Tom remained as exciting, weird and mercurial as ever. And *Doctor Who* could still satisfy some part of my imagination that nothing else could. The only reason I was playing *Star Wars* on the stairs is because the *Doctor Who* franchise didn't have anything like the same amount of toys available, and by this stage of my life, I'd moved beyond the realm of pure imagination and I needed some props.

For my eighth birthday, my parents gave me a red Palitoy Dalek; for my ninth, I got a Denys Fisher Fourth Doctor doll to go with it. I now know that a manufacturing cock-up meant that Tom Baker's head had to be substituted at the last minute with Gareth Hunt's from *The New Avengers*. This didn't bother me at the time as the head in question looked about as much like Tom Baker as it did Gareth Hunt (quality control on the *New Avengers* toys must have been half-hearted at best). There was a Denys Fisher TARDIS, too, but at £5.95 it was probably too steep for my parents' budget, and I never got the Denys Fisher Cyberman either – the only Cyberman with a nose.

Here are a few more *Doctor Who* toys and tie-ins that I did have:

- A board game entitled *War of the Daleks*. I remember that the little Dalek figures didn't have the right proportions – irritating – and I'd only had it a couple of months when one of the pseudo-Daleks went AWOL and the game was completely ruined.

- The Typhoo Tea and Weetabix card collections, which you'd get free in packets of tea and cereal. Free, unless you counted all the tea and cereal you had to consume to get at them. At one stage I was eating twelve Weetabix a day just to get my hands on more cards, and I hated Weetabix. However, looking back, this may be the most balanced diet I've ever had.

- Palitoy's talking K9. I hated K9. What was the point of him? The phrases the toy came out with included: 'Affirmative, Master', 'I cannot appear in this story because the floors are uneven' and 'You don't need me, you have a sonic screwdriver', although I may be recalling this wrong.

- The notorious *Doctor Who* underpants, which when worn showcased the classic 1970s Tom Baker face looming out of your crotch area. It is rumoured that Tom Baker himself sported these pants on his honeymoon night.

- Target novelisations of past adventures. We will come to them in the next chapter.

*

In 1979, Tom Baker's Doctor Who was arguably at his most popular. Just over 16 million people tuned in to watch the final episode of 'City of Death'. It helped that, although 'City of Death' is a wonderful story and Tom is magnificent throughout, there was nothing on the other side owing to industrial action at ITV. It was during this period of Baker's apotheosis that I went to live in New Zealand for five months.

We stayed with Auntie Angie and her husband, Uncle Mike, on their farm on the outskirts of Queenstown on the rural South Island. It was in the middle of nowhere – the nearest shop was miles away – but it was surrounded by beautiful countryside, there were gorgeous views of the mountains, and there were sheep. There were lots and lots of sheep. Plus, repeats of *Doctor Who* were on every day of the week.

I have so many wonderful memories of that time I spent in New Zealand: the tiny Honda motorcycle that I used to ride up and down the country lanes, pretending I was Poncherello from *CHiPs*; catching and killing my first fish (I cried when Uncle Mike told me to bash its head in); skiing on Coronet Peak; white-water rafting; flying in a helicopter for my tenth birthday. I was even a poster boy for a deer park while I was out there.

I kept a scrapbook of my holiday in New Zealand (and of the stopovers we made in Los Angeles and Singapore) and while the first half of this memento is filled with the sort of things you'd expect – sachets of thirty-three-year-old sugar from the plane that flew us there; a blurry photo of Jaws from the Universal Studios tour; a certificate that proves I successfully milked a cow – the second half is filled with black-and-white pictures of *Doctor Who*.

These images were carefully scissored from issues of *Doctor Who Weekly*. This was a brand-new magazine that was entirely devoted to the programme, and while I missed the first issue,

I must have started buying it the very moment we returned to the UK. Here are, variously, a portrait of the Second Doctor and an Ogron monster; Zygons attacking the Doctor; a pair of Sensorites; Davros's head and a colour poster for *Star Trek: The Motion Picture* (how the hell did that get in there?); a Krynoid in various stages of development (three of these) and a 1960s Dalek lurking under a bridge.

The pictures in this scrapbook do prove one thing, though. Despite what my mum would have you believe about my short-lived infatuation with *Star Wars* . . .

Mum: And *Battlestar Galactica*. You loved *Battlestar Galactica*.

Despite *brief flirtations with inferior franchises*, I remained faithful to Tom Baker and *Doctor Who*.

*

Tom Baker's final season introduced some radical changes to the programme's format, chief amongst them the demise of Tom Baker's Doctor. A new producer named John Nathan-Turner was now running the show. Out went the 1970s diamond-shaped logo and time vortex title sequence, and in came bent chrome and a glittering star field – this was a new decade. Out went the wide-eyed innocent face of Tom Baker and in came the knackered, jaded face of Tom Baker, who had now been in the role for seven years. Out went the classic theme music and in came a much brasher version, with less mystery and more sparkle.

Not that I knew anything about it. I was too busy watching *Buck Rogers in the 25th Century* on the other side.

Sue: Ooh, a new title sequence. The theme music is very techno. Why is Tom Baker snarling? Is he in pain? Is someone torturing him? Hmmm . . . It's very eighties, isn't it? It doesn't get any more eighties than chrome neon tubing. I'm sure it will grow on me. You have to move with the times. What did you think when you saw this episode's titles? Were you shocked?

Me: I didn't see it.

Sue: Were you still living in New Zealand?

Me: Erm . . . not quite.

Sue: What do you mean, not quite?

Me: I decided to watch something else instead.

Sue: You must be joking.

Me: I still feel bad about this but I switched to ITV. They were showing *Buck Rogers in the 25th Century* at exactly the same time, and because we didn't have a video recorder well, let's just say it was a very big decision.

Sue: Buck Rogers? Are you taking the piss?

There's a funereal feel to Tom Baker's final season and a sombre tone permeates every frame. It didn't matter if the Doctor was fighting vampires, marsh men or time-sensitive lions, he didn't seem to be his old self. Resigned, almost. Spent. Even as a kid, I knew something was wrong with him.

Buck Rogers, on the other hand, was fun. It had a disco-dancing hero in tight-fitting Lycra, there were exciting dogfights in space, just like in *Star Wars*, and the actress who played his sidekick, Wilma Deering, made me feel funny inside.

But on *Doctor Who*, we had long scenes of a grumpy Tom Baker staring at a BBC Micro computer while the universe was crushed to death by the grinding wheels of entropy – this really was the plot for every single episode of that series. The jokes that had replaced the violence had in turn been replaced by actual po-faced science.

Doctor Who was either growing old or growing up.

But that was OK. I was growing up, too.

*

Tom Baker's final story was called 'Logopolis'. At the end, the Doctor is forced to regenerate when he falls to his death from a radio telescope, or if you want to be really cynical about it, when somebody drops a Gareth Hunt doll off an Airfix model.

I cried.

Of course I cried.

I knew Tom was leaving long before he fell. But it wasn't my mum who spoiled it for me this time. Tom Baker had been on *Nationwide*, where he had looked very sad indeed, and he told me his time was up, but I mustn't worry, because *Doctor Who* would go on without him. *Doctor Who* would go on for ever. He promised.

And because he was Tom Baker, I believed him.

Five Faces

When I was growing up in the 1970s, I never thought I'd ever see an episode of *Doctor Who* with William Hartnell in it. They were in the past (even the ones set in the future). So when, in 1981, the BBC screened a trailer for something called *The Five Faces of Doctor Who* at the end of an episode of *Blake's 7*, I thought I had died and gone to heaven, or at the very least back to New Zealand.

> **BBC Announcer:** Starting in two weeks on BBC Two, *The Five Faces of Doctor Who* looks back in time to previous journeys of the TARDIS . . . The Doctor returns in five complete adventures over five weeks running from Monday to Thursday, beginning with the first episode of the first ever *Doctor Who*.

As noted above, in the days before the internet and VHS tapes or DVDs, it was almost impossible to see old episodes of *Doctor Who*, barring a few black-and-white clips which might accompany a feature on, say, *Blue Peter*. What few people knew at the time was that the BBC had wiped numerous episodes of the programme in order to reuse expensive videotape and save shelf space. So this season of repeats was, by some distance, An Event.

Only one thing stood between me and It: rugby practice.

I didn't like rugby. I couldn't even tell you what kind of rugby we were playing. I definitely didn't want to play it for the school team. But this was my first year at Big School, and I desperately wanted to fit in. So when I was plucked from a PE lesson to try out as a winger, I neglected to say, 'No thanks, I'd rather try out for basket weaving.' (Not an exaggeration, I really did weave baskets, and in fact I was the only boy at school who studied Home Economics.)

Actually, I was pretty good at rugby. But my ability to run like a Thal from a Dalek was fuelled entirely by a disinclination to being clattered into the mud by Ogron-like adolescents surely too burly and bloodthirsty to be called 'children', though they were all the same age as me. Plus none of them knew what Ogrons were.

On Monday 2 November 1981, the day of the first episode of *The Five Faces of Doctor Who*, I made sure I was the first player back in the changing room, out of my kit and into my clothes as speedily as if I were being pursued by a grunting prop forward. The programme began at 5.40 p.m. If I ran all the way, I could make it home in time.

But as I sprinted towards the exit, my right knee collided with the edge of a shower cubicle. My leg exploded with pain as a fragment of ceramic tile embedded itself in my flesh, right below the kneecap. I screamed, extremely loudly. A pool of blood formed around me and spread towards the door.

It must have been bad. Our rugby teacher, Mr Brown, not a man known for Florence Nightingale-like reverses of compassion, wanted to take me to A&E, although I could tell he wasn't thrilled by the prospect – he probably had other plans that night, though I doubt they included the first episode of *Doctor Who*.

Mr Brown: Get your stuff together, Perryman. We're
   going to the hospital.

Me: Do we have to?

Mr Brown: Why were you running on a wet floor
   without looking where you were going? A floor which
   is now covered in your blood, Perryman, and which
   will have to be cleaned. That wound needs serious
   attention.

Me: It's not *that* bad. My mum is a nurse. She could fix
   it.

Mr Brown: Well, if you are absolutely sure. Take this
   plaster and get out of my sight before I change my
   mind.

I limped home as fast as I could, which wasn't very, teeth
clenched in agony. Hobbling into the front room, blood
soaking through my new Farah trousers, I made straight for
the television, which I switched to BBC Two.

Dad: And what do you think you're doing?

Me: (*out of breath*) Doc . . . tor . . . Who.

Dad: Don't be stupid. It's Monday today. And what's
   wrong with your leg?

Me: It's . . . the first . . . episode . . . It's . . . on . . . now.

Dad: I'm watching the news.

Me: (*thinking fast, through haze of throbbing knee-pain*)
   If I promise to clean out the garage, can I watch it,
   please?

The *Doctor Who* theme music had already begun.

Me: *Please*, Dad. This is *really* important to me.

I could feel a river of blood trickling down my leg.

Dad: The whole garage? All of it? I don't want to hear any excuses about spiders, like last time. Oh, go on then.

Relieved, I collapsed onto the sofa and we watched 'An Unearthly Child' together.

Dad: What a load of old rubbish. I missed the news for *that*?
Me: The next episode might be better. It's on the same time tomorrow.
Dad: Oh no it isn't.
Me: Oh yes it is.
Dad: Would you like to bet on that?
Me: But old episodes of *Doctor Who* are on every day this week. And the week after that. And . . .
Dad: Trust me, it isn't. The news will be on. You can count on it, Son.

I didn't have the strength to argue. The pain in my knee was now more than I could bear, so I shuffled off to the kitchen to find my mum. She wrote a very stern letter to the school about the damage sustained to both her son and his expensive – and now ruined – trousers, as soon as she'd finished stitching the holes in my leg and slacks with the same piece of thread.

I missed the second episode. But thanks to a stroke of good fortune – for me – Dad went back to working nights at his factory, and this meant he had to be out of the house by 5.30 p.m.

Actually, Dad had not been wrong. That first episode was

too slow, too dark (as in we couldn't see anything) and too talky. Worse than that, the First Doctor was a *horrible man*. He was nothing like the Doctor I'd grown up with. Yes, that Doctor could be a bit scary at times, but he was never this strict and unapproachable and unpleasant.

Sadly, the third episode was even worse than the first.

Sue: What a c**t! Are we supposed to like the lead character? Because the show is doing a terrible job if we are supposed to root for this git.

---

*

You never forget your first Kroton.

No, not crouton, though I do actually remember my first crouton too; it was floating in a chicken and mushroom Cup-a-Soup. No, I'm talking about the Krotons, the race of quasi-organic tellurium-based crystals who appeared in the *Doctor Who* serial that the BBC chose to represent the Second Doctor's time in the TARDIS.

> **BBC Announcer**: The evening news on BBC One now is followed by the weather and then, at six o'clock, regional programmes nationwide. Here on BBC Two now, 'The Krotons', an adventure that involves the second of the five faces of *Doctor Who* . . .

If 'An Unearthly Child' was a letdown then the 'The Krotons' was a kick in the teeth. It was boring and difficult to follow. I remember thinking to myself: if this is the best story the BBC could find to show off the Second Doctor, how bad must the rest of his adventures be?

What I didn't realise then was that the BBC had thrown most of Patrick Troughton's stories into a skip, and the only four-part Second Doctor story left on their shelves was this one.

Sue's brother and daughter joined us for 'The Krotons' . . .

Gary: The robots have curling tongs and nutcrackers for hands. I just thought I should mention that.
Sue: I thought they were hiding the Krotons so they could ramp up the suspense; it turns out they were hiding them because they look dreadful.
Nicol: How do the Krotons get around?
Gary: They have a skirt made of waffles and that hides their legs. How can you watch this rubbish? The effects are terrible! *Lost in Space* and *Star Trek* were around at the same time and they looked better than this.
Sue: But *Doctor Who* didn't have their budget, Gary. And besides, it's part of *Doctor Who*'s charm.

When the Krotons are no more, the Gonds are ecstatic. 'We are free at last!' they cry.

Gary: Tell me about it.
Sue: It wasn't *that* bad.
Gary: Are you serious?
Sue: It was only four episodes long and it moved.
Nicol: You should see some of the stuff Neil makes my mam watch.

Sue: Some of the episodes don't exist and we still watch them.
Gary: You are both mad.

Two stories into *The Five Faces of Doctor Who*, I had to
face facts: old *Doctor Who* – *Doctor Who* made before I was
born – seemed to be absolutely rubbish. In fact, 'The Krotons' was so boring I didn't even make it to the final episode.

The truth is that many old episodes of *Doctor Who* were
better served by novelisations, and my young imagination,
than the shabby, black-and-white reality.

Hitherto, my image of the Second Doctor was based on
one of the many novelisations published by Target Books:
Doctor Who and the Web of Fear by Terrance Dicks, which
I remember reading in a caravan in Rhyl when I was eight
years old.

That book had one hell of a cover: a beautiful illustration
by Chris Achilleos of Patrick Troughton set against a spider-
web background. He's looking down at a fat, furry teddy bear
lassoing a soldier with a halo of bright yellow light, which
was cool, but not as cool as the realisation that the Second
Doctor's hair had been cut into the shape of a pudding bowl.
This made me feel a whole lot better about my own hairstyle,
the only difference being that my bowl was blond.

I tried to imagine what the Second Doctor was like – 'a
small man with untidy black hair and a gentle, humorous
face', according to Dicks – and as I read about his escapades
in the London Underground and his battle against the villainous Yeti (who turned out to be alien robots and not
homicidal teddy bears after all) I found it increasingly easy to

replace Tom Baker's face with my ideal of Patrick Troughton.

So when the time came for me to watch Patrick Troughton for real, I was expecting him to measure up to the Second Doctor of my imagination. And that's why it is with a very heavy heart that I have to confess the only thing I can remember about the November 1981 screening of 'The Krotons' is that I thought it was terrible.

*

And yet love of *Doctor Who*, like the Doctor himself, can regenerate after the deadliest of blows. Of all the repeats chosen to celebrate the Doctor's past in *The Five Faces of Doctor Who*, the one I was most looking forward to seeing was 'The Three Doctors'.

> **BBC Announcer**: On BBC One in five minutes
> there's the evening news and weather. In twenty-five
> minutes here on BBC Two, school uniforms become
> a controversial issue at *Grange Hill*. But now it's time
> for 'The Three Doctors', all called Who.

Of all the images I'd seen of earlier Doctors in books and magazines, there was one that stood out: a publicity photo of Pertwee, Troughton and Hartnell posing together to celebrate the programme's tenth birthday. I'd stare at this image for hours, trying to imagine what a story that featured three versions of the Doctor working together would possibly be like. Now I would get the chance to find out.

> **Sue**: Did you hate it? I bet you hated everything back
> then. You should probably blame your hormones.

It sounds to me like you were going through a very negative phase.

Me: No. I loved it.

Sue: Phew. I was starting to worry.

'The Three Doctors' was tremendous and Patrick Troughton was a revelation: the banter between him and his successor, Jon Pertwee, was priceless. Here was the Second Doctor of my imagination – playful and mischievous. And it was great to see the Brigadier, Sergeant Benton, and Jo Grant – the girl from the swamp – again too.

*

The BBC wrapped up *The Five Faces of Doctor Who* with a repeat of the Fourth Doctor's swansong, 'Logopolis'. I cried again, although I would have preferred something older – something *classic* – like 'Pyramids of Mars', 'The Brain of Morbius' or 'The Ark in Space'.

This season of repeats, though, is when I went from being a kid who liked *Doctor Who* to being a *Doctor Who* fan, for better or worse. For a fan, not liking *Doctor Who* can be just as much fun as liking it – like supporters of a conference league football team, you're in it for the long haul; if anyone is entitled to hurl abuse at lazy performances and shambolic set-pieces and poor managerial decisions, you are.

Besides, the season was called *Five Faces* because there was a fifth face – a new Doctor. His name was Peter Davison from *All Creatures Great and Small*. He's too young, I thought, when I heard he would be taking on the role, never imagining that one day I'd have to accept a Doctor almost twenty years *younger* than me. Also, how could anyone replace Tom Baker as the Doctor? I could barely remember a time when he wasn't a part of my childhood.

In a further shocking announcement, the BBC told us it was moving the Doctor out of his traditional Saturday tea-time slot to a new home on Monday and Tuesday evenings. This was sacrilege. It was like moving *Songs of Praise* to a Thursday or *Top of the Pops* to a Monday. I was only twelve but it sounded like what it was – slightly desperate.

I didn't like the Fifth Doctor at first. I thought he was pathetic.

Sue: Hormones.

It wasn't just the new Doctor I had a problem with: Peter Davison had inherited not one but three companions from his predecessor. Unfortunately, I wasn't very keen on two-thirds of them, either. There was Tegan, the Australian air hostess who never stopped whingeing, and Nyssa, a telebio-geneticist/princess from the planet Traken, though certainly pretty, was a bit too prissy and stuck-up for me. But I did like the Doctor's third companion. His name was Adric.

Adric was both a teenage mathematical genius from the planet Alzarius and the quintessential nerd. He seemed perpetually ill at ease. No one took him seriously, not even the Doctor. If the Master wasn't torturing him, the Australian air hostess was picking on him. Adric was played by an inexperienced young actor called Matthew Waterhouse, who stood awkwardly and never seemed to know where to put his hands. Coupled with being made to wear clothes he didn't like – Adric's costume was a never-changing set of green and yellow pyjamas – I found I could identify strongly with this character, which was a new development in my relationship with *Doctor Who*. Except for the maths part. I was rubbish at maths.

Nobody wanted to talk about *Doctor Who* at Big School. It was the love that dared not speak its name, and I found it hard to moderate my enthusiasm and pedantry to acceptable levels.

Them: Knock, knock!

Me: Who's there?

Them: Doctor!

Me: Doctor who?

Them: Exactly!

Me: That doesn't work though, does it? The programme may be called *Doctor Who* but the character is called the Doctor. So the joke should really go 'Knock, knock!' 'Who's there?' 'The Doctor!' 'The Doctor who?' 'The Doctor who is a Time Lord from the planet Gallifrey, has two hearts, and travels with his companions in a battered-looking blue police box called the TARDIS, which stands for Time and Relative Dimension in Space.'

Them: Fuck off.

Aside from the pyjamas, Adric had it easy. At least he had his maths.

*

The Fifth Doctor's first year is pretty terrible. Peter Davison warms to the part – and I warmed to him as the series went on – but most of the adventures were rickety in both concept and execution. At least it wasn't going out on Saturday nights. However, there is one great story in that season. It's called 'Earthshock'.

Doctor Who never usually bothered to hide the identity of its villains. In fact, the opposite was usually true; if you're watching something called 'Death to the Daleks', you can't be surprised when some Daleks turn up and then die. But 'Earthshock' wasn't playing by the same rules.

The first shock in 'Earthshock' arrived at the climax to the opening episode, which, up to that point, was a standard runaround with some faceless androids as the bad guys. But then, without any warning whatsoever, something truly wonderful happened:

INTERIOR: Console room, spaceship. Some Cybermen are studying a holographic image of the Doctor.

Cyberleader: Destroy them! Destroy them at once!
Me: CYBERMEN!

I slipped out of my chair and onto my knees. I was twelve years old. The last time I'd seen Cybermen was half my lifetime ago, but I recognised them instantly. It didn't matter that these Cybermen didn't look or sound anything like the Cybermen of old, or that there wasn't a single line of dialogue to confirm that they definitely *were* Cybermen; even though they were on screen for less than ten seconds, *I knew*.

The other surprise was less welcome. Do you remember when my mum told me the Doctor's friends never died?

She lied.

The Cyberleader blasts the TARDIS console.

Sue: Noooo! They've killed the TARDIS!

The Doctor retaliates by shooting the Cyberleader at point-blank range.

Sue: Bloody hell, the Doctor just shot a Cyberman!

Bang!

Sue: He just shot him twice!

Bang!

Sue: Three times!

The Doctor tries to rescue Adric but it's too late and his companion doesn't make it out alive.

Sue: I'm shocked.
Me: You're Earthshocked.

This was the second shock in 'Earthshock': the death of a companion. Suddenly, the Doctor was fallible. Yes, scores of innocent people had been killed over the course of his adventures, but those deaths might be considered collateral damage (and guest stars and extras didn't really count). This time, the Doctor had failed to save someone who was close to him.

The really worrying thing about this, though, was I had begun to feel like I cared more about the death of Adric than the people who were making the programme did. And with this, my metamorphosis into a true fan was complete.

Words I Learned from *Doctor Who*

Colin Baker once said that it was part of *Doctor Who*'s job to send children scurrying off to their dictionaries when the Doctor uses a word they don't understand. And even though he was being a bit sesquipedalian about it, and if a child had taken his advice they would have missed half the episode he was in (and he wasn't in that many), he was also right. Because over six years, ITV's answer to *Doctor Who* – *The Tomorrow People* – only managed to teach me three words, all beginning with the letter T: telepathy, telekinesis and teleportation. *Doctor Who*, on the other hand, is still expanding my vocabulary in new and exciting ways today.

Bohemian – One of the many words I learned from Terrance Dicks, who would use it to describe the Fourth Doctor in every Target novelisation he ever wrote. According to Dicks, the Doctor wore 'vaguely Bohemian looking garments'; I spent most of my formative years believing that the word meant 'badly fitting'.

Dalekanium – The material from which the perfidious Daleks are made and which is impervious to absolutely nothing.

Entropy – Everybody is going to die. Slowly.

Hiatus – An enforced break and *not* a paid holiday where you sit around on your backside doing nothing for eighteen months.

Homunculus – A homicidal robot with the brain of a pig. This is not exactly correct but it sounds more like what something called a homunculus ought to be than the definition you'll find in the dictionary.

Isomorphic – This has nothing to do with energy drinks. The word explains why the only person who can fly the Doctor's TARDIS is the Doctor. (See James Bond's gun in *Skyfall* for a blatant rip-off of this idea.)

Megabyte Modem – back in 1986, this was a genuine sci-fi term for a futuristically fast internet connection. These days we all have megabyte modems, apart from the perfidious customer complaints department of British Telecom, apparently.

Penultimate – I learned this word not from *Doctor Who*, but from the BBC continuity announcers who would regularly use it when they were introducing the third part of a four-part story. It was a word I came to dislike: the penultimate episode was usually the dullest one.

Perfidious – Deceitful and untrustworthy. I frequently utilised perfidious in school essays to impress the reader and I am still using it today. QED.

Radiophonic – Electronic music that sounds odd and/or disturbing and has been composed in a BBC basement with no windows. See also: Tangerine Dream (page 61).

Robophobia – An inexplicable fear of killer robots.

Serendipity – *Doctor Who*'s excuse for a plot riddled with coincidences.

Timey-wimey – *Doctor Who*'s excuse for a plot that has long since stopped making sense.

Whovian – Please refer to this book's glossary (page 259).

1983

1983 was a brilliant year to be a *Doctor Who* fan. It was the twentieth anniversary of the show, which meant there were lots of things to collect – lavish coffee-table books, *Doctor Who* wallpaper, Dalek Easter Eggs, LPs of the background music, *Peter Davison's Book of Alien Planets*, TARDIS tents, T-shirts, mugs. There was even an academic book written on the subject, entitled *The Unfolding Text* (sample chapter: 'Regeneration: Narrative Similarity and Difference'). Best of all, there was a videocassette of 'Revenge of the Cybermen' starring Tom Baker, but it cost an eye-watering £40 and we didn't have a VCR to play it on.

There were also two very special anniversary events planned for 1983. One was a television special. The other . . .

> **BBC Continuity Announcer:** To celebrate twenty years of *Doctor Who*, BBC Enterprises are holding a *Doctor Who* celebration at Longleat in Wiltshire on Easter Bank Holiday, Sunday 3 and Monday 4 April. It will include stars and characters from the series, and displays of BBC make-up, costumes and visual effects. For further information please send a stamped addressed envelope to BBC Enterprises . . .

Ah, Longleat. I wasn't allowed to go. I wasn't even allowed to send a stamped addressed envelope to the BBC for further information. I was informed in no uncertain terms that we would not be visiting Longleat to help celebrate twenty years of *Doctor Who*, and that was final. I blame my sister. Joanne didn't like *Doctor Who*.* If Mum and Dad had to take one of us to Longleat, we all had to go to Longleat, guaranteeing that at least three-quarters of our party would have a thoroughly miserable time.

Anyway, thanks to my selfish sister, readers of this book are deprived of my memories of Longleat, perhaps *the* pivotal event in the history of *Doctor Who* fandom. Famously, Mark Strickson, the actor who played Adric's replacement on the programme, had appeared on *Saturday Superstore* a few weeks earlier, where he told viewers not to bother buying tickets in advance. 'Just turn up on the day,' he said.

Thanks to Mark, Longleat was a glorious shambles. BBC Enterprises had expected 10,000 fans to show up, so when 40,000 descended on the site, they had to lock the doors and turn people away. The roads around the estate became gridlocked, the makeshift parking area turned into a mud bath, and people were obliged to stand in line for five hours just to get a glimpse of Tom Baker in a tent. The toilets overflowed, the food ran out and the Red Cross had to be called in to airlift small children out of a talk given by Jeremy Bentham on the history of TARDIS design variations.

Sounds awful, doesn't it? Yet I would have sold my own sister to attend. I cannot recall precisely what I did on the

---

* When I began writing this book, I asked my sister to share her memories of *Doctor Who* with me, and this is what she came up with: 'It was too scary. I didn't like it very much. I remember Daleks and Cybermen being in it, if that's any help.' This is why she doesn't feature in this book very much, which is a lucky escape for Joanne, I expect.

afternoon of Sunday 3 April, while the Longleat celebration was happening without me, but whatever it was, I cannot imagine I did it with good grace.

Fortunately, Longleat was not the highlight of *Doctor Who*'s twentieth-anniversary celebrations. That honour fell to 'The Five Doctors', a movie-length multi-Doctor anniversary special that would feature every incarnation of the Time Lord, lots of companions, and loads of monsters. Or if you were me in 1983, the best thing in the world ever.

The build-up to the programme is almost as memorable to me as the episode itself. The hype was unprecedented. Everywhere I looked, people were talking about *Doctor Who* on 'normal telly', even the news. There was a special *Radio Times* cover, a painting of all five Doctors and the Master, which made my heart miss a beat when I saw it in the newsagent's on Southbank Road. Furthermore, I was allowed to buy it – an unheard-of indulgence in a house where the *Radio Times* was normally seen only at Christmas.

'The Five Doctors' was scheduled for transmission as part of BBC One's *Children in Need* coverage. I can remember thinking at the time how nice it was that the Corporation was giving those poor urchins a special episode of *Doctor Who*. That'll cheer them up, I thought, though I confess I was worried that they'd keep cutting away from the Daleks, Wirrn etc. every fifteen minutes so they could show videos of homeless kids sleeping rough on the streets, which would spoil it for me.

In the event, 'The Five Doctors' was everything I wanted it to be and more. OK, the ticker at the bottom of the screen constantly asking for donations got on my nerves after a

while, and Tom Baker wasn't in it very much, but that didn't
seem to matter because he hadn't been gone that long, and
besides, I was much more excited about seeing Jon Pertwee,
Patrick Troughton and William Hartnell together again.
Except it wasn't William Hartnell, it was just somebody who
looked like him. Did I know this at the time? Probably. Did
I care? Not a bit, not when I had Daleks, Cybermen, and a
Yeti to distract me. There was also an amazing new monster,
a sleek, silver killing machine that went by the name of the
Raston Warrior Robot.

Sue: That's scary. I like that. Is this new? It's not an Auton, is
it?

Me: No, it's a new monster.

Sue: I thought so. I wouldn't have forgotten that in a hurry.
Nice arse.

The Cybermen advance on the Third Doctor and Sarah . . .

Sue: Look at that! This is brilliant.

The Raston Warrior Robot makes short work of the Cybermen.

Sue: I love it. I just wish his poles were a bit shorter. I don't
see how he could keep them up his arms like that. There's no
room for them.

Me: Maybe he runs over to his cave to get another spear
and then he runs back to throw it. Because he's quantum
locked, you can't see him when he's running backwards and
forwards.

Sue: Bullshit.

As I've said earlier, 1983 was a brilliant year. I was proud to be a *Doctor Who* fan in 1983. I didn't care if my friends and family weren't interested in the show; if they wanted to miss out on the best television programme ever made, that was their lookout.

At school the Monday after 'The Five Doctors', I was approached by a couple of bigger lads in the playground.

Them: Oi, Perryman! You like *Doctor Who*, don't you?
Me: (*uncertainly*) Yes . . .
Them: That robot with the missiles coming out of his hands . . .
Me: The Raston Warrior Robot?
Them: Yeah, that was pretty cool, actually.

I didn't say I told you so. But I told you so.

I Wasn't a Teenage Whovian

In early 1984 I began to get interested in girls. Perhaps not coincidentally, at around the same time, I stopped watching *Doctor Who* for three years. Final childhood memory of the show: Ingrid Pitt karate-kicking a sea monster called the Myrka in the face. After that . . . nothing. It was becoming increasingly difficult to reconcile the demands of early adolescence with the exact and opposite demands of being a teenage Whovian. At this point in history, being a teenage Whovian was just about the worst thing it was possible to be.

It was the Myrka's fault. *Doctor Who*'s past is littered with ropey special effects and unrealistic monsters, though that had never bothered me before. But there was something arrestingly, preternaturally dire about the Myrka. It was operated by the same men who brought Dobbin the pantomime horse to life in *Rentaghost*, but Dobbin was a far scarier prospect than the floppy green waddlefuck that staggered along a corridor, bumping into the walls, in episode 2 of the story 'Warriors of the Deep'.

The faces of the Doctor and Tegan register fear and horror at the approach of the Myrka. And then after all that build up . . .

Sue: Oh dear.

At least she has something to take her mind off it:

Sue: The door is even worse than the monster. Is it made from marshmallow?
Me: This story's nickname is 'Warriors on the Cheap'.
Sue: I'm not surprised. I don't understand why they need this stupid Myrka thing anyway. They've already got the Silurians and the Sea Devils. How many monsters do they need?

The Doctor throws an ammunition magazine at the Myrka and the blast disorientates the beast.

Tegan: It's blinded!
Sue: They should have blinded the audience. That would have been more merciful.

I was thirteen when I started noticing the female of our species. Up until then, the only girls I'd been interested in were the Doctor's assistants, and that was purely platonic. But then one day – practically overnight – girls stopped being my classmates with the funny clothes, long silly hair and giggly voices, and they became the most alluring creatures on this or any other planet. I'd even been on a date with a girl, if you can call paying for Sharon Wilkins to watch *E.T.: The Extra Terrestrial* at the local ABC fleapit as long as she agrees to sit next to you, a date.

It wasn't just a conspicuous love of *Doctor Who* that was cramping my style. My physical appearance definitely contributed to my failure to make any headway with the opposite sex: my pudding-bowl haircut (cheers, Mum), my squashed boxer's nose (thanks for that, Dad), and my delightfully spotty face (nice one, Curly Wurlys). In addition to which, my Mum, in an effort to save some money, took it upon herself to kit me out in a pair of safety boots that she'd liberated from the factory where Dad worked. The first time I wore them to school, my classmates took it in turns to sing UB40's 'One In Ten' at me. I didn't get it at first, and they had to explain it was because I walked around with a size-one foot in a size-ten shoe. This went on for about a year.

So to recap: comedy shoes, Mr Logic hair, chronic acne and a big squashed nose. Where girls were concerned, I could ill afford the additional handicap of a deep enthusiasm for, and encyclopaedic knowledge of, *Doctor Who*. So *Doctor Who* had to go.

One night in 1984 Amanda Williams, the girl of my dreams, asked me round to her house to watch *Lace*. *Lace* was a very steamy (at least by 1984 standards) television mini-series based on the equally steamy novel by Shirley Conran, the *Fifty Shades of Grey* of its day. It would have been a fantastic opportunity for a quick fumble if Amanda's mum and dad hadn't been sitting in the same room as us. I made it as far as the second ad-break before sheer blushing discomfiture got the better of me and I had to make my excuses and leave. When I got home, I was too embarrassed to tell my mum where I'd been, and she only got the truth out of me when she threatened to take my ZX Spectrum away.

Ah yes, my ZX Spectrum, another reason for abandoning *Doctor Who*. I loved my Spectrum like the girlfriend I didn't have. While Peter Davison was fighting Daleks and the combined uselessness of the BBC prop department, I was copying reams of machine code into a cheap lump of plastic, just so I could play an electronic version of Hangman on it several hours later, instead of using, say, the pencil and paper right next to me. And when I wasn't doing that, I was painstakingly transcribing pages from the *Daily Mirror* newspaper onto our television screen in BASIC, because no one had invented the World Wide Web yet. But most of the time, I just played games on it.

*

And so, time passed. I chased girls and learned the trumpet. I took my O levels and visited America. I graduated from the Spectrum to a Commodore 64. But what I didn't do for the next three years was watch – or even think much about – *Doctor Who*. So I missed Peter Davison's regeneration into Colin Baker, and then I missed Colin Baker.

I didn't really notice that the programme was circling failure in a rapidly decaying orbit and so wasn't much bothered when it was announced that it would be going 'on hiatus' for a year – even the BBC had noticed the show wasn't attracting anything like the audience numbers of yesteryear. I didn't really care about any of it because I had been on hiatus from *Doctor Who* for quite some time myself.

And then everything started to fall apart at home . . .

My parents divorced in 1987. However, instead of going their separate ways, they carried on sharing the house, in different rooms, with individual rotas for the kitchen and the bathroom; it was like a bad eighties sitcom, but without the laughter track. My sister and I continued to live at home, where we would occasionally be used as weapons in our parents' ongoing war of attrition. Christmas that year was especially grim. You don't easily forget sitting down to eat a roast turkey dinner with all the trimmings while your dad cooks beans on toast for himself in the kitchen next door. Happy days.

I now realise that my parents must have been going through a terrible ordeal, but all I can remember about this period of my life is a long string of pointless arguments between me and them. Arguments about failing to return my library books, arguments about money, arguments about curfews, arguments about the number of biscuits I'd left in the barrel; even the colour of the sky wasn't off-limits. On my eighteenth birthday, the whole family had a massive fight because I had forgotten to post a letter for my sister. I can't remember what was in that letter now, or why it was so important, but it must have been a big deal because two days later, after threatening to put my fist through the wall, I packed my bags and left home.

After I left, Mum threw out my red Palitoy Dalek, my Denys Fisher Tom Baker, my Target novelisations, my back issues of *Doctor Who Weekly* and my talking K9 (so it wasn't all bad). She did not do this out of malice, but because all the evidence suggested I had grown out of *Doctor Who* and wasn't coming back.

As so often before, she was only half-right.

Six Things I Love (not including Sue and *Doctor Who*)

Amazingly, I don't just love *Doctor Who* and my wife. There's enough room left in my life to obsess about a handful of other things as well.

1. Tangerine Dream

My friend Jonathan Grove introduced me to the work of the German pioneers of electronic music Tangerine Dream after school one day. Their 1982 album, *White Eagle*, with its hypnotic, futuristic and slightly haunting electronic sound-scapes, sounded like the sort of music Drashigs would dance to. I was hooked and I went straight to Coventry's lending library to borrow everything I could find with their name on it. And there was a lot.

Tangerine Dream have a ridiculously large back catalogue – 137 official albums at the last count. Some of these albums are seminal (the eerie, pulsing polyphony of *Phaedra*, or the majestic, repetitive beauty of *Ricochet*), but most of them aren't. Nevertheless, I have bought and listened to them all. When my time comes, I would like their 1972 double-album *Zeit* played – in full – at my funeral. After a while, although people will still be crying, they will have forgotten why.

2. Cats and Dogs

According to *Ghostbusters*, when cats and dogs live together it's a sure sign of the Apocalypse. But I disagree. Yes, you read me right. *I disagree with* Ghostbusters.

The thing is, cats are great and so are dogs. I love both animals dearly and I couldn't possibly choose between the two, which is why Sue and I own three cats and a dog. With the dog I get adulation, loyalty and affection. With the cats I get passive aggression, a sense of entitlement and suspicion. If I'm feeling sad and lonely, I'll give the dog a fuss; if I'm feeling confident and playful, I'll worry a cat. So what if I can't go on holiday any more, that the house stinks of damp fur, and friends with cat allergies stay away? It's worth it for the silent companionship.

Please note: cats and dogs will also watch *anything* with you on television, even Tess Daly.

3. Jaws

Not only is *Jaws* the best film ever made, you can use it to teach a person everything they need to know about the art of film-making. I know this to be true because that's exactly what I did when I worked as a university lecturer. My students would get hung up on the rubber shark and the film's lack of nudity, but what did they know? Nothing. That's why I made the sonsofbitches watch *Jaws* every week.

The direction, editing, lighting, writing, acting, music – *Jaws* is a masterclass from start to finish. It may have traumatised me as a child, and I'll never swim in the sea or go near a yellow barrel again, but it's more than made up for it. *Jaws* is the perfect film. If you told me that you didn't like *Jaws*, or, even worse, that you hadn't seen it yet, I couldn't, in all good conscience, be your friend.

4. Walking

I know this is what people put on their CVs when they can't come up with an interesting interest, but I've recently taken up walking. It's not that I didn't – or couldn't – walk before, I just decided to take it more seriously. And by seriously, I mean spending over £500 on a waterproof Berghaus jacket and another £50 on a pair of hiking socks.

This passion for ludicrously expensive walking began in 2008, when I was going through my inevitable mid-life crisis. I couldn't afford a sports car (and I can't drive), and a love affair was completely out of the question (as I said, I can't drive), so I climbed Mount Kilimanjaro for charity instead. Why did you climb Kilimanjaro, Neil? Because, like Tangerine Dream's back catalogue, it was there. I trained for a year, which mainly consisted of me walking up and down a country lane for hours on end, sometimes with the dog, listening to the *Risky Business* soundtrack on my iPod.

Walking up Mount Kilimanjaro was relatively easy. As a committed smoker, my lungs weren't bothered by lack of oxygen when our expedition reached the most dangerous stages, which must have annoyed the trail of ultra-fit vegans who were vomiting and fainting behind me. I planted a scale model Cyberman on the summit of the mountain, 20,000 feet up in the air, where, I like to think, impervious to the cold, he is plotting the next great Cyber-assault on we puny humans. Just spare the cats and dogs, OK?

5. My PS3

You remember how I felt about my ZX Spectrum as a teen-ager? Thirty years later, my PlayStation 3 inspires a similarly intense rush of feeling. You can do almost anything with a PS3. You can watch DVDs and Blu Rays with it, you can stream digital photos from your computer to it, you can even use it to play music files other than those by Tangerine Dream.

You can play games on it too. My favourite PS3 game is *Call of Duty*, a first-person shooter that lets you blast complete strangers in the face with an M16 rifle without fear of arrest. You can even taunt them about it later over a Bluetooth headset. Nothing beats the thrill of reducing an American teenager to tears when you interrupt their buzz kill.

My PS3 is very old – its fan stopped working six months ago, which means it now reaches temperatures as hot as the sun, and sometimes, usually in the middle of a film, it sounds as if a Boeing jet engine is idling in the corner of our living room. But I still love my PS3, and it will be a very sad day indeed when I bin it for the forthcoming PS4, which I already know I will without a backwards glance.

6. My friends

I know I may have painted a self-portrait of an isolated loner who can only relate to animals, violent videogames and gory films – neighbours say I am a quiet man who keeps himself to himself – so I think I should also point out that I actually have quite a lot of friends and not all of them are imaginary or from the internet.

In fact my idea of heaven is watching *Jaws* on my PS3 with a cat on my lap, my dog at my feet and my closest friends by my side. When the shark has been blown to smithereens, we will go for a serious walk, where we'll discuss our favourite moments from the film (I like the bit where Chief Brody's son copies him). I won't inflict any Tangerine Dream on them, though, not even Jonathan Grove. I love them all too much for that.

Resurrection

Doctor Who walked back into my life – or I walked back into *Doctor Who* – in October 1988.

Despite a pronounced lack of study and a self-imposed bout of homelessness, I had still managed to pass all my exams and had been accepted into the prestigious grove of academe that was Sunderland Polytechnic.

It was Wednesday night at 7.30 p.m. In the communal television room of my hall of residence, a handful of freshers had gathered to watch *Coronation Street*. Having already spent all my money for that week on subsidised beer, I took a seat, watching *Coronation Street* being marginally better than sitting alone in my room feeling homesick.

But a few minutes later, a denim-clad student in the front row stood up to change the channel. Immediately, another student, this one dressed in a bloodstained rugby shirt, stood up and changed it back. After a brief pause, Denim Man got up and changed it back again, only this time he stayed on his feet and shielded the television's controls with the palm of his hand.

Rugby Man: What the fuck is this?
Denim Man: What the fuck does it look like?
Rugby Man: *TISWAS*, mate. Put *Corrie* back on.
Smart Blazer Man at the back of the room: No, wait.
Leave this on.

Denim Man: Yeah, leave it alone. Let's watch this instead.

'This' was *Doctor Who*. Rugby Man looked furious but sat down, crossed his arms and waited for 'Remembrance of the Daleks' to impress him.

I hadn't seen an episode of *Doctor Who* since the Myrka fiasco four years earlier.

First impressions weren't great. Did this new Doctor – Sylvester McCoy – really have to roll his 'Rs' quite so much? Why was his pullover covered in question marks? You can't be much of an enigma if you have to advertise the fact, surely? Was this impish incarnation of the Time Lord brilliantly unorthodox or a complete prat? To this day I'm still not sure. And then there was the incidental music, which sounded like it had been composed by me on a ZX Spectrum.

When the programme had finished, Rugby Man stood up.

Rugby Man: Well, that was bloody shit.

But Rugby Man was wrong. It was a little bit shit but I enjoyed it. I enjoyed it a lot.

The Doctor is trapped in the cellar with a Dalek. He runs up the stairs . . .

Sue: F**king hell! A Dalek is flying up the stairs!

And then the theme music crashes in.

Sue: *That's* how you do a cliffhanger.

Me: 'Remembrance of the Daleks', part 1 got me back into
Doctor Who. It was the first episode I'd seen in four years. I
saw it by accident, in a halls of residence TV common room
in my first week away from home in the north-east. It was the
cliffhanger that pulled me back in.

Sue: I can see why. It's really good.

Me: If I'd been a child prodigy, and I'd gone to university a
year earlier, I would have walked in on 'Time and the Rani'
instead, which you gave a score of minus 1 to.

Sue: And we wouldn't be sitting here now, doing this.

Me: And I would have no friends or any interests to speak of.
Yeah, 1988 was a big year for me.

Sue: I gave birth to Nicol in 1988 so I think I win that one.

*

The thing about 'Remembrance of the Daleks' is that it had
obviously been made by fans of the show. So not only did
the story feature the Doctor's deadliest enemies, it also took
place in November 1963, the month *Doctor Who* was born.
It even featured the same Shoreditch School from that first
episode, 'An Unearthly Child'. The show was treating its
own history with a slightly stalkerish kind of affection. I was
impressed. The Doctor's new companion, Ace, wasn't bad
looking either.

I bought the latest issue of *Doctor Who Magazine* the very
next day, my first since 1984. I found the issue in the children's comic rack, sandwiched between *Jackie* and *Bunty*.
Kneeling down to rummage through the children's section
of WHSmith felt reassuring somehow. It harked back to a

much less complicated time. I should add that I bought the *Guardian* as well.

The following week in the TV room, I faced down a challenge from Rugby Man, who had brought along a few burly mates to back him up. However, the majority managed to watch episode 2 of 'Remembrance of the Daleks' in a tightly anxious silence, certain that at any minute the opposing group would rush to the front and form a scrum around the TV. As a result, as soon as the episode had finished, I was so relieved I could hardly remember anything about it. But once again, I felt like I had enjoyed it.

I may have fallen under the Doctor's spell again because I was feeling vulnerable and homesick. Maybe I was grasping for a connection to my childhood, something reassuring that I could fall back on because my new student life was stressful and unfamiliar. And it wasn't like I could go home – with Mum and Dad divorcing, home wasn't really there to go to.

Sue: Or maybe you just really liked Daleks?

She's right, of course – some things are better with the Daleks. As soon as my student grant cheque turned up the following week, I bought a second-hand portable colour television, and as a result I saw the Doctor blow up the Daleks' home planet, Skaro, I grappled with the left-wing allegory of 'The Happiness Patrol', I thrilled to the celebratory pomp of 'Silver Nemesis', and tried to forget the surreal postmodernism of 'The Greatest Show in the Galaxy', without having to worry about a challenge from the First XV. And in between all that, I even found time to lose my virginity.

Sue: You just can't help yourself, can you? You want to
tell everyone that it's possible to have sex and watch
Doctor Who at the same time. Well, not at the same
time exactly, but you know what I mean.

When I moved into rented accommodation the following
year, my flatmates couldn't have cared less about *Doctor Who*.
Not that they ever mocked it – that would have required
them giving it a second thought. They didn't even comment
when I hung a poster of Tom Baker and some Sontarans on
the door to my room (a free gift with *Doctor Who Magazine*). They probably thought I was being ironic.

So, alone in my room, I watched *Doctor Who* on my
trusty portable and, without irony, I was happy.

I was happy until I saw 'Ghost Light'.

Broadcast over three weeks in October 1989, 'Ghost
Light' seriously messed with my head. It didn't make any
sense. Not even remotely. Not in a 'this doesn't make any
sense and is therefore complete rubbish' sort of way, but in
a 'this doesn't make any sense in the same way that a David
Lynch film doesn't make sense, so it must be amazing' sort
of way.

'Ghost Light' was made for the video generation. It was
so complex, it had to be watched again, so it could be ana-
lysed, dissected and, well, made sense of, I suppose. And
this would have been great if I'd owned a video recorder,
because analysing *Doctor Who* came naturally to me. I'd
just spent a year being trained in the basics of semiotics
and postmodernism, so 'Ghost Light' came along at exactly the right time. I'd even read *The Unfolding Text* and not

found it particularly silly. I knew it was possible to treat the programme as a serious subject, and if there was ever a story ripe for serious discussion, 'Ghost Light' was it.

Sue: OK, I've definitely got it, now. This isn't a real house. It's a time travelling zoo. They are actually travelling backwards in time and that's why all the dead animals are coming back to life and the ghosts think they exist, when they don't. It's not that hard to work out when you put your mind to it.

And then a few seconds later . . .

Sue: Actually, maybe I'm wrong. I can't get my head around this.
Me: Stop guessing, then.
Sue: I hope this makes sense in the end. That's all I'm saying.

When Ace and Inspector Mackenzie explore the attic, they find Mrs Pritchard and Gwendoline hidden under some sheets.

Ace: They're just toys. They're just Josiah's toys.
Sue: Oh, I get it. They're robots.
Me: Stop guessing!
Sue: OK, I give up. I'm lost. It doesn't make any bloody sense.

But I had no one to share my theories with. Nobody wanted to discuss the mysterious life cycle of Josiah Smith and how the story's over-arching theme of change was a metaphor for the series as a whole. *Not a single person.* Even when I was in a room filled with people who were funded by the taxpayer to talk about nothing but television morning, noon and night, no one wanted to talk about *Doctor Who*, and that included my first serious girlfriend, Candice.

Sue: Did Candice like *Doctor Who*?
Me: We never really talked about it.
Sue: Were you ashamed of it?
Me: A little.
Sue: Oh. I was joking.

I tell a lie. There was this one time when I tried to convince Candice that the Doctor's companion, Ace, was a feminist role model:

Me: *Doctor Who* is very progressive these days. It's
    nothing like it used to be. The companions don't
    scream at the monsters any more – they throw high
    explosives at them instead. In fact, the companion is
    almost as important as the Doctor.
Candice: Sorry, what? I wasn't listening.

I do have one abiding memory of watching *Doctor Who* with Candice, though. Well, perhaps not *with*; she was in the same room as me when the final episode of the classic series was broadcast in December 1989. It was in her flat and she was packing for our Christmas break. In fact, I'm sure I missed large chunks of that episode because Candice kept asking me for my advice about which clothes to take with her. And because I was a good boyfriend, I tried to give her my undivided attention, even when the Doctor and the Master were engaged in a fight to the death just a few inches away from her.

This memory is tinged with sadness, though. Not just because I lost touch with Candice and the last time I heard from her she was well on her way to becoming a multimillionaire. No, it was because when 'Survival', part 3 finished, and Sylvester McCoy's Doctor walked off into the sunset with Ace, I knew they weren't coming back.

Sue: I know you are going to kill me for saying this, but the speech at the end sounded like it was cobbled together at the last minute. Sorry.

Me: I really like it. It's optimistic.

Sue: I can see why you were upset about *Doctor Who* finishing at this point. Just when it was good again. It also explains why you were still banging on about it when I met you. I'll never be a fan, but they shouldn't have stopped it there.

The BBC had really gone and done it. They had cancelled *Doctor Who*.

And yet twenty-six years was a remarkable achievement. The show had left its mark on millions of young viewers and on the wider popular culture: the Daleks, the Cybermen, the TARDIS, long scarves and paper bags full of jelly babies, women running up and down corridors screaming, giant maggots, floppy green waddlefucks . . . and Drashigs. Who could possibly forget the Drashigs?

Doctor Who was over. However, my life was just beginning. It was time to move on. I was twenty years old; perhaps the moment had at last come for me to put away childish things. So I did.

But I put them somewhere I could find them.

Part Two

Fan love is not like real love. Fan love never dies.
— TOM BAKER, THE FOURTH DOCTOR

Sue's Chapter

The first time I met Neil Perry was when he accosted me in a corridor in 1993. He was looking for someone to interview for the university's student radio station, and because someone had let him down at the last minute, he was desperate. 'Do you know anything about road movies?' he pleaded as I passed him on my way to a semiotics seminar. The panicked look on his face made me feel sorry for him – plus I didn't really want to go to the semiotics seminar – so I pretended I was an expert, which is when he first told me that he wanted to kiss me.

I accompanied him to a deserted classroom where he pointed a microphone at me and I told him everything I could about *Thelma & Louise*. He laughed in all the right places and he was overjoyed that he wouldn't need to edit my interview that much. I don't know why this made me feel special but it did. I was getting up to leave when he began bumping his gums about something else, but I wasn't listening to what he was saying. I was much more struck by the *tone* of his voice, the way he laughed, and the passion he had for whatever it was he was banging on about; knowing Neil it was probably something pretentious. I tried to locate his accent. He didn't seem to have an accent. That made him even more interesting.

We got to know each other better over the next few weeks, mainly because we were both heavy smokers. Whenever we stepped out of the edit suites on the first floor of the media department for a cigarette, we seemed to bump into each other. I was finishing my final-year video project, while Neil, who had just been offered the position as a part-time lecturer in video production, was training himself to use the equipment in the room next door. He was very nervous about his new job; understandable really, because he didn't know what he was doing. One day he couldn't get his equipment to work and I had to tell him it was because he'd removed the tab from the VHS tape, which meant he couldn't record over it any more. Seriously, who offered this numpty a job?

We were puffing away one day when Neil proudly told me that he was a 'new man'. That's OK, I thought, I was starting a new life and a new man was just what I was looking for. He was a little younger than me, and a bit of a flirt, but we really hit it off, which is surprising because we had practically nothing in common. I told him that I wanted to make furniture for a living. He told me that he was the only boy at his school who studied Home Economics because the tools in the woodwork block intimidated him. I liked football and tennis; Neil liked to read and talk. I was good with my hands; Neil was good with his head. I was divorced; Neil swore to me that he would never get married. But we made each other laugh and we both knew how to use an edit suite. Well, I did.

He didn't even back off when I told him that I had a four-year-old daughter. I was one of the 1 per cent of single parents studying at a university, and Neil seemed genuinely interested in some of the challenges this posed – he could be a bit patronising with it but he meant well. Most people clammed up or didn't know what to say.

When he told me that his name was actually Neil Perry-*man*, I just laughed. He explained to me that his ex-girlfriend had been a radical feminist and it had been her idea to ditch the patriarchal part of his surname. He also told me that he was a feminist sympathiser; I thought this meant that he felt sorry for feminists. But on the plus side, if a girl could convince him to change his surname, then asking him to leave the toilet seat down shouldn't be a problem.

The thing is, right, Neil was different from every man I'd met up to then. Most of the men in my life had been, let's say, *butcher* than Neil, and that includes my gay brother, Gary. Neil was very earnest when it came to discussing gender politics, which he did a lot, but his heart seemed to be in the right place. Having said that, his hair was a mess. He had a tuft of fuzz poking out of his forehead that was one of the stupidest things I'd ever seen. He looked like a cross between a sex pest and a unicorn. I'd trained to be a professional hairdresser, so every time I spoke to him I wanted to rush at him with a pair of scissors. When I pressed him about it, he told me that he'd woken one day with some chewing gum stuck to his head. But rather than wash it out like any sane, rational, normal person, Neil had cut it out with a razor blade. Every time the hair grew back, he had to hack at it again, but sometimes he'd forget, and when he did forget I couldn't look at him without staring at the ridiculous *thing* sprouting from the top of his head. It was especially noticeable when Neil tied his hair back in a ponytail – it was like he had one ponytail at the back and a second, rival one at the front. I know it sounds silly but I wanted to fix it for him.

That Easter, we went to Whitby together. I was one of a number of students on a university field trip while Neil was there to look after us. This was ridiculous because Neil could barely look after himself. We had supposedly come to the seaside resort to visit some of the locations that featured in Bram Stoker's *Dracula*, which we were studying in one of our classes, but everybody knew that these trips were just an excuse for a very competitive pool tournament in a pub on the quayside. Neil didn't have a partner for the pool tournament, so I teamed up with him before he could find one. Sadly, he couldn't play pool to save his life, but thanks to my misspent youth we still got to the final. I did everything I could to keep Neil away from the table as much as possible, but when it came to the deciding game it was his turn to pot the black. He was snookered behind the opponent's yellow and he had given up the shot as a lost cause before he'd finished chalking his cue. I told him not to be so hasty as I pointed to the cushion at the far end of the table, which set him up for a spectacular trick shot. Not only did Neil hit the black ball, he potted it. Neil has subsequently told me that this was when he fell in love with me; I don't blame him, that shot was sweet. Or maybe it was when I told him I'd been a contestant on *Bullseye*? I've asked him about it for this chapter and he says he can't remember the precise moment because he was so drunk – but he does recall that we accidentally left two of his students behind in Whitby at the end of the night.

So, a raving feminist who looked like Jesus, who couldn't

hold his drink, who was hopeless at pool, and who couldn't count people back onto a bus. Yes, Neil was quite a catch. Even so, I still invited him back to my home in Hartlepool for a meal. I probably would have done it sooner but my parents had been living with me while they rented out their house to some lodgers. But this was the day they were finally moving out, and because my parents were also looking after Nicol that night, we would have the place to ourselves. I definitely wasn't going to introduce Neil to my family until I was sure about him. You know what they say. The gentle, funny, unicorn ones are always the worst.

Christopher Street

As we approached Hartlepool, I was expecting the worst. Sue was a single parent who lived in a council house in the north of England. I imagined burning cars on the pavement, damp on the walls and a kitchen infested with cockroaches. As Sue drove us down a small terraced street, with a beautiful wrought-iron lamppost, exquisitely arranged flowerboxes and neatly polished doors, I didn't think we'd be stopping. Suddenly, Sue jammed on the brakes.

Sue: Oh, no.
Me: What's wrong?
Sue: My parents are here.

I panicked. You met a girl's parents after the fourth, fifth or six hundredth date. You definitely didn't meet the parents if you hadn't slept with their daughter yet. A woman was waving at us from the kerb. This must be Sue's mum. I couldn't put my finger on it but there was something oddly familiar about her. Sue was already out of the car before I could unbuckle my seatbelt.

Sue's mam: Hiya, chuck. The lodgers have decided to stay at ours for a few more weeks so we'll have to move back in again. You don't mind, do you? I told your father that you wouldn't mind. Who's this?

Sue tapped on the passenger window so I reluctantly

stepped out of the car. I couldn't believe it. Sue's mother was the spitting double of Jon Pertwee. All she needed was a crushed velvet cape.

Sue: This is Neil. He's a friend from university.

Sue's mam: That's nice. Anyway, you're just in time. I'm off to the bingo with your father. Give us a fiver and I'll go halves if we win.

We were now joined outside the house by the snooker player Dennis Taylor. This was Sue's dad.

Sue's mam: Nicol's inside and she hasn't had her tea yet. It looks like you could do with some scran inside you as well, young man.

Sue's mother poked my ribcage with her finger. I half-expected her to cry '*HAI!*'

Sue's mam: There's nowt on him.

And with that, Jon Pertwee and Dennis Taylor walked arm in arm towards the Mecca.

*

Sue likes to say that I only agreed to go back to her place that first time because she had cable television. I admit that when I realised the channel UK Gold was broadcasting late-night repeats of *Doctor Who* – episodes I'd never seen before – Hartlepool suddenly seemed as exciting as New Zealand. And I also admit that I placed a blank VHS tape in the pocket of my donkey jacket, just in case, during my stay, the opportunity arose to record an episode or

two. But Sue fascinated me. She was unlike any woman I'd
ever met. She drank pints for a start – not because she was
a feminist, she just drank pints. And yes, I fancied her. I
fancied her like mad. It didn't bother me that she was older
than me, or that she was a single parent. I wasn't looking for a serious relationship; besides, knowing my luck,
I'd almost certainly mess things up long before I met her
daughter.

But it turned out Sue's daughter was waiting for us in the
living room.

Nicol: Do you want a sweet?

This was the first thing that Nicol Malapert Thompson
ever said to me.

Me: No, thank you.
Nicol: Do you want a sweet?

It was also the second, third, fourth and fifth thing she
ever said to me.

Nicol: Do you want a sweet?
Me: No, I'm fine. Really.
Nicol: Do you want a sweet?
Sue: Just tell her that you want a sweet. It's her new
    joke. Humour her.
Nicol: Do you want a sweet?
Me: Yes, Nicol. I would love a sweet. Thank you very
    much.
Nicol: Then suck your feet!

Sue's daughter roared with laughter. I wanted to join in

but how could I? Her so-called joke didn't make any sense. What did the sucking of feet have to do with sweets? It wasn't even remotely funny.

Sue: She's four, Neil. This is Monty Python to a four-year-old.

Nicol clambered onto the sofa, paused for effect, and then yelled at the top of her lungs:

Nicol: DO YOU WANT A SWEET?

Every time Sue led Nicol up the wooden hill to bed, the little comedienne would creep down again a few minutes later; we could hear her giggling as she tiptoed towards the living-room door, preparing to deliver her killer punchline for the umpteenth time. This went on for about an hour, until Sue gave in and Nicol was allowed to sit with us while we watched the *Nine O'Clock News*.

Sue: If you ignore her, she'll fall asleep eventually.
Nicol: What's a Bosnian Muslim, Mam?
Me: I know, why don't we watch a video instead? That might be fun.
Nicol: Yes! *The Little Mermaid!*
Sue: We can't, chick. The video recorder's still broken.

I glanced at the rectangular bulge in my donkey jacket and sighed.

Sue decided to stay with Nicol in her bedroom until she fell asleep. She told me that she'd come back downstairs again later – if she could stay awake. I glanced at the clock on the mantelpiece. It was 11.20 p.m.; *Doctor Who* was due to start in ten minutes. I told her not to worry about me and to get some sleep.

With Sue gone, I urgently flicked through the channels on her cable box – past the German quiz shows and the racy Italian movies – until I found UK Gold. As I waited for part 2 of 'The Curse of Peladon' (Jon Pertwee, season 9, 1972) to begin I could feel butterflies in the pit of my stomach. This was partly because upstairs were two people I instinctively knew were going to become the most important of my adult life, but mostly it was because I'd never seen 'The Curse of Peladon' before.

The Doctor assumes that the Ice Warriors must be the bad guys, and when it turns out that they aren't, Sue isn't very happy, to put it mildly.

Sue: That makes the Doctor a little bit racist, doesn't it? I expect a lot more from him. It should be him convincing everyone else that *they* are prejudiced, not the other way round. That's not good at all.
Me: I don't care what you say, this episode is still very important to me. This is the episode that was playing on UK Gold the first night you brought me home to meet Nicol. It was Tuesday 13 April 1993.
Sue: What was she wearing?
Me: I beg your pardon?
Sue: You can remember which episode of *Doctor Who* was on telly that night, but you can't remember what Nicol was wearing. Why am I not surprised?

It was 11.28 p.m. when the living room door opened again.

Sue: It's only me.
Me: I thought you'd gone to bed.
Sue: Nicol is fast asleep. I've come to keep you
    company. What are you doing?
Me: Oh, nothing. Just watching TV.

Sue knelt on the floor in front of the sofa, obstructing my view of the television.

Announcer: And now on UK Gold, it's time for the Doctor
    to continue his adventure on the planet Peladon . . .

Sue moved closer. As the theme music swelled to its familiar crescendo, she prised the remote from my hand.

Sue: Give that to me. I've just thought of something else
    we could do.

And without breaking eye contact, she aimed it behind her back and switched off the television.

Then Sue is introduced to Alpha Centauri.

Sue: Oh, *purlease!* What's *that* supposed to be?

Sue is struck dumb while her mind attempts to process the image. But she gets there in the end.

Sue: It's a giant penis. (*Pause*) It's a giant green penis in a shower curtain.
Me: Just be thankful Alpha Centauri wasn't pink.

The Collector Gene

In 1975, when Weetabix's *Doctor Who* promotion was over and you couldn't buy the special packets in the shops any more, I threw my Weetabix cards away. I find this thoughtless act quite difficult to write about. My collector gene hadn't been activated yet. However, shortly after this, I found myself strangely drawn to the checklist I'd found on the first page of the Target novelisation of *The Three Doctors*. As I scanned this list of the other titles in the series, something inside me clicked – or cracked. In that moment, I knew with absolute certainty that I would have to possess every single last one of these books, and if I didn't, I would never be whole again.

As I've said elsewhere in this book, there wasn't that much *Doctor Who* stuff around to collect when I was growing up in the 1970s. I now realise that this was probably for the best. If the same amount of merchandise that's available today had been around when I was a boy, I would have bankrupted my parents. Thirty years later, I've almost bankrupted myself.

I suspect that this gene may be hereditary. My mum had a thing for Lladró porcelain and my sister owned one of the biggest collections of Sindy dolls West Coventry has ever seen. In the late 1980s, when *Doctor Who* was coming to an end, I mostly collected records by Tangerine Dream; but I also steadfastly acquired each new Target novelisation – there were now over a hundred – and, of course, old episodes of

Doctor Who on videocassette. As many fans of a certain age will tell you, *Doctor Who* VHS tapes never lined up on the shelf properly. The diamond-shaped logo would move up and down willy-nilly on the spine of the box. Sometimes it was vertical, other times it was horizontal. And for the show's thirtieth anniversary in 1993, the logo changed completely, which only made things worse. *Doctor Who* fans would be entitled to launch a legal claim for compensation against BBC Enterprises for knowingly encouraging chronic hoarding for financial gain, leading in turn to the mental anguish of rampant obsessive-compulsive disorder.

I am currently addicted to collecting a new range of classic *Doctor Who* action figures. These are the toys I so desperately craved as a child but which nobody ever got round to manufacturing for me. If only my younger self could see the carnival of monsters camped out on my bookshelves: fully articulated Zygons, difficult-to-balance Ice Warriors, a string-vested Sea Devil, and the shape-shifting robot Kamelion, who is disguised as the Master, and not the Master at all, despite what it says on the box. Furthermore, these figures look amazing. There are no Gareth Hunt lookalikes here.

Am I being exploited? Say, for example, I want a 'Destiny of the Daleks' Dalek to complete my collection of Daleks. I have to fork out for Tom Baker Doctor at the same time – he's part of the set. Or maybe I've got my eye on a Sontaran spaceship. Just as long as I don't mind paying extra for another Tom – he's part of the set. And then there's the Jagaroth from 'City of Death', and a Krynoid from 'The Seeds of Doom'. That's two more Toms, thank you very much. As a result, I now have more Tom Baker action figures than I have Daleks. I've got Tom in a hat and I've got Tom without a hat. I've got Tom in a burgundy-coloured coat, Tom in an oatmeal coat, and Tom in a waistcoat. I've even got a unique Tom with no head; I think one of our cats ate it.

And then there's the spectre of eBay. Oh, look, some Weetabix cards with the original cereal boxes still intact – a bargain at £76. Before you know it, a trip down memory lane has turned into a time-consuming, money-draining quest for completism – because you are not trying simply to complete a set of books or toys or Weetabix cards, you are trying to complete yourself, to get back to the whole person you were before, as a child, before the obstructions and compromises of adulthood got in the way. And yet, all you are really doing is accumulating a pile of crap, souvenirs of the futility of the quest. Thanks very much, collector gene.

All that being true, if anyone reading this can help me plug the hole in my Target book collection by sending me a copy of *The Wheel In Space*, I'd be eternally grateful. I haven't slept since 1988.

Introducing *Doctor Who*

Sue discovered that I was a functioning *Doctor Who* fan the day I moved in with her and Nicol. Up until then, I'd managed to keep it under wraps.

I didn't bring that many possessions with me when I moved into Christopher Street in July 1993. All I had was a suitcase, two carrier bags and a small collection of cardboard boxes. When I asked Sue if I could store them in her attic, she demanded to know what was inside them. I think she suspected they might be full of pornography.

Before I could explain, Nicol had already tipped the contents of the nearest box onto the floor.

Nicol: What's this?

She was waving a VHS cassette in her hand.

Me: That, Nicol, is a Dalek.

She was holding 'Day of the Daleks' to be precise. (Infuriatingly, the BBC had edited out all the cliffhangers, but there was no need to burden her with that right now.)

Sue: So, how many tapes like this have you got?
Me: Oh, about six boxes.
Sue: But you've only brought six boxes with you.

Given the look on Sue's face as Nicol systematically unpacked my boxes, I wish they had contained pornography.

It would have been easier to explain and marginally less embarrassing. So again I asked Sue if I could store these tapes in her attic. Her reply surprised me:

Sue: I could put some shelves up if you like.

I stared at my tapes, which Nicol was stacking into neat piles on the carpet. I didn't think Sue's shelving suggestion was a trap, but I wasn't sure. Her home was gorgeous, and it was obvious that a lot of time and effort had gone into making it look just so. You didn't need to be an interior designer to know that my distended tape collection would create quite the wrong impression.

Nicol was now arranging my tapes into a single quivering tower of plastic. As I watched her play, I thought about putting away childish things again. If I was going to be a father figure to Nicol, maybe this was an opportunity to make a fresh start. Maybe now was the time to stop worrying about continuity errors in 'Mawdryn Undead'. Maybe the moment had come to grow up.

Sue: Or I could get the stepladders and you can store them in the attic. It's your choice.

Wait a minute, this felt like an increasingly momentous decision. How damp was her attic? I didn't want my tapes to go mouldy up there. And what happened if I decided to buy more? Would I have to hide them in the attic after I'd watched them? That would be a bit weird. Or did it mean that I wouldn't be buying any more tapes? I wasn't thrilled about that, either. And then there was my plan to become a fully formed adult in the near future to consider.

Then it hit me: maybe I could watch these tapes with Nicol while we bonded as stepfather and stepdaughter! I started watching *Doctor Who* when I was Nicol's age and it had never done me any harm, possibly. The Doctor had been a wonderful role model. He taught me to oppose violence (when he wasn't committing genocide) and to embrace justice, equality, curiosity and compassion. In fact, I decided, I would be neglecting my duties as a responsible parent if I *didn't* show these stories to Nicol. When I met her, Nicol was destined to grow up without a Doctor to call her own. But I could fix that. With my help, Nicol would grow up with *seven* Doctors to call her own – and I would just grow up.

Sue put up some shelves.

*

Although I didn't bring that many possessions with me when I moved into Christopher Street, I did have plenty of baggage, the sort of baggage that made it difficult for me to adjust to my new role as a responsible stepfather.

I was too strict with Nicol, for a start. My own parents weren't exactly draconian, but they did have some very clear ideas when it came to boundaries and discipline. As far as I could tell, Nicol was allowed to do anything she liked, whenever she liked. I'm not saying she was spoiled – she wasn't demanding as such – but she did have a ridiculous amount of freedom when it came to what she ate for dinner, what time she went to bed, and, most importantly of all, what she watched on TV.

One night Nicol and I had an argument about something or other – I forget the details now but it probably had something to do with her not eating her vegetables – and in a spectacularly childish move I removed the plug from her television set to teach her a lesson. Sue wasn't very happy with me when she came home to find her daughter in tears because she couldn't watch her favourite movies all night. Sorry, Nic.

However, let's take a look at Nicol's videos when I moved in, shall we? *The Breakfast Club, Sixteen Candles, Ferris Bueller's Day Off, Pretty in Pink* and *Weird Science*. Yes, Nicol was a John Hughes junkie – and there's nothing wrong with that – I just didn't think these movies were suitable for a four-year-old child.

> **Me:** Have you actually seen *The Breakfast Club*, Susan? Everyone takes drugs in it. *Ferris Bueller* glorifies truancy, for God's sake. Is this really the kind of film that Nicol should be watching at this impressionable age? I'm just relieved that she hasn't got a copy of *She's Having a Baby*.
>
> **Sue:** She has. She's lent it to next-door.
>
> **Me:** Look, Nicol shouldn't be watching television at this hour. She should be asleep. And if she is going to watch something, it should something more appropriate. She's four, not fourteen. *Weird Science* is not for kids.
>
> **Sue:** So what do you suggest? Wait . . . Don't tell me. One of your *Doctor Who* videos, I suppose?
>
> **Me:** Why not? There's never any teenage pregnancies in *Doctor Who*. And you never see anyone taking drugs.

(This isn't strictly true. In 'The Talons of Weng-Chiang'

one of the story's villains chases the dragon in an opium den; in 'Nightmare of Eden', the aliens turn out to be an addictive narcotic; and in 'Snakedance', the Fifth Doctor enjoys a hallucinatory trip after being bitten on the wrist by a snake. Also, the Sixth Doctor's hideous multicoloured frock coat can only have been dreamed up by someone on drugs. Ketamine, probably.)

While Sue was busy rewiring Nicol's television, I studied my VHS tape collection for the perfect story to show her daughter. With Sue calling me upstairs, I instinctively grabbed 'Day of the Daleks'. This was the tape that Nicol waved at me the day I moved in with her. I took this for a sign and hoped for the best.

Sue and her daughter were cuddling each other on Nicol's bed when I joined them. Simple Minds were belting out 'Don't You Forget About Me'.

> **Sue**: Listen, Nicol. Neil has something he wants to share with you. He thought it would be nice if you watched something together for a change. Something you haven't seen before.

I dropped the VHS tape into Nicol's lap.

> **Me**: It's 'Day of the Daleks'. It's very good.
> **Nicol**: I'm watching *The Breakfast Club*.
> **Me**: *The Breakfast Club* has finished. Look, it's the credits.
> **Nicol**: I want to watch it again.
> **Sue**: Why don't you watch something else with Neil? You never know, it might be fun.

Nicol: But I want to watch *The Breakfast Club*.
Me: It's OK. Forget it. It doesn't matter.

I headed for the bedroom door.

Sue: I know! Why don't you watch *The Breakfast Club*
together instead?

*

The next day, Nicol sidled up to me while I was chopping
potatoes in the kitchen. When she tugged at my sleeve, I
almost sliced my index finger off.

Nicol: Can I watch *Doctor Who* with you tonight, Neil?
Me: Your mum sent you in here to ask me that, didn't
she?
Nicol: Yes.
Me: You don't have to do this, Nicol. Honestly, you
don't.
Nicol: What is *Doctor Who* anyway?
Me: You really want to know?
Nicol: Yes. Tell me.
Me: Well, it's about a man – well, alien – who can travel
through space and time. He's called the Doctor . . .
Nicol: Doctor Who.
Me: No, *Doctor Who* is the name of the programme.
Nobody knows what the Doctor's real name is.
Nicol: (*giggling*) Don't be silly. What's his name? Tell
me.
Me: I honestly don't know. It's a mystery.
Nicol: Do you find out at the end?

Me: At the end of this story? No.

Nicol: Can we watch the one where we do find out?

Me: I haven't got that one. Anyway, the Doctor has a
   spaceship called the TARDIS, which stands for Time
   and Relative Dimension in Space. It looks like a
   police telephone box . . .

Nicol: What's a police telephone box?

Me: It's a telephone box that only policemen can use.

Nicol: Like a post box?

Me: No, it's a lot bigger than a post box and it's blue.
   Look, it doesn't matter. The TARDIS exterior isn't
   even in this one.

Nicol: I want to see it.

Me: Look, why don't we just watch this story first. Trust
   me, it's great.

I pressed Play on her top-loading VCR and Nicol crossed
her arms and waited for 'Day of the Daleks' to impress her.

Nicol: Who's that?

Me: That's the Doctor.

She shouted with laughter.

Nicol: Big nose!

Me: Don't you think he looks like your grandma? Please
   don't tell her I said that.

The episode begins with a terrorist from the future
attempting to assassinate a political figure from the past.

Nicol: Who's that?

Me: That's a guerrilla.

Nicol: Don't be silly! That's a man! A gorilla is a big
    monkey. Who's he?
Me: That's a politician.
Nicol: What does that mean?
Me: It doesn't matter. Look, this is the Brigadier . . .
Nicol: That's a silly name.

Three minutes in and she's already beginning to fidget.

Nicol: I'm bored. Nothing's happening.
Me: Look, the Doctor is trying to fix a bit of the
    TARDIS.
Nicol: Why is it broken?
Me: Well, it's complicated. You see, the Doctor comes
    from a planet called Gallifrey and he's been a very
    naughty boy, so his parents took his toy away from
    him because he wouldn't listen to his betters and do
    as he was told. Ring any bells? Anyway, they basically
    took the plug off his TARDIS and now he can't go
    anywhere.
Nicol: That's *boring*.
Me: Not really. Lots of monsters come to Earth, so he
    doesn't really need his TARDIS any more.
Nicol: So why is he fixing it?

I quickly change the subject:

Me: That's Jo Grant. Isn't she lovely?

*

I knew it was hopeless when Nicol started to kick the covers
off her bed, a sure sign she was restless. Another sign was she

had stopped asking questions. She didn't even ask me if the ape-like Ogrons were gorillas.

Maybe Nicol was too young to appreciate *Doctor Who* after all. And it was very late; she was probably tired. I told myself that it wouldn't have mattered what we were watching that night, she would have reacted exactly the same way. She just needed a good night's sleep. And besides, Nicol shouldn't be watching television at this hour anyway.

I'd really hoped to see Nicol's eyes light up with wonder and joy that night – the same wonder and joy I experienced when I encountered *Doctor Who* for the first time. What I wasn't expecting was she'd have that joyful look on her face when I offered to switch *Doctor Who* off. We were only ten minutes into the first episode; she didn't even get to see a Dalek.

I offered to read *The Little Mermaid* to her but Nicol declined. As I headed downstairs again to join Sue, I heard *The Breakfast Club* rewinding in her VCR. She was still watching it when I went to bed an hour later.

*

Once the shelves were up, my video cassettes became part of the furniture, but my girlfriend proved as adept as her daughter at ignoring *Doctor Who* and my clumsy attempts to insinuate it into our unmarried life. Whenever I'd suggest it might be fun to watch, say, 'The Seeds of Death' or 'The Ambassadors of Death' or 'The Robots of Death' or even the comparatively light-hearted 'City of Death' together, the answer was always 'no'.

Occasionally I would ask her for her memories of the programme.

Sue: We didn't watch the BBC when I was growing up.
I lived in an ITV house. Sport was the only exception.

Me: So you never watched *Doctor Who*?

Sue: Oh, I knew what *Doctor Who* was. Everybody did.
One of the Doctors had a scarf.

Me: What about Jon Pertwee?

Sue: Oh, I definitely remember him. He was Worzel
Gummidge. The scarecrow.

Me: You don't remember Jon Pertwee in *Doctor Who*?

Sue: I know Jon Pertwee was one of the Doctor Whos,
but I didn't watch it. How many more times do I have
to tell you this?

Me: You were fourteen when Tom Baker took over.

Sue: You won't let this go, will you? Tom Baker was the
one with the scarf. I'm not completely stupid.

Me: Can you name any of the actors who played the
Doctor before Tom Baker?

Sue: I don't know. Jon Pertwee? How many other
Doctors were there?

Me: Two.

Sue: Hold on. The old feller with the white hair . . .
Peter Cushing. And whatshisname, that little feller . . .
(*triumphantly*) Charlie Drake!

Me: Patrick Troughton!

Sue: Well, he looked like Charlie Drake.

Seriously, what was the point in going out with an older
woman if she couldn't remember 'The Web of Fear' – and
even if she did remember it, thought the lead actor battling
Yeti on the London Underground was Charlie Drake?

Eventually, Sue gave in and agreed to watch one of the all-time classic *Doctor Who* adventures with me, the gritty and intelligent 'Genesis of the Daleks'.

Sue: It's really good, this. Proper scary. I can almost understand why you like this programme. Are all the Tom Baker stories as good as this one?

It would be another eighteen years before she found out. In the meantime, my new female housemates and I soon settled into a domestic routine which suited all of us. I kept watching, reading about and obsessing over every tiny detail of *Doctor Who*. And they left me to it.

Hiatus 2: This Time It's Personal

I would like to reassure *Doctor Who* devotees that there
are no plans to axe *Doctor Who*. There may be a little
longer between this series and the next than usual, but I
very much hope that it will continue to be as successful
in the 90s as it has been for the last twenty-six years.
Peter Cregeen, BBC Head of Series, 1989

The BBC first tried to axe *Doctor Who* in 1985. Back then,
the outcry from fans and the popular press – not to mention 'Doctor in Distress', a terrible protest record featuring
Bobby G from Bucks Fizz; 'Listener in Distress' would have
been more accurate – forced the BBC to capitulate, and
what had originally been intended as an irreversible cancellation was instead converted to an 'eighteen-month hiatus',
which is where I first heard that deathly word.

So when, in 1989, the BBC decided to cancel the show
again, they did it quietly. There was nothing to worry about,
they told us. *Doctor Who* wasn't dead, it was just resting.
This was the line repeatedly trotted out by the perfidious
Peter Cregeen, the BBC's Head of Series, when he was asked
about the show's future. His words are etched on my memory like a Dear John letter from an ex-girlfriend.

In truth, this hiatus was intended to be an indefinite one,
the sort of hiatus from which no Time Lord returns. There was
no official cancellation announcement this time. There were

no protests, no petitions and, mercifully, no one contacted Bobby G. The tabloids weren't interested in headlines about a TV show that was having some time off, and the viewing public didn't seem to care that the only time they saw *Doctor Who* these days was via a clip on an episode of *Telly Addicts*.

And so a great darkness fell upon the land.

Then in 1993 came the news we'd been waiting so desperately for: *Doctor Who* was coming back. There was going to be a one-off special called 'The Dark Dimension'. It sounded fantastic. Apparently, all the surviving Doctors were going to be in it – even Tom Baker had agreed to show up this time – and they would unite against an army of classic monsters: Daleks, Cybermen, Autons, the lot. If everything went well and the ratings were good, I thought, the BBC would have no choice but to revive *Doctor Who* as a proper series. There was still a chance that Nicol would grow up with a Doctor to call her own.

But two months later, the BBC abruptly aborted the project, citing budgetary concerns. I was livid. In fact, I got so worked up about it I wrote a protest letter. I typed it out on Sue's second-hand Olivetti and I sent it to a semi-professional fanzine called *DreamWatch Bulletin* (formerly *Doctor Who Bulletin*). By semi-professional I mean the magazine was printed on glossy paper and you could buy it in specialist shops like Forbidden Planet, but also that it was a not wholly professional enterprise. *DWB* was full of inaccuracies, insane theorising and wild, libellous rumour and in some ways can be said to have invented the concept of *Doctor Who* online forums several years before the rise of the internet.

Reading this letter now, I think I must have been going through Kübler-Ross's five stages of grief.

It was nice while it lasted but it's time to face up to the inevitable: Doctor Who *is dead.*

Clearly I skipped the first stage of grief – denial – fairly quickly.

The final nail in the coffin was unceremoniously hammered in on Friday 11 July by the faceless BBC Board of Management. They have acted like an evil, selfish parent who have (sic) taken away our present from under the tree on Christmas Eve.

Or a plug off a TV, eh me-in-1993? This is clearly anger, the second stage, expressed in grammatically uncertain terms. But I has learnt a lot since then.

How long can a fan-based network sustain itself with no new product to dissect and discuss?

Oh, about sixteen years, give or take.

What exactly is the point in petitioning the BBC? First we get Eldorado *and now this debacle, what makes you think anything will change? It's over. No amount of post mortems will change this sad fact, and no witch-hunts will result in a U-turn. It will merely create new false hopes to be stamped upon. I know when it's time to get out of this vicious circle, and that time is now.*

Hmm, the anger here is spinning out of control. Not only do I really have it in for *Eldorado*, I seem to be trapped in a vicious circle of mixed metaphors from which no amount of post mortems will result in a U-turn.

Maybe it was Colin Baker's revenge against a corporation that had betrayed and humiliated him and then had the audacity to ask him for his co-operation in such a project; maybe it was a cunning plan on behalf of Alan Yentob and the BBC to shut the fans up once and for all; maybe the script was crap; maybe, maybe, maybe . . .

Welcome to the third stage: bargaining. If only, if only, if only . . .

This is all academic. I know when I am beaten.

Stage four: depression, leading to . . .

I know when it's time to move on.

Finally, I have reached the acceptance stage. But acceptance came at a cost:

My attention has now turned to Star Trek: The Next Generation, *not because it is a better show but it does have one thing going for it – new episodes.*

OK, that's quite enough of that. I then go on and on about how wonderful *Star Trek: The Next Generation* is for several pages, but I can't bring myself to reprint it here.

Sue looked over the letter before I posted it.

Sue: You're very passionate about this, aren't you?
Me: It drives me up the wall. *Doctor Who* makes more
    money in overseas sales and merchandising than it

costs to produce. The BBC's decision not to make
Doctor Who doesn't make any financial sense!

Sue: You should put that in your letter instead of all that
Star Trek rubbish.

*

I can't remember now if the *Children in Need* special
'Dimensions in Time' was always planned as a fundraiser
for homeless children or whether it was intended to pla-
cate hopeless fans who had had their spirits crushed by the
'Dark Dimension' debacle – two equally worthy causes, in
my view. However, when I learned that all the Doctors and
his companions would be teaming up to face the cast of
EastEnders in a time-warped Albert Square – in 3D, no less
– my heart sank. I just hoped that the homeless kids would
get something out of it, because the fans' new false hopes
were surely about to be stamped upon. Again.

In order to view 'Dimensions in Time' in 3D, you needed
a special pair of 3D glasses; and in order to get hold of the
3D glasses, you had to buy a copy of the *Radio Times*. Of
course, I stupidly decided to leave it to the day of the broadcast before trying to obtain a pair, by which time the special
Radio Times had sold out and there were no glasses to be had
anywhere – not at the newsagent's, not at the supermarket
and especially not at the opticians. ('I don't suppose you sell
3D glasses as well, do you . . . ?') With less than half an
hour to go before the transmission – just as I was consider-
ing making my own specs out of a couple of Quality Street
wrappers – Sue disappeared. She returned twenty minutes
later with a pair of 3D glasses and no *Radio Times*.

Sue: I knocked on every door in the street until I found someone who would part with a pair. I had to give them two quid for the glasses and I've promised to donate at least another fiver to *Children in Need*. Here you go.

Me: But what about you and Nicol? We need three pairs of glasses if we're going to watch it together.

Sue: Don't push it, Neil.

Sue returned to the living room when it was all over.

Sue: Why are you crying?

Me: I'm fine. I just saw a sad film about some poor homeless kids. It really brings it home to you in 3D.

Suddenly there's a flash and then Ace finds herself in the East End of London with the Sixth Doctor. There's a lot for Sue to process and the penny only drops when . . .

Sue: Gita! It's Gita and Sanjay from *EastEnders*!

Me: Finally, she gets it.

Another flash and the Sixth Doctor and Ace are replaced by the Third Doctor and . . .

Sue: That's Bonnie Langford. I need a drink when Bonnie is on screen.

Romana: Have you seen the Doctor?

Phil Mitchell: Doctor Legg is the only doctor round here, love.

Romana: Doctor who?

Sue: I bet Steven Moffat loves 'Dimensions in Time'. It's timey-wimey and it's got his favourite joke in it.

Later on the Seventh Doctor is joined by . . .

Sue: K9!
Me: Yes, but which version?
Sue: Oh, f**k off.
The Seventh Doctor: I'm trying to overload the Rani's computer, enhance the power of the time tunnel to pull her TARDIS in and not me.
Sue: Does anybody actually understand this? Sober, I mean.
Me: No.
Sue: What a shambles. The BBC should have lost the rights to make *Doctor Who* when that went out. No wonder you were in such a foul mood that week. You must have found it really painful to watch. Oh well, *Doctor Who* came back in the end and everything worked out fine. And it could have been a lot worse. It could have been *Eldorado*.

'Dimensions in Time' was so mind-bendingly, humiliatingly dreadful the BBC didn't dare broadcast the whole thing in one go. They were probably worried that *Children in Need* viewers would start withdrawing their pledges. The second part was transmitted the next day, in the middle of *Noel's House Party*. Even Noel Edmonds – a man whose career was built on his seeming *unembarrassabilty* – introduced the segment and then turned his head away in shame. It was the final proof that the BBC didn't just dislike *Doctor Who*; they were actively seeking to destroy it.

As if by way of an apology, BBC One broadcast a hastily commissioned documentary on the night of *Doctor Who's* thirtieth anniversary in November 1993 – 'Thirty Years in the TARDIS', which was actually surprisingly good. But with no new episodes in sight, it felt like I had been invited to attend a posthumous birthday party for a murdered relative by the very person who had killed them. The programme concluded with a tight-lipped Alan Yentob teasing a possible comeback for the Doctor. But I didn't believe him. Thanks to the BBC, *Doctor Who* had become the thing that nobody liked any more.

Except for the fans. If the Doctor wasn't going to return to television any time soon, he would have to survive in other media – comics, books, videos. This wasn't anything new for *Doctor Who*. From the very beginning the character has appeared in spin-off comic strips – *TV Action*, *Countdown* etc. – and this tradition still continues in the official *Doctor Who Magazine* to this day. But the comic strips were just one strand. The most exciting development was the launch of a brand-new series of books called the New Adventures.

When Virgin's publishing arm ran out of Target novelisations to reprint in 1990, and with no new novelisations on the horizon thanks to the programme being 'rested', the company decided to plug the gap with a series of original novels. These novels were called the New Adventures and they were, to all intents and purposes, the continuing exploits of the Seventh Doctor and Ace, no longer limited by budget or special effects. Described as being too broad and deep for the small screen, they certainly lived up to the claim, with many of them containing strong violence, swearing and even sex, the last of which, for many readers, demanded the biggest imaginative leap of all.

But these adventures weren't constrained to the printed page. Industrious fans with access to increasingly affordable video technology managed to convince *Doctor Who* cast members to play subtly different versions of themselves for direct-to-VHS releases. So, Sixth Doctor Colin Baker took on the role of a pan-dimensional hero called the Stranger, while Nicola Bryant, best known for playing his companion Perpugilliam Brown, portrayed Miss, erm, Brown. The BBC's lawyers were naturally suspicious, showing that when it came to protecting their intellectual property, perhaps the corporation did care about *Doctor Who* after all. However, the fans also knew that the BBC didn't own the whole Whoniverse. They didn't own the rights to the Daleks, for a start; Terry Nation's agent was famous for driving a hard bargain whenever the programme wanted to use them. There were other cheaper monsters and characters not owned by the BBC, too. All of a sudden, if you wanted to make a sequel to 'Terror of the Zygons', say, and you could raise the funds, there was little to stop you except your own lack of competence and talent. And, as it turned out, this was easily overcome.

The result was a series of amateur fan videos like *Wartime*, which saw U.N.I.T.'s Sergeant Benton confront his haunted past; *Shakedown*, which featured Sontarans battling the cast of *Blake's 7*; and *Downtime*, where the Brigadier took on the Yeti for the third and final time. And these videos didn't have to include the words 'Time' or 'Down' in the title, either. For example, in *The Airzone Solution*, four actors who have played the Doctor team up for an edgy eco-thriller, although it's probably best remembered – or forgotten – for the bit where Colin Baker climbs into bed with Nicola Bryant for a quick fumble, something that definitely never happened in 'Attack of the Cybermen', though no less frightening.

Sue: So what are you putting me through tonight?

Me: Tonight I'm going to give you a taste of how desperate *Doctor Who* fans were in 1995.

Sue: A desperate *Doctor Who* fan. Sounds wonderful.

Me: So I'm going to show you a fan film.

Sue: Haven't I suffered enough?

Me: The fans grew tired of waiting for the BBC to bring *Doctor Who* back, so they did it themselves. Fans are like that.

Sue: But how could they afford it? Kickstarter didn't exist then. They must have had more money than sense.

These videos were not very good – some of them were barely legal – but none of them were as shameful as 'Dimensions in Time'. The books, comics and videos were produced by the fans for the fans. *Doctor Who* was the thing that nobody liked, least of all the BBC; nevertheless we cherished it, we nurtured it, and we ultimately spent a fortune on it. But it was worth every penny because, for better or worse, *Doctor Who* belonged to us now.

Which is when the BBC decided to take it back.

Before We Get to the 1996 TV Movie, Six Other Things I Hate

1. Mayonnaise

Of course I hate the things that most people hate – injustice, world hunger, the Liberal Democrats – but there is a special place in hell reserved for mayonnaise. 'Mayo' is the bane of my existence. In fact, I have thought about forming a lobby group called 'Hold the Mayo' to get it outlawed. It's not just that I don't like it; the horrible gunk is *everywhere*. Imagine that you fancy a sandwich but you don't want it smothered in liquefied egg. Now look at the choices you have left. If you're lucky, you might find a packet of Simply Ham at the back of the chiller. The sandwich company is basically saying, if you don't like mayonnaise, you can't be trusted with anything else – tomatoes, say, or a little bit of salad. It's an outrage.

I appreciate this may seem rather trivial to those of you who are fighting homophobia or racism – or who don't buy your sandwiches from the all-night garage – but as far as I'm concerned, this blatant pro-mayo discrimination is, to quote Bender from Matt Groening's *Futurama*, the worst kind of discrimination: the kind against me.

2. New Year's Eve

I hate New Year's Eve. I feel like it's my duty as a human being to at least try to have a good time. But it's freezing cold outside; you can't book a taxi; all the decent parties sold out months ago; post-Christmas ennui is in full effect; and on the stroke of midnight, drunks will attempt forcibly to kiss you on the lips. If I want that, I can get it at home. And all that palaver to usher in the gloomiest month of the year.

The worst New Year's Eve of all was Millennium Eve. We hadn't planned on going out that night – I thought I'd be too busy avoiding planes dropping out of the sky to party like it was 1999 – but when I realised that a computer bug wasn't going to bring civilisation to its knees after all, I felt we ought to at least make an effort to mark the big occasion. We had plenty of bottled water and tinned fruit under the stairs but no alcohol. So we got into Sue's car and headed for Newcastle, thinking we might see some fireworks. No such luck. Tickets for the Quayside had sold out weeks ago so we stood shivering on the outskirts of the city with the rest of the cheapskates, staring up at an empty sky. It was cold, overcrowded and anti-climactic, but cold, overcrowded and anti-climactic in a special, once-in-a-millennium sort of way.

The most memorable moment was when, on the stroke of midnight, someone in the crowd proposed to their girl-friend. I'll never forget his words to her after she'd slapped him across the face: 'It'll be another thousand years before I ask you again, you bitch.'

3. Michael Bublé

Sue loves Michael Bublé. She won't stop playing his sani-tised, soulless pop at me, no matter how much I plead with her to turn it off. Everywhere I turn, he's there: in the car, in the kitchen, the garden, the bathroom and, if Sue had her way, our bedroom too. The chubby-cheeked crooner has been compared to Frank Sinatra by people who don't know what they are talking about. Bublé is to Sinatra what a Care Bear is to a grizzly, only even more irresistibly punchable. Given half a chance, I would cheerfully smack him in the face myself. I just haven't met him yet.

4. Jaws 4: The Revenge

The tagline for the third sequel to the best film ever made is: 'This time it's personal'. When I saw it – alone – in Coventry's ABC cinema in 1987, that's exactly how it felt to me: personal. In much the same way that finding out someone had eaten your cat with mayonnaise would feel personal.

Jaws 4 is so bad it makes *Jaws 3* look like *Jaws 2*. The sequels prior to this one had been exponentially dire; surely the bottom of the yellow barrel had been scraped with the previous film, which had been made in 3D. But no. The movie begins when Chief Brody dies – off-screen – from a cardiac arrest, a clogged artery succeeding where two giant sharks had failed. Nonetheless, his widow Ellen blames the Great White for her husband's demise, convinced that it is pursuing a bloody vendetta against her and her grieving family. (NB This is the actual plot. It grows less credible from there.)

The film is set in the Bahamas and stars Michael Caine as a cheeky, Michael Caine-ish airline pilot. Caine is fond of saying that although he knew *Jaws 4* was going to be a terrible film, he very much enjoyed the house it built. Of course, as a *Jaws* completist – and notwithstanding the fact that I hate it – I own three copies of *Jaws 4*, as part of various VHS and DVD box sets, which means every time I buy another copy, I am probably helping redecorate the bathroom of that house. I am literally a hostage to Michael Caine's fortune.

5. Smoking

I smoke a pack of Marlboro Lights every single day. If I'm stressed, which is most of the time, I'll break open a second pack. I *hate* the fact that I'm writing this paragraph with a cigarette dangling from my lips. What I hate even more is that if you took this fag away from me, I'd curl up in the corner of the room and cry. I'm going to stop smoking just as soon as I finish this book. No, that is a lie. Who am I kidding? I'm going to smoke until I die and then be cremated so someone else can inhale me. You know, to give something back.

The problem is I desperately need the cigarettes to help me cope with . . .

6. Other People

Yes, I know I said I loved other people elsewhere in this book but I was talking about my wife and my friends. It's everybody else I have a problem with – and not just the mayonnaise-loving, New-Year-revelling *Jaws 4* apologists, either. Take you, for instance, reading this book. You're all right I suppose, though the chances are you probably like *Doctor Who*, which makes you a bit suspect in my eyes. Don't you think you ought to grow out of it? I bet you loved *The TV Movie* too, didn't you? People like you always do. Don't you get it? *The TV Movie* is shit! It's SHIT!

I need a cigarette.

1996

It's 9.30 a.m. and I am on the horns of a dilemma. Not for the first time this morning, I let my fingers play across Paul McGann's handsome, shrink-wrapped face.

Am I dreaming? Is *Doctor Who* really coming back? Did the BBC really manage to negotiate a multimillion-dollar US co-production deal, and did they really cast one of the best actors of our generation – and Sylvester McCoy – to play the Doctor? And if I wanted to, could I really remove this videocassette from its box, slide the tape into my VCR, and watch a brand-new episode of my favourite TV show for the first time in six and a half years, right now?

No, I couldn't. Not yet.

Not until Sue gets home.

Her parting words to me as she left for work this morning:

Sue: Whatever you do, don't watch it without me.

I was down at Woolworths before they opened. I didn't want to run the risk that the shop would be swamped with eager fans like me and they might sell out of stock, and, sure enough, a small crowd had already gathered when I got there. But as it happened, I was the only one queuing outside the doors who didn't work for Woolworths. Copies of the tape hadn't even made it to the shelves yet, and the staff suggested I go for a walk while they hunted through their stock room. I declined. After a tense fifteen-minute wait – still no other fans around – I returned home, £12.99 poorer, to begin the longer, no less agonising wait for Sue.

I studied the box again. Paul McGann was wearing a stiff-looking wig and a frock coat. Well, there was no shame in that. After all, William Hartnell had worn a wig and a frock coat too. (Jon Pertwee's bouffant and Tom Baker's curls only looked like wigs.) I scanned the blurb on the back of the box again, just in case I'd missed something vitally important the seventeen times I read it previously, and I thought about removing the shrink-wrap and just staring at the cassette for a bit.

Sue: Whatever you do, don't watch it without me.

I decide to leave the shrink-wrap alone.

To be honest, I was anxious about this new *Doctor Who*. The omens weren't good. And it wasn't just the wig and the frock coat – everything about the BBC's intended reboot of the franchise seemed slightly off. They hadn't even come up with a proper title for it, not 'Return of the Doctor' or 'The Deadly Regeneration' or anything like that, just *The TV Movie*. Worse still, the movie had been shown in America and Canada already. I mean, seriously, *Canada*? I wouldn't have minded so much if the BBC had released the VHS a week earlier, like they'd promised to, but last-minute editing delayed its release until it eventually went on sale just a few days before it was due to be broadcast on BBC One. Or as Sue put it:

Sue: Why not save your money and wait for it to turn up on the telly for free?

Because that's not how we Whovians roll, as no one said in 1996.

Furthermore, this unexpected delay severely disrupted my dream of sharing the return of *Doctor Who* with Sue.

This had been the original plan: because I couldn't drive, Sue would take me to the special midnight opening at HMV in Newcastle. I would queue from 9 p.m. and she would visit her brother, Gary, who lived in nearby Gateshead. She would return for me at 12.15 a.m. and we would be home by 1 a.m., and we would watch the first new *Doctor Who* to be produced since its cancellation in 1989 together. And it would definitely be brilliant.

It didn't turn out that way. Instead, the tape's release got pushed back to a date when Sue was working, and the only midnight opening still scheduled to take place was down in London; I did ask Sue if it might be possible for her to drive me to the capital in her battered Renault Clio, but her answer was both unequivocal and peppered with four-letter words, none of which were 'okay', 'sure' or 'good idea'.

So here I am. It's 10 a.m. and there are another eight hours to wait until Sue gets home.

Sue: Whatever you do, don't watch it without me.

What did Sue mean by that, I wondered. Did it mean she was as excited about *Doctor Who*'s imminent return as I was? Was her display of total indifference in the weeks leading up to its release just a clever smokescreen? Was it possible she was losing as much sleep over the return of the show as I was? Or – and this was much more likely – was she taking the piss? If she was taking the piss, I could go ahead and watch it without her, no harm done. But what if she wasn't taking the piss? What if it was a sincere romantic gesture on her part?

Hmm. Maybe it was possible to re-seal shrink-wrap with wood glue or something. Or maybe I could return to Woolies to buy a second copy. If I watched that one instead, I'd still have a pristine, shrink-wrapped tape in my hands when she returned. Money was tight, though, and even if I could afford two copies, could I really go three days without a cigarette? Plus, while we watched it together, I would have to pretend that I hadn't already seen it earlier in the day, probably several times, and feign spontaneous surprise or suspense or delight at this new Doctor's adventures, and that seemed wrong somehow – like cheating.

Behind his plastic prison, Paul McGann sure looks tempting. But it's no good. I can't do it.

I want to watch it with Sue.

*

My heart skips a beat when I hear Sue's car pull up outside just after 7 p.m. In just a few minutes we will be watching new *Doctor Who* together. Thankfully, Nicol is staying at a friend's tonight. I wasn't that upset to learn she'd miss Paul McGann's debut as the Doctor as she'd only spend the evening throwing salt and vinegar hula-hoops at his face, because right now she's only eight.

I wave the tape in Sue's face as she takes her coat off. Its shrink-wrap is still unblemished, except for a very small tear where I'd rubbed Paul's face a little *too* hard.

Me: I haven't watched it yet. Look, it's still in its
wrapper.

Sue: That's nice, love, I thought you'd have worn it out
by now.

Me: But . . . but you told me to wait for you.

Sue: I was joking, you idiot. But it was very sweet of
you to wait . . . Hang on a minute – you didn't buy
two copies, did you?

Me: The thought never even crossed my mind. Now,
can we just sit down and watch it? *Please?*

Sue: Can I get something to eat first? I'll only be a minute.

She sat down next to me on the sofa forty-five minutes
later, a plate of lasagne balanced delicately on her knee.
Swallowing a mouthful of pasta, she motioned towards the
television with her fork.

Sue: Off you go, then.

Me: But you won't be able to concentrate on the plot if
you're eating at the same time.

Sue: I'm fine. I can listen to it. Press Play.

Ninety minutes later . . .

Sue: That wasn't bad.

Me: Yes it was. It was a disaster!

Sue: Don't worry. I'm sure they'll get it right when it
goes to a series.

The Master: The Doctor is half human!

Sue: Eh? Since when?

I pause the DVD.

Me: What do you make of that, then?
Sue: It makes sense, I suppose.
Me: WHAT?
Sue: Well, he's obsessed with Earth. He can't keep away from the place. Why isn't he saving Mars every week? There has to be a reason for it and that's a good enough reason as any.
Me: So, do you think Paul McGann counts?
Sue: Of course he f**king counts. Why wouldn't he?

*

When Sue went to bed, I stayed up and watched *The TV Movie* again, just to be sure. Yes, the Americans had achieved the seemingly impossible – they had taken the thing that nobody liked very much and ruined it.

It wasn't just that the Doctor was being played by someone good looking or that the character was half-human all of a sudden. This Doctor kissed women on the lips. His TARDIS could bring people back from the dead. The plot felt both rushed and too complicated. The music was blaring and intrusive. The whole production looked unsustainably expensive. There was no way this version of *Doctor Who*, or one like it, would ever go to a series.

It was time to face up to it. The hiatus was back on – possibly for ever. And do you know something? I was almost relieved. There was some stuff I had to get on with.

Hiatus 3: Living Without *Doctor Who*

Sue: You remember how Neil only agreed to come back to my place that time so he could watch repeats of *Doctor Who* on UK Gold? Well the only reason he asked me to marry him in 1999 is because he thought the world was about to end. He says he became convinced civilisation was on the brink of collapse shortly after they showed that *Doctor Who* movie with Paul McGann. I thought he might be having a breakdown or something but he says he just really hated it. (I don't know why, I thought it was OK.) Anyway, he says it was an article about the Millennium Bug in an in-flight magazine that did it. The one that said brilliant technologists from Silicon Valley were building shelters in the middle of the desert to prepare for the effects of a computer bug that would bring society to its knees.

Me: I completely fell for it. These were intelligent people, or at least that's what I thought, so they had to know something we didn't. And then the media got hold of it and everywhere you turned there were tales of impending doom, from documentaries outlining how to survive societal disintegration to scaremongering leaflets being posted through letterboxes. By the middle of December 1999 I had stockpiled enough tinned soup, bottled water and

candles to survive just about anything except New
Year's Eve (*see above*).

Sue: And that's why, in July, Neil decided to marry me.
He thought it was only going to last six months.

Me: Which would still have been longer than your first
marriage.

Sue: Fair enough.

Me: But we both know there was more to it than that.
There was Nicol to consider.

*

Nicol has never called me Dad; I've always been Neil to her.
And I'm OK with that, because she's never once screamed,
'You can't tell me what to do, you're not my real dad!' in my
face either. For this and numerous other reasons, I'm a lucky
man.

It's never bothered me that Nicol isn't my biological
daughter. For example, in the unhappy event that she was
diagnosed with a hereditary disease, Sue couldn't blame me
for it – result! And from my perspective, I arrived in Nic's
life at just the right time, having missed the sleepless nights,
the dirty nappies and the 'terrible twos'.

Did it take me longer to bond with Nicol because I wasn't
around to see her take her first steps or hear her first words?
Probably. The truth is it took me ages to get to grips with
being a responsible Neil. One minute I was an unattached,
decidedly immature twenty-three-year-old, the next I was
attending parent evenings, dressing up as Santa Claus and
developing coping mechanisms for multiple episodes of
Rugrats. But slowly we got there. In fact, I have only two

regrets when I look back on Nicol's childhood: (1) she never gave *Doctor Who* a fair chance, and (2) she never tested my uncertain skills as a parent.

Sue insisted that we give Nicol as much freedom as possible when she was growing up. I just kept waiting for something to go wrong. Maybe Nicol would fall in with the wrong crowd. Maybe she'd be bullied. Or maybe she actually would fall prey to a terrible illness. Nothing. Not so much as a broken bone or a bad school report. In fact, all I have are happy, carefree memories of Nicol's childhood: our trip to Disneyland, cheering her on at sports days, taking her trick-or-treating, explaining terrorism to her (actually, that wasn't so pleasant) and being there for her when the Spice Girls split up. And *Rugrats* is pretty good once you get into it.

So Nicol – and Sue – made parenthood ridiculously easy. I'd already decided I wanted to spend the rest of my life with them long before I proposed. I couldn't imagine the world without them in it – unless the world came to an abrupt end, of course. But I wasn't crazy about the concept of marriage; I think anyone whose parents are divorced has a tendency to feel this way. Marriage was just a piece of paper, it didn't mean anything. What finally changed my mind was Nicol.

In 1998 Sue lost her dad to cancer; her mum had passed away eighteen months earlier, doing what she loved – she was going for double top in a darts tournament and suffered a massive heart attack. For the first time, I started to worry about what might happen to Nicol if anything happened to Sue; Sue loved darts. And it dawned on me that a piece of paper can mean a lot.

So I asked Nicol if I could adopt her. And after I'd explained to her what adopt meant, she flung her arms around me and said yes. It would not be an exaggeration to describe this as the best moment of my life because it was the best moment of my life. And then I asked her if it was OK if I married her mam as well, and all she wanted to know was what colour her bridesmaid's dress would be. When I told her she'd be changing her surname to Perryman, she wasn't so thrilled.

Sue and I were married in a register office in Hartlepool on Friday 23 July 1999. The bride wore cream and the bridesmaid wore cream too. The registrar asked Sue to take me as her lawfully wedded wife and she agreed before he could correct himself. It's still legally binding, I think.

> **Sue:** I suggested Neil change his name to Perrywoman but he wasn't having it.

*

In the summer of 2000 – the summer I feared would never come – I experienced an epiphany. I was reading a *Doctor Who* novel in bed one night when it suddenly occurred to me that I was thirty years old and I hadn't read any Dostoevsky yet – seventy-one novels by Terrance Dicks, yes, but not one by Tolstoy, Hemingway or a woman.* I had to broaden my horizons before it was too late.

I never finished that *Doctor Who* book – which ends, I believe, with the Eighth Doctor destroying his home planet, Gallifrey (like that would ever happen in the TV series) – and

---

* Strictly speaking, this is untrue. I had read at least five novels penned by a woman, specifically the five New Adventures written by Kate Orman, the lone female contributor to the series.

when I placed it neatly on my bookshelf to gather dust I felt like the proverbial weight had lifted from my shoulders. No longer would I have to keep up with the BBC's punishing release schedule, which left me both out of pocket and with little time to do anything else. At last, I was letting go.

One day, I sold half my *Doctor Who* tapes to a friend. I didn't do this because I needed the money – in fact, I let them go cheaply. The rest of my *Doctor Who* VHS collection went in the attic; by the time they came back out again, the format, a bit like my passion for *Doctor Who*, was on the wane – or at least, at a manageable level. As Sue liked to say, I had more important things to worry about now.

Since 1993 I had been a part-time university lecturer.* My teaching career didn't get off to an auspicious start. During my first seminar I was so nervous, I opened the camera case upside down and as a £3,000 camcorder bounced off the linoleum floor, I had to pretend that I'd done it on purpose so the students wouldn't repeat the same mistake. Camcorder safely secured to a tripod, I thought I'd show them how to focus the camera and adjust its lens and, because it seemed to be going reasonably well, I decided to toss in a gag.

Me: And this is what we call a crash zoom. Or, if you're a *Doctor Who* fan, a Dalek just turned up!

Silence.

When the students filed out of the room at the end of the lesson, I breathed a huge sigh of relief. But then I noticed

* Happily, the institution became a university when Sunderland was awarded city status in 1992. A polytechnic lecturer doesn't have quite the same cachet.

that one of them had stayed behind. Was he was going to complain about my teaching methods? In my nervousness, had I spoken too fast for him to keep up?

The student glanced furtively around the room, as if to make sure that we were alone.

> **Student:** I was just wondering . . . Are you by any chance? You know . . . I just thought you might be . . . Well, erm . . .

I swallowed hard. I'd read about this sort of thing. He was going to ask me out.

> **Student:** It's just that . . . OK, I'm just going to come right out and say it. Are you a *Doctor Who* fan?

And that's how I met John Paul Green. We were to become firm – though platonic – friends. We were a similar age, we both came from the West Midlands and his appreciation for 1970s *Doctor Who* was almost as limitless as mine. It seemed a bit weird that he was my student and I was his mentor, not least when I had to fail him for leaving his tripod's base plate on a bus. It was even weirder when he slept with my sister. Nevertheless, six years later he was our best man; and we didn't make him wear cream.

*

Between 1993 and 1999 I screened *Jaws* to my students so many times I wore the tape out and the university had to buy me a new one. I discovered I loved teaching, and not just because I got to watch *Jaws* a lot; it felt like I'd accidentally stumbled into a vocation.

By rights, I should have been a terrible teacher. I wasn't really a 'people person' and I found students irritating even when I was one myself. But I worked hard to compensate for my lack of experience and, with lots of help from Sue, I got quite good at it. Teaching is part knowledge transfer, part performance art; what I lacked in the former, I made up for in the latter. In 1997, despite breaking down in tears during the interview because I so *desperately* wanted it to go well, I was made a full-time member of staff.

One of my responsibilities as a full-time university lecturer was that I had to be 'research active'. This basically meant I was expected to commit to a PhD immediately. So the first thing I had to decide was what subject I was going to study in depth. I cast around for an alternative to *Jaws*, about which I knew an awful lot. Naturally, there was only one.

I can still remember Sue's first words after I told her I planned to take a PhD in *Doctor Who* – her first words after she stopped laughing, anyway.

> **Sue:** I tell you what, Neil, it'll be worth five years of hard work just so you can tell people at dinner parties you're a Doctor in *Doctor Who*.

For this reason alone, she still hasn't forgiven me for jacking it in.

I first suspected that I might not complete my PhD during the training day I was forced to attend a few weeks into my studies. As part of an obligatory icebreaker session we were told to turn to the stranger sitting next to us and explain to them what our PhD was all about and what its impact on society at large would be. I was sitting next to a budding scientist and he went first. I couldn't follow every detail of what he was saying but it definitely had something to do with enzymes and finding a cure for cancer.

When he was finished, he turned to me.

Him: So what's yours about?

Me: Well, in a nutshell, and this is quite tricky to explain to a lay person, I am looking at the ways in which metatextual, erm, texts, impact on the parent text *vis-à-vis* the complex relationships between the, erm, semiotic thickness of the, erm, oh dear, text, and the burgeoning use of converging technologies, which have quantifiably altered the ways in which the audience interact with the, erm, text.

Though I had skilfully avoided two important words beginning with D and W, the scientist clearly wasn't too impressed with my waffle and with good reason. I had made my PhD sound like a complete waste of time.

I tried to ignore the warning signs and ploughed on with my studies. I got as far as being published a couple of times. However, it could take anything up to two years between the completion of a paper and its eventual publication. In my field of study, the subject could regenerate in the amount of time it took for my research to see print – sometimes twice – so when my work did appear, it already felt woefully out of date. In the age of the internet, where information was instantaneous and accessible, academic research felt strangely archaic and limited. It was careful, methodical and deeply frustrating.

It was around this time that I started to branch out into

teaching more theoretical subjects, and as luck would have it, most of the modules I taught on were run by my friend and former student John Paul. Just like me, John Paul didn't know what do with the rest of his life after he graduated and, just like me, he enrolled on an MA. And then, after a short stint as a technician in the drama department, he started working as a visiting lecturer in the same faculty as me, and by the turn of the millennium he was responsible for running several modules on the history of broadcasting. And that's when he came up to me one day with an exciting proposition: how would I like to be paid to teach *Doctor Who*?

Big mistake.

*

'It's very slow.'

'Are all the old episodes as boring as this one?'

'The actors didn't know their lines.'

'That was *Doctor Poo*.'

'It looked like it was a rehearsal.'

'Was the Doctor really wearing a wig?'

'What a load of old shit.'

Enthusiasm is supposed to be infectious, or at least that's what they told me when I was training to be a teacher. What nonsense. It didn't matter how passionate I became when I talked to my students about early episodes of *Doctor Who*, their response was always the same: sheer indifference. In fact, the more passionate and animated I got about it, the more determined they seemed to wear me down. It's as if they had sensed my weak spot and they instinctively knew how to exploit it.

Timetabling the screenings at 9 a.m. on a Monday probably didn't help. Who wanted to watch a black-and-white episode of *Doctor Who* first thing in the morning? Even I didn't want to do that. So I'd sneak off for a cup of tea after I'd hit the Play button in the lecture theatre, but when I returned a few minutes later, it was always the same story: students checking their email; students tweeting and texting; students updating their Facebook statuses ('dr who . . . its SO BORING . . . LOLZ . . .').

I wouldn't have minded so much if their criticisms of early *Doctor Who* had been in any way constructive or perceptive, but more often than not they simply focused on the show's less-than-special special effects. When I told them that criticising a television programme for not including any computer graphics when computer graphics hadn't actually been invented yet was an untenable position, they shrugged their collective shoulders and asked me how long it would take before we got to *Stargate SG-1*.

And after a day of this, I would return home to the prospect of watching *Doctor Who* and writing about *Doctor Who* and thinking thoughts about *Doctor Who* that no one had thought before for a PhD that I knew in my heart would increase the sum of human knowledge not one iota.

Each man kills the thing he loves, wrote Oscar Wilde in one of the books I still haven't read. But the combination of simultaneously both studying *and* teaching *Doctor Who* was proving almost fatal; I started to feel like the thing I loved was killing me.

Every time a student completes a module, they are invited to send anonymous feedback to their lecturer, just in case their apathetic silence in the seminars hasn't sent a clear enough message. This is just a small selection of responses from the students who took my Science Fiction module:

- Too much *Doctor Who* and not enough *Third Rock from the Sun*.
- More vampires please.
- I couldn't find the reading list until the day after the deadline past (*sic*).
- Change the time of the screening. Some of us have lives.
- Only one episode of *Red Dwarf*? Smeg.
- Neil Perryman is a sad wanker who watches far too much *Dr Who*.

It was that last one that did it. For the final time, it isn't *Dr Who* – it's *Doctor Who*!

I stopped teaching on this module the same day I packed in my PhD. I wouldn't make the same mistake twice.

Then I wondered what the hell I was going to do next.

Doctor Who and the Woman from Hartlepool

Wednesday 7 February 2001

Sue loves a good television-shopping channel. When I suggested that we watch QVC together that night, she must have thought her luck was in. It was only when she realised that Tom Baker was plugging a *Doctor Who* book for two solid hours that the scales fell from her eyes. Still, she attempted to make the best of it.

Sue: Should I get this book for you? It sounds like a good deal to me.

Me: According to you, everything on QVC sounds like a good deal. We're still paying for that Pilates machine you never use. And those paint rollers. And the apple-corer.

Sue: Go on, you should order it. They might let you speak to Tom Baker.

Me: I don't want to speak to Tom Baker.

Sue: You do, Neil. What would you like to ask him?

Me: Nothing. You know I don't like speaking to celebrities. Just thinking about it makes me uncomfortable.

Sue: Go on. There must be something you'd like to ask him.

Me: I don't know. I'd probably ask him why he hasn't agreed to make a Big Finish audio yet.* Even Paul

* Big Finish is a company that produces new, officially licensed *Doctor Who* stories on CD and download.

McGann has done one, and he barely counts.
Sue: I'm just popping out for a smoke. I'll be back in a
    minute.

Sue leaves me to enjoy another rambling Tom Baker
anecdote. While Tom's stories are entertainingly louche,
they are also impeding QVC's ability to shift enough copies
of the book he was sent there to promote. The shopping
channel's male presenter has to keep steering things back
on track.

QVC: I know, Tom, let's go to one of our callers. Let's
    talk to Susan on the phone.
Tom: Susan?
QVC: Susan's just bought the book and she's phoned
    through.
Sue: Hello, Tom? Is that you, Tom?

I feel like my stomach has just dropped through the floor.

Tom: Is that Susan Barrett?
Sue: No, it's Susan Perryman.

Tom is confused and disappointed. I am confused and
horrified.

Tom: Oh, hello, Susan.
Sue: Listen, Tom, I'm going to ask you a big question
    on behalf of your fans.

Tom is clearly nonplussed. He can't decipher Sue's thick
regional accent and the QVC presenter has to repeat the
question.

> QVC: Susan is going to ask you a big question on behalf
>   of all your fans.
> Tom: Oh. Go on, then.
> Sue: Would you ever consider coming back as the best
>   Doctor ever?
> Tom: Would I *WHAT*?
> QVC: Susan wants to know, would you ever consider
>   coming back as the best Doctor ever?
> Tom: Well, I would if you were in charge of it, Susan. If
>   the fans were in charge, of course I would.

Suddenly I get it. Tom thinks my wife is some sort of super-fan. But of course he does. Only a *Doctor Who* fan would telephone a shopping channel for the chance to quiz an actor about something that is obviously never going to happen and over which they have little or no control. I notice that Tom has segued into a very familiar – and very long – anecdote, so I seize the opportunity to rush upstairs. I find Sue in our bedroom, giggling down the phone. She holds up a single finger to hush me and I stand there in impotent silence, watching my wife nodding along with Tom Baker on the other end of the line. And then I realise that even standing in the same room where this phone call is taking place is making me feel sick with nerves, so I race downstairs again, just in time to witness Tom suggesting that he could play the Doctor's arch-enemy, the Master. Sue laughs politely and pretends to know who the Master is.

> Sue: That would be wonderful. Maybe one day, eh? My
>   other question . . . If all the other surviving Doctors

have come back to do these new audio adventures, why haven't you?

Tom shifts uncomfortably in his seat.

Tom: I don't know, really . . . (*to the QVC presenter*)
   What have the other Doctors been up to?
QVC: I have no idea.
Sue: You know, Tom . . . the . . . erm . . . new audio
   adventures?

I grab a pen and hurry back upstairs, scrawling the words BIG FINISH on my palm as I go, which I then wave frantically in Sue's face. She thinks I must be telling her to wrap things up with a gesture everyone will remember – a song maybe – and emphatically shakes her head. Thankfully, Tom has finally remembered something about the audio adventures.

Tom: Ah yes, I know! It's because they haven't produced
   a script that I like. And if they do produce a script
   that I like, I'll do it. I can't speak for the other fellows.
   Who are they? I only found out recently that there
   were other Doctors. I didn't know that.
Sue: Well, Paul McGann's done it . . .
Tom: Oh, really?
Sue: Yes, and you have a much better voice than him.
Tom: Oh Susan, who knows what to say!

And finally, to my huge relief, Tom unleashes one of his trademark toothy grins.

QVC: Well, Sue, thanks so much for taking the time

and effort to call through to talk to us tonight.

Tom: Goodbye, Susan! Goodbye!

Sue comes back downstairs and sits down.

Sue: Did you enjoy that, Neil? I did.

And the thing is, I have to admit, I had quite enjoyed it. Sue was brilliant. Instead of being intimidated, she just went ahead and did it. It's one of the reasons I married her – or she married me – her determination to get on with it and make things happen.

Which brings us back to the caravan.

Caravan of Love

Me: OK, so where is it?

Sue: You're standing in it. Just think, this could all be ours. All you have to do is say yes.

Me: But it's a cowshed. Is the property on the other side of the building? Is it through this door?

Sue: No, *this is it*. What do you think? Do you like it? Please say yes.

Me: You must be joking.

Sue: You need to use your imagination.

Me: My imagination? There's nothing here but cow shit and dead chickens. And I'm pretty sure that roof is made from asbestos.

Sue had wanted to build a house since I met her. She tirelessly searched for the right location for several years until she finally found the perfect property fifteen minutes down the road in County Durham. But there was a twist. Building a single house would have been too easy for Sue. Anybody could do that, she told me. No, Sue wanted to build *five* houses.

She made it sound straightforward enough: the enormous cowshed would be divided between us, Sue's two brothers and her younger brother's best friend. The fifth property would be finished and sold first, which would help us to fund the completion of the other four. And even though it sounded like a huge undertaking, with considerable risks involved, Sue assured me that the building work would take a year at most.

I wasn't that keen, to be honest. I enjoyed my home comforts too much. We'd just installed something called Sky+ at home – you could rewind live TV and everything – whereas this location was so remote, it didn't even have a phone. The nearest shop was twenty minutes away by car (I still didn't drive), there was no water supply (we would have to drill for it) and, worst of all, I would have to live in a static caravan for twelve months.

Still, it was only a year. And I owed Sue so much. She had given me a family, a home and a life to be proud of. She'd humoured me when I'd thought the world was going to end and consoled me when it hadn't. Whenever I needed them, she'd put up more shelves. As we navigated our way through the cowpats and chicken entrails, I couldn't say no to her. How could I?

Me: OK, let's do it.

How hard could it be?

*

We put our home on the market and prayed for a quick sale. A consortium of professional developers had taken an interest in the cowshed and our window of opportunity was closing fast. And then the sale of our house fell through, thanks to somebody being gazumped further down our chain, and it looked as if Sue's dream would be over before it could even begin. But Sue didn't give up. She picked up the phone and she didn't put it down again until she'd made a series of offers, counter-offers, deals and complicated promises. The paperwork was signed forty-eight hours later.

The next day, we bought the Lyndhurst 2000. It had two bedrooms, an en-suite toilet, a modest kitchen and a decent-sized living room. It seemed quite spacious when we paid for it, though once it was filled with two adults, a teenager, a fully grown Labrador and a cat it was a little on the cramped side. Or, as Sue insisted, 'bijou'.

We moved into this caravan on 18 July 2004, the same day the BBC began principal photography on a brand-new series of *Doctor Who*. Experts believe the four most stressful situations in life are bereavement, divorce, moving house and making a new series of *Doctor Who*, so let's just say the day was rather tense for all concerned.

And then everything started to go wrong. In our rush to complete the sale, we – and by we, I mean Sue – hadn't checked the paperwork properly, and we discovered that there was a right-of-way issue with one of the farmers which meant we wouldn't be able to transport any raw materials onto the site to build our houses until the dispute was resolved.

That would take more than a year.

*

We were driving to work one morning when Sue hit me with a spectacularly unexpected question.

Sue: Do you want to hear my theory about Rose Tyler?

No, I did not. How would she like it if I suddenly had a theory about bathroom fittings or the dimensions of our still-theoretical new kitchen? That was her domain. *Doctor Who* was mine.

For ten years, I kept *Doctor Who* and Sue apart – unless you include *The TV Movie* fiasco and that time she rang Tom Baker on QVC. *Doctor Who* was *my* thing. And while it's true that I was on the cusp of giving it up for dead when the BBC suddenly decided to bring it back to life again, I still felt very possessive and protective of the programme. I suppose this is what it would feel like if Tangerine Dream had a Number One hit record and overnight everyone started using it for ringtones and adverts. So when my wife suddenly starting asking complicated questions about the Doctor's past, it felt awkward. She desperately wanted to know who had started the Time War and why the Doctor had to destroy Gallifrey. If I hadn't stopped reading the novels, I might have had an answer for her.

For the record, Sue's theory was 100 per cent correct: Bad Wolf was Rose Tyler all along. I was hoping for the Master myself.

At least Nicol's indifference was consistent. One Saturday she walked in on me when I was blubbing my eyes out over the episode where K9 is blown to smithereens (and I don't even like K9).

Nicol: Mam! Mam! Neil's having a nervous breakdown.

When Rose Tyler left the programme under tragic circumstances a few weeks later, I paid Nicol to go to the cinema so she wouldn't have to witness a grown man weeping again.

It was becoming embarrassing. You were compelled to cry only very occasionally when you watched the old series (e.g. Adric) but the new series tugged at the tear ducts every week. If Rose's dad wasn't being run over, the Doctor's girlfriend was dying of a broken heart. Yes, *his girlfriend*. Things were different now.

John Paul was the only person I could talk to about *Doctor Who* without feeling self-conscious and odd. The plaudits from the press and the public surprised him as much as they did me. Everything seemed too good to be true. Even though Christopher Eccleston resigned the day after his first episode was broadcast, his successor was a self-confessed fan-boy named David Tennant and people couldn't get enough of him. I would meet John Paul for a cigarette between our university classes to discuss the latest developments and we would shake our heads in disbelief. I told him that I'd heard the Cybermen were coming back and we both snickered like schoolboys just thinking about it.

*

Saturday 13 May 2006: County Durham

I can't remember for the life of me what the argument was about now, only that it was bad enough for me to storm off in a huff and lock myself in the site caravan. This was a cheap, dilapidated wreck we'd bought so the builders would have somewhere to store their tools and facilitate their endless tea breaks. It was bloody freezing, even with all four bars blazing on its portable electric heater, but I'd be damned if I was going to slope back to the Lyndhurst and apologise to Sue for whatever it was I had done wrong.

We were supposed to be attending a party at John Paul's house that night, and he sounded very disappointed when I called to tell him we wouldn't be coming. I pretended Sue wasn't feeling very well, instead of the truth, which was that we weren't talking to each other and probably wouldn't be for several hours yet. This was because the site caravan had a portable TV. If it hadn't, I would have been forced to swallow my pride and return to the Lyndhurst a lot earlier than I did, because there was no way I was about to miss tonight's episode of *Doctor Who*, no matter how angry I was with my wife.

I was especially excited because tonight's episode was called 'Rise of the Cybermen'. There's a title that doesn't muck about, I thought. You know exactly where you are with a title like that. This wouldn't be another 'Earthshock'. You wouldn't see me falling out of my chair this time.

But about twenty minutes into the episode, I fell out of my chair – well, off my stool; I was still shivering in the caravan. The Doctor and Rose Tyler are strolling through a busy thoroughfare on a parallel Earth, when suddenly, as if by magic, every pedestrian is halted in their tracks by a signal beamed directly into their ears. Perplexed, our heroes make their way through this frozen crowd towards a man in a dark blue suit . . .

That's funny, I thought. The man in the dark blue suit looks like John Paul. Actually, he looks *a lot* like John Paul.

I grabbed my mobile phone and composed a text to my friend.

> Are you watching Who? Somebody looks exactly like u. LOL.

Before I could press the send button, my phone buzzed. It was a text from my friend Damon:

> Is JP on Dr Who?

A text from Jonathan Grove followed a few seconds later:

> Is that John Paul on the telly?

And then another, this time from Sue in the Lyndhurst:

> Fucking hell. Are you watching this?

Then the phone rang. It was John Paul. He told me not to hate him.

I didn't hate him. I envied him. My best friend was sharing the screen with a bloody Doctor and he wasn't even an actor. He told me that a journalist had tipped him off that the show was looking for extras to appear in a crowd scene in Cardiff, and he thought he'd end up as an unrecognisable blur in the background. But then the director Graeme Harper picked him to appear in a dramatic close-up where Billie Piper has to stare meaningfully into somebody's ear for several minutes. So John Paul was on screen for *ages*. In fact he's so prominent that I thought they might bring out an action figure of him.

So *that's* why he was throwing a party tonight. It all made sense now.

John Paul: Oh, one last thing. I'm in another episode later on. Don't tell anyone but it's got the Daleks in it. Bye!

I hurried back to the Lyndhurst to confirm Sue's suspicions. It was the first time *Doctor Who* had ever brought us closer together, because in all the excitement the row was forgotten and never mentioned again.

*

A year after we moved into our caravan, building work began on our new home. Two and a half years after that, we moved in.

It took me a little while to readjust to life in a real house. Not only was it safe to flush the toilet in cold weather, I also had a working internet connection again. Cooking in a separate room felt almost decadent. And for the first time in years I actually got a good night's sleep when it rained. Of course, I loved it. Sue had built a magnificent house – no, five houses – as I always knew she would. OK, it's too big for us, it's impossible to keep clean and it's infested with spiders, but I loved it then and I still love it now. And the TV is *massive*.

During our bleakest moments in that caravan – not being able to cook Christmas dinner when the Calor gas tank froze was a lowlight – Sue always promised that she would pay me back one day. She told me that I could choose any project I liked when the house was finished. As long as I was following my dream, she said, she would support me every step of the way. After all, it was only watching TV. How hard could it be?

Now, where did I put those childish things?

Part Three

I tried to get my wife to watch 'Genesis of the Daleks' once.

STEVEN MOFFAT, writer and producer of *Doctor Who*

Cyberspace Backslash Flashback Backlash

In 1995, I had a life changing experience I needed to share with Sue.

> **Me:** It's this thing called the internet. You use it to talk to people from all over the world on a computer. It's incredible. I was talking to a man from Austin, Texas about cattle farming yesterday. Can you believe it?
>
> **Sue:** What do you know about cattle farming?
>
> **Me:** More than I did yesterday.
>
> **Sue:** I don't see the point. If you want to talk to someone, talk to me.
>
> **Me:** OK. Did you know there's a type of agricultural fertiliser sold by the city of Austin, Texas wastewater department that contains actual human sewage sludge?
>
> **Sue:** I didn't, no. What's this thing called again?
>
> **Me:** The internet.
>
> **Sue:** I can see why it might appeal to you. You love talking shite.

I admit most of the online conversations I had when I first discovered the internet were banal at best. The pattern was always the same: small talk about the weather followed by a discussion about the time difference – everyone I talked to seemed to be American back then. But it didn't really matter because I was making the impossible happen. I was communicating with someone on a different continent with real-time text. It didn't get much more sci-fi than that in 1995.

>   **Sue**: You do realise that half these people aren't who they say they are. That woman you are talking to right now is probably a man.

This didn't concern me in the slightest. The idea that on the internet you could be anybody you wanted to be – younger, older, sexier, wiser, even a different gender – intrigued me but it also seemed like an awful lot of effort; I couldn't be bothered.

>   **Me**: *Hi, I'm Neil from England. I teach video production at a university. What's the weather like where you are? It's 1 p.m. over here.* You should try this, Sue, it's brilliant!
>   **Sue**: Jesus, what are you going be like when you find out about the telephone?

One of my first one-to-one online chats was with a law student from Ohio. We were discussing capital punishment when the name Jeremy Bentham came up. Several minutes later, I realised that we were chatting at cross-purposes: he was referring to the renowned eighteenth-century English philosopher while I was talking about the co-founder of the *Doctor Who Appreciation Society*. In fact, Bentham the Younger is a descendent of Bentham the Elder; and, perhaps unsurprisingly given the feeding pool of internet early adopters, the American law student had been through this rigmarole before. And that's how he came to give me the directions to a special place on the internet where I could discuss *Doctor Who* to my heart's content. It was here – in the *rec.arts.drwho* newsgroup – that I finally found true fandom.

I knew that other *Doctor Who* fans existed before this, of course. I was aware there was a Doctor Who Appreciation Society, though I had never joined it; and I knew that there were conventions and local clubs, but I never had the guts to go to either, mainly because I suspected that most of the people who went to them were nutcases.*

But *rec.arts.drwho* was the perfect compromise. I had stumbled into the world's largest room of like-minded people but I could leave whenever I wanted. I didn't even have to say anything – I could just eavesdrop at the back of the room on the virtual conversations that were already under way without anyone giving me so much as a funny look (or

---

* Someone calling themselves 'bombonstilts' recently posted the following reminiscence at an internet forum called Roobarbs, neatly summing up what I feared all such meetings would be like:

'I went to a local group occasionally when I was about twelve or so. The first time I went, the only people there for the first hour (apart from me) were . . . developmentally and mentally challenged is probably the least loaded way of putting it. Without wishing to speak ill of anyone, I was expecting to meet with likeminded people and discuss the show I liked, rather than being stuck with people a few of whom I had actually seen shouting at nothing in the centre of town.

'After an hour the Guy With The Videos showed up with his clearly terrified wife and dropped off his *n*th generation copy of *The Time Warrior* and scarpered. Luckily the place where they met was slap bang in the middle of the red light district so my mum came to pick me up before it got too late, but that was the longest and most awkward two hours of my life up to that point.

'Not the best introduction to fandom.

'The second time I went someone asked me if I'd let Sarah Jane shit on my chest. But then I did also win a calendar, so it wasn't all bad.'

(www.zetaminor.com/roobarb/showthread.php?30454-Meeting-grumpy-Who-stars&p=898810&viewfull=1#post898810)

emoticon). Many of these conversations were bewildering at first: debates about Sylvester McCoy's Scottish accent, fiery arguments over the U.N.I.T. Dating Controversy, whatever that was, and endless exegeses about which Dalek story was the best one. Needless to say, I was immediately hooked.

After several weeks of lurking, I finally summoned up enough courage to post something myself:

> **To**: rec.arts.drwho
> **From**: Neil Perryman
> **Date**: 31 March 1995
> **Subject**: Functionaries
> *Is it just me or are the Functionaries from 'Carnival of Monsters' the worst example of make-up in the entire history of the series? I nearly fell off my chair in shock when they first shambled onto the set. Bits of latex flapping around like no one's business! And it wasn't just one of them – all of them were flapping about! It was unbelievable!*

It doesn't surprise me that my first internet post was about *Doctor Who*. What does surprise me is just how bitchy it was. I was being unkind to 'Carnival of Monsters', the first *Doctor Who* story I ever saw and the source of my first childhood memory.

> *Did Angela Seyfang (the make-up artist, and I use the term loosely) ever work again?*

Wow. That was a bit harsh. And just for the record, she did. Regularly.

There are two possible excuses for my behaviour. The first is that I genuinely felt upset when I wrote those words. My post coincides with the release of 'Carnival of Monsters' on

VHS, and it would have been the first time that I'd seen this particular story since the 'Five Faces' repeat in 1981. I was still in a period of adjustment – old stories rarely measure up to your childhood memories of them and 'Carnival of Monsters' had looked somewhat *cheaper* than I remembered. The second possibility is that I'd convinced myself that the best way to make an impression on this newsgroup was to wade in with a bold, opinionated statement, featuring plenty of exclamation marks, sarcasm and cynicism. And that's because my earliest memories of *rec.arts.drwho* is as a place where everyone was a little on the grumpy side.

I sat back and waited for the debate to begin. But nobody replied to my first post. After that disappointment, I didn't contribute to the newsgroup again for quite some time – the language labs were locked over the Easter holidays. However, when I returned in May I dove right back in and, soon enough, I was swimming with the grumpy sharks, trading cynical, sarcastic jibes with the best and worst of them. The smiliest smiley cannot express how much I loved it.

It was in the *rec.arts.drwho* newsgroup that I learned which directors were OK to like and which ones I should dismiss out of hand; which authors to praise and which ones to scorn; which actors to follow and which ones to avoid at all costs, especially if you ran into them at a convention bar. It was here that I learned how to use words like 'rad' and 'trad' without blushing, where I tried to make sense of something called the Cartmel Master Plan, and where I took my side in the infernal Pertwee versus McCoy flame war. It was also in this newsgroup that I learned about the Tavern, a pub in Fitzrovia where a powerful cabal of fans would gather

on the first Thursday of every month to plan for the day
when they would control the programme themselves and,
on a good night, fight each other in the street to decide who
would get first dibs on being producer; the T in Russell T.
Davies stands for Toughnut.

But newsgroups and chatrooms were just the beginning.
There were also FTP archives, where you could download
images of Leela in her loincloth or TARDIS dematerialisa-
tion sound effects (whatever floated your boat), and there
was the World Wide Web, where I found *Doctor Who*
episode guides, fan-fiction and some TARDIS-based pornography that I'd rather not discuss. I spent so much time in
the university language labs between 1995 and 1996 that
Sue finally decided it would be for the best if we bought our
own PC so we could connect to the internet at home. That
way, at least she'd get to spend some time with me, even if
she was staring at the back of my head while I argued with
some moron from Montreal about the merits – merits! – of
The TV Movie.

I tried to convince my bosses at the university that we
should be teaching the internet to our students but they
seemed to think it was just a passing fad. I didn't listen to
them; instead I spent every spare hour I could learning how
to build webpages by hand, with raw HTML code at first
and then with increasingly sophisticated software. It took
me several years and countless sleepless nights but in the
end I got to grips with it. I soon became master of my own
domain, which I bought for £1.50 from supernames.co.uk.

In 2001, the university finally saw the light. They asked
me to design an undergraduate syllabus that would cover

both the theory of the internet as well as the practical side of building websites. Coincidentally, this was also the year I won *rec.arts.drwho*'s coveted Rookie of the Year Award (I neglected to remind them that I'd been hanging around the place for five). NB I didn't win this award because I had anything particularly interesting to say about *Doctor Who*. I won this award because of all the websites I'd devoted to it.

Cue list.

Six (not very successful) Websites

1. Views from the Gallery (1998–1999)

My first website was dedicated to the American science-fiction series *Babylon 5*. The site used such cutting-edge technologies as framed navigation, blinking text and animated GIFs. However, what it lacked in aesthetics it more than made up for in content. Because I couldn't be bothered to review every single episode of the space opera myself, I recruited like-minded fans from the internet to write them for me. This collaborative approach not only saved me time and effort, it also resulted in the formation of a close community of virtual friends – virtual friends being the best kind, i.e. ones you never have to meet.

2. The Eclipse Café (1998–2001)

My old school pal Jonathan Grove and I were running our very own online social network long before Facebook came along and 'stole' our idea. Jon, who was as obsessed with the internet as I was, had invested some money in his own private server and he wanted to experiment with some virtual community software that he'd bought. However, while Jon had the technical know-how, he didn't have a ready-made community to test it on, and that's where I came in. I convinced my *Babylon 5* friends to join the new network, which they then used to swap intimate details about their private lives. Sadly, unlike Facebook, the Eclipse Café peaked at nineteen members, the intimate details of a group of *Babylon 5* fans proving to be not merely a hermetically closed circle but one with nothing very interesting in the middle of it.

3. Tachyon TV (2001–2006)

Tachyon TV was supposed to be like The Onion for science-fiction fans. It was basically a monthly website with a single page of topical spoof news stories but with a telefantasy twist. *DOCTOR WHO* LOGO DESIGNERS FOUND HIDING IN FALLUJAH was one hilarious headline; IS SADDAM HUSSEIN SECRETLY BUILDING IMPER-IAL AT-AT WALKERS? was another. It hasn't aged very well, mostly because it was pretty old to begin with.

Despite Tachyon TV's shameless derivativeness, the site built up a small but loyal audience, until one day it caught the attention of a TV production company. They invited me to a meeting in their offices to discuss a Top Secret project with them, so I bought a new suit and caught the first train to London. The brief they gave me was, well, brief: watch the news on television for a whole week and then write some funny jokes about it. The week I was assigned to watch the news was the week of the Soham murders. On the Friday night, I submitted five pages of gags to the production com-pany. I never heard from them again.

It was a valuable learning experience. Nowadays, I could easily sell that material to Frankie Boyle.

4. Watching Too Much Telly (2003–2005)

I took up blogging because I figured if I wrote something new every day, I'd eventually get better at it. I didn't really care if anyone read what I had to say or not, and not a lot of people did, but the routine I set myself – to write at least five hundred words about a TV programme I'd seen the night before – felt like it might lead somewhere eventually. Occasionally I would post something other than a review – usually a rant about living in a caravan, building a house or my never-ending battles with BT's Customer Complaints Department – but most of the time I just published withering commentaries about the latest series of *Big Brother* or that week's *EastEnders*. And then one day, I posted a review of a documentary about the art of parkouring, or as I put it:

If you ever find yourself facing an obstacle when you are running down the street, don't go around it – jump over it! But only if said obstacle is really, really small and it makes you look like a right prat.

I was lucky if any of my blog posts attracted a couple of comments at most, but this particular review ended up with ninety-one responses. The parkouring community was furious with me. In hindsight, I shouldn't have described them as 'demented baboons in hoodies'. I tried to shrug off their virtual vitriol, but there was one comment that really got under my skin:

YOU SPEND EVERY WAKING SECOND NO DOUBT ON YOUR FAT ARSE!

The commentator then imagined what would happen if I ever attempted to parkour myself:

I believe that you would bounce . . . roll to a halt and fucking

cry like a fat motherfucking tard while he sucks his fat mother-
fucking thumb then gets hungry and fucking eats his thumb.

Something in me snapped. I persuaded Sue to photograph me jumping through our building site. I leapt from
beams, hurdled over tractors and rolled through dried-up
cow dung. This would show those parkouring baboons! I
ended up on the roof of our caravan where, as I was waiting
for Sue to bring me a stepladder so I could get back down
again, I tripped over some loose felt and plummeted to the
ground, breaking both ankles. I cried like a motherfucking tard and was crippled for months but I still posted the
photos. And no one has ever called me Fat Boy again.

5. Behind the Sofa (2005–2011)

I was still blogging when *Doctor Who* returned to television
in 2005, so it felt natural to combine my two interests. Once
again, I recruited like-minded souls from across the internet
to help share the workload, and this allowed me to stagger
reviews of a single episode over a whole week, which meant
that people kept coming back for more. In fact Behind the
Sofa became so popular it made numerous recommended
lists on TV websites, and when one of the new series writers,
Steven Moffat, left a very nice comment on a review, I remember thinking that blogging couldn't get any better than this.

6. Tachyon TV 2.0 (2006–2011)

One of Behind the Sofa's most prolific contributors was a
man named Damon Querry, and because he lived just a
few miles away from me, and because he didn't sound like

he was a total nutter, I suggested that we meet each other face-to-face. We chose a local *Doctor Who* convention in Stockton-on-Tees as neutral territory and Damon brought a friend along with him for moral support. This man's name was John Williams. Not only was John an expert on soap operas set in the north of England – he still insists on calling *Emmerdale*, *Emmerdale Farm* – he was, and remains, the funniest man I have ever met. The three of us decided to join forces and re-launch Tachyon TV as a weekly series of irreverent *Doctor Who*-themed podcasts, the hot new medium. If we could make each other laugh, maybe we could make other fans laugh too.

When we ran out of amusing things to say about classic episodes of *Doctor Who*, we branched out into interviewing celebrities instead – though this might be pushing the term 'celebrities' past its breaking point. One Thursday at the Tavern in Fitzrovia, we plied Bentham the Younger with lemonade until he admitted – on the record, no less – that *Torchwood* was 'a mistake'. Step aside, Woodward and Bernstein! And we chatted to actors and producers and writers from the classic era and the new series and no one called anyone a motherfucking tard, at least not when the mic was on.

I loved working on Tachyon TV but, as with all my previous online projects, I started getting restless after a while. There are only so many times someone who knows everything about *Doctor Who* can ask someone else who knows everything about *Doctor Who* a question fans who know everything about *Doctor Who* already know the answer to.

I needed a new challenge, a new domain to conquer and legally register. It was time for the Adventure to begin . . .

Spoiler Warning

Congratulations! You have reached the part of the book where Sue's epic journey through twenty-six years of *Doctor Who*, and my two-year battle with a blog about it, really begins. While you don't have to have read our blog to understand, and hopefully enjoy, what follows, readers should know that I reveal many of Sue's episode scores and opinions along the way, plus most of the endings of every *Doctor Who* story ever made. If you've never visited our blog before – or if you'd prefer to discover these things on the blog first – now might be a good time to find a bookmark, pop it in here, and head over to www.wifeinspace.com. It's only half a million words so it shouldn't take you that long to get up to speed. We'll wait here until you get back.

The Experiment Begins

Done? Let's go!

It wasn't my intention to watch *Doctor Who* from the very beginning with Sue, or with anyone else for that matter. I planned to go it alone for a new blog.

I had been thinking about re-watching the classic series ever since I read the first volume of Toby Hadoke and Rob Shearman's *Running Through Corridors*, where the pair watch and review every episode of *Doctor Who* in chronological order. Because Hadoke and Shearman are funny, engaging writers, reading this book was a thoroughly entertaining experience. But it also reminded me that, although I called myself a *Doctor Who* fan, and other people called me a Whovian, there were quite a few episodes of *Doctor Who* I had never actually seen.

> **John Williams:** The first rule of watching *Doctor Who* from the beginning is you don't watch *Doctor Who* from the beginning. You start with 'The Dalek Invasion of Earth'. *Everybody* gives up in the middle of 'The Sensorites'.
>
> **Me:** But if I start with the tenth story, won't that be cheating?
>
> **John:** Look, do you want to do this or not? You can watch the first nine stories at the end if it bothers you. If you get that far. How are you going to watch them?

Me: When Sue's gone to bed, I suppose.

John: That will never work. If you watch them late
    at night, you'll fall asleep before you reach the first
    cliffhanger. If I were you, I would follow Andrew
    Pixley's* advice. He watched them while he was
    having his tea.

Me: If I do embark on this marathon, I might write it
    up for Tachyon TV. I could make it a regular feature.

John: Really? What could you possibly say about *Doctor
    Who* that hasn't been said a million times before?

John was right, of course – the last thing the world needed
was another *Doctor Who* blog. But I couldn't get the idea of
blogging a television series from the very beginning out of
my head, though I baulked at John's suggestion of '*Emmerdale Farm*'. And, perhaps arrogantly, I couldn't shake the
feeling that *Doctor Who* had some mileage left in it. There
had to be an angle that nobody had considered before, I just
had to find it.

And then . . .

Sue: Haven't you got a DVD we could watch instead?
    This is terrible.

She had a point, *Downton Abbey* was awful.

Me: We could watch *Doctor Who*.

The rest, as Neil Perry would have said, is herstory.

*

* Esteemed television historian, renowned *Doctor Who* archivist and
thoroughly nice man.

I made sure that the viewing conditions were just right the night we started our experiment: the curtains were drawn, the cats and dog had been fed, our phones were switched off, our ashtrays were empty and our lighters were full. Sue was cradling a mug of tea and I was nursing a stiff drink.

I reached for the remote control and pressed Play . . .

DOCTOR WHO: AN UNEARTHLY CHILD BY ANTHONY COBURN

Twenty-five minutes later . . .

Sue: Eh?

Sue absorbed the first episode of Doctor Who *in respectful silence and this was her first audible reaction to it as the credits rolled.*

Me: Is that all you've got?
Sue: I thought it would be a lot longer than that.

Of all the opening gambits I could have expected – from a gushing 'Wow! Now I understand why you love this show!' to a rueful 'We missed The One Show *for that?' – that wasn't on my list.*

Me: So what did you think, then? It's a classic, so no pressure.

She sighed deeply, and then she told me she was shocked by William Hartnell's curt, abrasive manner, and how it was hard for her to believe that this Doctor was the same character played by David Tennant and Matt Smith.

Sue: The Doctor was arrogant, snide and spiteful. He's a bit creepy, to be honest.

Sue awarded an 'An Unearthly Child' 7 out of 10.

The idea of awarding scores for episodes or stories was meant to be a joke – the sort of thing one might expect from a stat-obsessed Whovian. But I was rather irritated by this 7. Many fans – myself included – would argue that 'An Unearthly Child' is as good as 1960s *Doctor Who* ever gets. A 7 out of 10 didn't inspire confidence because the scores would only get lower from here.

Sure enough, the next three episodes, which featured hirsute cavemen questing for fire, only scored 4 out of 10 apiece. But that was all right because those episodes aren't very good. But then it was the turn of 'The Daleks'. This is the story that introduced an unsuspecting public to the eponymous villains for the first time, and, practically overnight, the bungalow loving bastards transformed *Doctor Who* from an offbeat curiosity on the brink of cancellation into a *bona fide* phenomenon.

Sue gave 'The Daleks' 3 out of 10.

Sue: Is that score too low? Will the fans be upset with me?
Me: Forget about them. I want to record your honest reactions.
Sue: 2/10, then.
Me: Are you joking?
Sue: I don't have anything to compare it to, apart from the new series. And 'Genesis of the Daleks', which this story seems to contradict, I might add.

Getting into Dalek chronology right now could be fatal, so I
sulk instead.

Sue: OK, OK. I'll give it . . . 3/10.
Me: You do realise that if it wasn't for this story, the series
would have been cancelled after just a handful of episodes.
We wouldn't be watching *Doctor Who* today if it wasn't for
'The Daleks'.
Sue: Can I change my score back to a 2?

The scores were low and the commentary was withering.
However, Sue was clearly enjoying herself. My favourite part
of the experiment so far was not watching the episodes but
writing them up for the blog afterwards. I knew it was working – not only was it funny, Sue was genuinely saying things
no one had said about *Doctor Who* before – at least not outside of a 1960s living room.

However, I was still a little worried. It wasn't the
thought of seven hundred episodes of *Doctor Who* that
bothered me (that would come later), it was how Sue
might be treated by the *Doctor Who* fan community.
Years had passed since *rec.arts.drwho* but they were no
less grumpy and cynical – in fact they were worse. I hesitated before publishing Sue's lukewarm assessment of 'An
Unearthly Child' because I knew when I did I would be
offering up my wife to ridicule, scorn and possibly the
odd death threat. And I still went ahead and published
it anyway.

And then the feedback started:

This is superb. You have to keep her at it, regardless of the effect on your marriage.

Keep going. This is more fun than watching The Persuaders.

Susan must have the patience of a saint! Your Susan that is, not the unearthly one.

Laugh out loud hilarious. Please keep up the experiment.

I love it! (You're not really going to inflict the recons on her, though, surely?)

There was a warning, too:

I think that you should look up the statistics on this before you seriously think of continuing. Do you know that one in three marriages fail before the 'Ambassadors of Death'?

Really? I thought it would be a lot higher than that.

Sue pretended not to care about the comments until I caught her reading some of them one night. She told me that the positive reactions had surprised her – she thought the fans would be appalled by her lack of respect. I told her to take nothing for granted and that she should wait until I published her review of 'The Daleks', which was even more contentious.

Sue: If this was a modern Doctor, you'd just assume that he was playing with them and he had a plan up his sleeve, but with this git you really believe that he'll sell everyone out just to get away. What a total knob. They should have called the show *Ian*. 3/10.

But I needn't have worried:

I think her score is spot on! Good on you, Sue.

I don't blame her for giving it a 3. I love it to bits but I'm looking at it through rose tinted specs.

Sue seems a sensible and wise individual.

I look forward to her reactions to 'The Web Planet', which I recall is 246 episodes long.

Sue is my new Perfect Woman™

Sue liked that last comment *a lot*.

Thirteen episodes down, only another six-hundred and eighty-four to go! But we were about to head into uncharted territory.

Here Be Recons

When I told Sue that more than a hundred black-and-white episodes of *Doctor Who* no longer existed, she was delighted.

Sue: What a relief.

Suffice to say, this is not what fans think of the BBC's policy of wiping much of its archive of classic television during the 1960s and 70s. *Doctor Who* fans consider it to be at best a short-sighted business decision and at worst an act of cultural vandalism and betrayal. But Sue was not a *Doctor Who* fan.

Sue: It means we can skip about a hundred episodes, doesn't it? I don't know what you were worrying about, Neil. This is going to be a piece of piss.

I told Sue that, unfortunately for her, we wouldn't have to skip any missing episodes if we didn't want to.

Sue: I'm not reading any of your books. You can forget about that for a start.
Me: Don't worry. You won't have to read anything, although you will have to concentrate quite hard.
Sue: I get it. You're going to read the books to me one-by-one, I'm going to imagine them in my head, then I'll tell you what I think about the imaginary acting, writing and carpentry, give it a mark out of ten and you'll write it all down.

Me: To be honest, that sounds more fun.

Although these episodes no longer existed on videotape or film, fans had resourcefully combined black-and-white photos taken in front of the TV and domestic audio recordings made during the programmes' original transmission in the 1960s – the family dog can occasionally be heard barking in the background – with modern computer technology to produce rough approximations of what the stories may have been like.

> **Sue**: Are these the reconstructions that everyone keeps going on about on the blog? Rob Shearman says we shouldn't watch them. He says it's too dangerous.
>
> **Me**: You don't even know who Rob Shearman is.

Rob Shearman was correct, though. It could be a step too far. The best recon could only ever be a shadow of its former self; and if the original story wasn't up to much, any recon, no matter how skilfully or lovingly rendered, could only be worse – much worse. If I didn't fancy wading through 106 black-and-white slide shows to the accompaniment of the muffled barking of a long-dead dog, I was pretty certain that Sue would feel the same way.

So I compromised. For a DVD release, the BBC had edited the missing seven-part story 'Marco Polo' into a single thirty-minute episode, which meant that Sue could both experience a reconstruction – referred to by hip Whovians as 'recons' – and a notoriously long historical saga – referred to by hip Whovians as 'historicals' – in one fell swoop.

Sue: I'm enjoying this a lot more than some of the others I've seen. It's a lot faster for a start.
Me: To be fair, the original version would be a lot slower than this. This is three hours edited down to thirty minutes.
Sue: Can we watch all of them like this? It would save us a lot of time.

She is convinced that the lack of moving pictures improves things because she isn't distracted by poor camera work and flimsy sets.

Sue: I really enjoyed that. I also think it helps that these are real, historical people, and not silly cavemen or aliens.
Me: So, how do you feel about us watching more recons?
Sue: Not a problem. Bring 'em on.

'Marco Polo' proved to be an early turning point in the progress of the blog. When I told Sue that most of the fans I knew had never sat through a single recon, she took it as a challenge to watch more. When I told her that those fans included her own husband, she was incredulous.

> **Sue**: Fucking hell, Neil! And you call yourself a
> Whovian!
> **Me**: I don't, actually.
> **Sue**: Quite right too. All these years, I've been married
> to a lightweight. It's like I don't even know you.

In my life as a *Doctor Who* fan, recons had always felt like something I would get round to later. I didn't have the patience to sit through episodes that no longer existed, especially when there were plenty that did. And in truth, reading the novelisations of missing stories was both easier and kinder; the acting, writing and carpentry of my imagination were likely to be of a far higher standard than the fuzzy, jerry-built reality.

Sue told me in no uncertain terms that I was a wimp. Skipping the recons would be cheating, she said; if something was worth doing, it was worth doing laboriously.

> **Me:** I'll remind you of that when we reach 'The Space
> Pirates', assuming our marriage survives that long.
> **Sue:** Come on, Neil. If Rob fucking Shearman can do
> it, so can we.

So in the end, it wasn't me who made Sue watch more than a hundred black-and-white episodes of *Doctor Who* that no longer existed; typically, it was she who made me do it.

~~Five~~ Six More Things Sue Has Made Me Do

1. She made me jump out of a plane
When a group of her students pitched a documentary about parachuting to Sue, she didn't hesitate to volunteer me as its subject. She told them that my fear of heights alone would give them everything they needed to make a compelling television programme. There's no way I'm going anywhere near a plane, a parachute, an airfield or any of your students, I told her. The next thing I know I'm clinging on to the wing of a Cessna 3,500 feet in the air, while an ex-army sergeant yells in my face to let go.

2. She made me jump out of a plane again
Unfortunately, the students who were supposed to be documenting my jump into the wild blue yonder were drinking coffee in the aerodrome's cafeteria when the instructors finally prised my fingers off the fuselage and I fell, screaming every inch of the way. As a result they failed to get any footage of me crashing to earth in a nearby field, which meant that I had to jump out of the plane again. Sue insisted on this because she didn't want her students to fail and also she was the one who suggested that they go for a coffee in the first place.

3. She made me take my dad on honeymoon with us
Sue was adamant that Nicol come with us on our honeymoon to Florida, which meant that my dad had to come along too.

We lounged by the pool, with my dad. We went on Space Mountain at Disneyland, with my dad. We dined beneath the twinkling stars, with my dad. To be fair, it was a memorable family holiday but it was not especially romantic.

Now that Nicol has grown up and left home, in order finally to experience the joy of a proper honeymoon I have suggested to Sue that we renew our wedding vows somewhere idyllic – a beach in Hawaii, maybe, or a balcony overlooking Niagara Falls – but she says it won't feel the same without an old man standing next to us, chain smoking and complaining about his IBS.

4. She made me dress as a woman
One day, when Nicol was six, she was feeling poorly and down in the dumps so Sue asked me to cheer her up. I wanted to show her *Monty Python and the Holy Grail* but Sue had a much better idea. And that's why I ended up parading around the living room in Sue's bra and skirt as if it was the most natural thing in the world. It did the trick, though – Nicol thought it was the funniest thing she had ever seen and everybody laughed. And yes, I enjoyed it too. It felt like a nice thing to do. Making Nicol laugh I mean, not the dressing-up part.

But Nicol wouldn't let it lie. In the weeks that followed she told *everyone* that I liked to walk round the house in women's clothing – her friends, her friends' parents, her teachers, even our neighbours – until half of Christopher Street thought Nicol and her mum were living with Norman Bates.

It's an unfunny joke that has run for twenty years. Every time *Psycho* is on; every time Vic and Bob said 'Are you looking at my bra?'; every time a hard-hitting documentary about transvestism appeared on television; every time David Beckham wore a sarong or we were served in a café by a waitress with big hands – oh, how they laughed.

I have tried reminding them what Norman Bates liked to do when he dressed up in women's clothing but to no effect.

5. She made me quit my job

One day, Sue sat me down and told me that, if teaching wasn't fun any more, if my heart wasn't in it, then I should get out and let somebody else have a go. She was fed up with hearing me moan every single day on the way to work about the current state of higher education and how it isn't like it used to be. Unlike me, Sue has lost none of her enthusiasm for teaching and none of her commitment to her students. She would chuck someone out of a plane – twice – if she thought it might help them achieve their goals. And she must be doing something right, because her students keep winning awards.

Sue is a great motivator. She made me believe I could do anything. Obviously, the blog would not have been a success without her – we never would have got past the recons, for a start – and I certainly would never have finished this book without her standing at my shoulder, urging me on.

6. She made me think of another thing she made me do

Sue: Couldn't you come up with six things? All the other lists in this book come in sixes.

The Miserable Git and the Scruffy Drunk

The wife went through a lot in those first six months. She dealt with giant insects ('Did that ant really just run head-long into that camera?'); she visited Swinging London in the sixties ('Are the Pink Floyd in this one?'); she watched the Daleks' Master Plan fall apart ('Twelve parts. Twelve. Bloody. Parts.'); and she couldn't understand why nobody ever mentioned the Time War ('The last time I was this lost, I was watching *Lost*.').

The one constant through all this was the irascible presence of William Hartnell's Doctor – or as Sue christened him, the Miserable Git.

Sue didn't like the First Doctor very much and the truth is, neither did I. Seen in relatively quick succession, his behaviour in these early stories was often inexplicably appalling – he was startlingly rude and he kept trying to ditch his companions, or on one occasion kill them. He abandoned his own granddaughter on the Dalek-ravaged ruins of future Earth without even asking her if she minded. Matt Smith he wasn't.

Sue: They should have called the lead actor William Heartless.

There was also another problem. Some of the Miserable Git's so-called adventures were just so . . . *dull*. Take 'The Sensorites', for example. I had attempted to watch 'The

Sensorites' several times over the years but without success;
I had never even managed to crawl to the end of the first
episode – and 'The Sensorites' is six episodes long.

Sue: This reminds me of *Avatar*.

Me: *Avatar*? *AVATAR*! Are you taking the piss?

Sue: Well, it's not in 3D, obviously, and the aliens aren't
blue . . .

Me: Their costumes might have been blue, actually.

Sue: Well there you go, then. I don't understand why you've
been so reluctant to watch this one. It's not that bad. You
should keep an open mind.

Sue gave 'The Sensorites' 5 out of 10, so either she's much
more forgiving than I am or she's completely insane. I would
have scored it significantly lower and that was before she
made me sit through the whole thing.

I think this is one of the reasons why Sue's episode commentaries became so popular so quickly. If she'd hated
everything, then the blog would have been a soulless and
predictable chore, not only for us, but for our readers as
well. But she didn't hate everything. Far from it: she actively
enjoyed 'The Aztecs'; she liked 'Planet of Giants' and nobody
likes that one; she even went so far as to call 'The Time
Meddler' 'superb' and 'The Myth Makers' 'excellent . . . very
funny but still very bleak'. And that was a recon.

It wasn't all plain sailing. 'The Celestial Toymaker' was so
appalling (and possibly racist) that she refused even to score
it. The only reason the ant-based epic 'The Web Planet'

achieved 1 out of a possible 10 was because the Spanish dub of episode 6 made her laugh. However, she kept coming back for more. And when my head went down or I questioned whether it was worth going on, she was always there with the same response.

Sue: I thought you said you liked *Doctor Who*.

That's right, I had to keep reminding myself; I thought I did.

*

When the time came for us to watch the second Peter Cushing Dalek movie, I decided to do something a bit different. Instead of presenting Sue's opinions to the world via the medium of transcribed prose, I would make her speak to our audience directly.

I'd wanted to record a podcast commentary for ages, if only to prove to everybody that my wife actually existed. No one had accused me directly of conjuring up an imaginary wife – I am a *Doctor Who* fan, after all – but even I thought this new *Who*-munching version of Sue seemed too good to be true. It was time to put her to the test.

Sue: I'm sorry, but you want me to do what?
Me: I want you to watch this film, and I want you to talk over it while you watch it. Oh, and I want you to record everything you say.
Sue: And where will you be while I'm doing this?
Me: Nicol is taking me shopping. You'll be fine. Here, have a glass of wine.

Sue telephoned me forty-five minutes later.

Me: What's wrong? You can't have finished it already.
Sue: Look, I had to stop the film. There's this bit where the Doctor can't see a note his granddaughter has left for him on a door, EVEN THOUGH IT'S RIGHT THERE IN FRONT OF HIM! It's fucking ridiculous, Neil. Seriously.

Five minutes later, she rang again.

Sue: Do I have to do this? This doesn't feel right to me. This is supposed to be Adventures *with* the Wife in Space so where the hell are you? I sound drunk. And sweary.
Me: Good.

When I returned home, Sue was very merry indeed, which explains why in her commentary she believes that Neil Tennant played the Tenth Doctor. But it did prove one thing: not only did my wife exist, if something happened to me she should be able to complete the experiment without me.

*

And then, after eighty-six episodes, thirty-three recons and two films that don't count, we reached the experiment's first milestone. The Miserable Git was about to regenerate into Charlie Drake.

Sue: That should have been brilliant. It's got the Cybermen in it, it's got the very first regeneration in it, and you've been

banging on about the missing episode for almost twenty years. And it was shit! I definitely would have stopped watching *Doctor Who* if I had been a kid back then.
Me: But you were a kid back then.
Sue: Shut it.

When we began our experiment, the Second Doctor's first twelve episodes did not exist in the archives; Sue didn't see Charlie – or Patrick Troughton, to give him his birth name – move properly for two whole weeks. Even then it took her a while to warm to him. She thought he was too silly and too dishevelled to take seriously.

>   **Sue**: What's he doing, Neil? He's playing it like a scruffy drunk.

It wasn't until Troughton's sixth story, 'The Faceless Ones', that everything seemed to click into place.

The Doctor enters into a peaceful negotiation with the alien interlopers.

Sue: He's definitely the Doctor now. He didn't just blow the bad guys up and he didn't watch somebody else blow them up, either. He showed great humanity and forgiveness. And that's what the Doctor is all about, isn't he?
Me: Is this the point where you feel like you are watching real *Doctor Who*?
Sue: Yes. Yes, I think it is.

From that point on, even if the story wasn't very good, Sue didn't have a bad word to say about the Scruffy Drunk. It didn't matter if he was fighting Daleks ('You can't take your eyes off him'), Cybermen ('Troughton's *great*') or Yeti ('He's very good, which definitely goes without saying now'), his performance was always sublime. She even forgave him when he played a Mexican doppelgänger in 'Enemy of the World' with a disgracefully fruity accent ('It's Inspector Clouseau meets Speedy Gonzales').

When we reached 'The Krotons' – the same lousy story I couldn't finish when I was twelve – I decided the time had come to shake things up a bit. I invited Sue's brother, Gary, to join us on the sofa.

Gary: I saw most of the William Hartnells but I don't remember watching this one. I think I'd grown out of *Doctor Who* by the time I was twelve.
Me: You weren't a fan of Patrick Troughton, then?
Gary: No, I was probably watching *Lost in Space*. It was much better. There was a robot called Robby the Robot in it. What more do you want?

I didn't have the heart to tell him that the robot in Lost in Space *wasn't called Robby. It wasn't called anything.*

Gary: This is shit.
Sue: Leave it alone.

Later . . .

Gary: The robots have the same arms as Robby the Robot!

Me: Are you sure you weren't watching this after all, Gary?
Gary: The pain! The pain!

Sue gave 'The Krotons' a generous 6 out of 10; her brother was less impressed and awarded it a 1. And even though Gary's assessment was much fairer than Sue's – 'The Krotons' only seems to get worse as the years go by – his opinions didn't go down very well on the blog.

Don't invite Gary round ever again, not even for Christmas Dinner.

Gary manages to suck the joy out of everything. He really brings the mood down. I'm quite angry about it, actually.

Tell Gary to get lost. In space, preferably.

Who's (sic) stupid idea was it to invite this moron round? He knows nothing.

Your brother-in-law is a massive c**t.

When I launched a website survey a few weeks later and asked our readers if there was anything they didn't like about the blog, 32 per cent simply said: Gary.

This was one of those moments where writing the blog and its effect on our real lives intersected in quite an uncomfortable way. We shielded Gary from the ensuing backlash. He didn't discover total strangers were calling him a massive c**t until three months later when it was casually mentioned on local BBC radio. Sue was appearing on the station to talk about the experiment so far when she admitted to the show's host, Bob Fischer, that Gary was loathed and despised by the vast majority of our readers.

Later that night, I apologised to Gary and asked him if he felt OK about it.

Gary: It's fine, Neil. You should hear what the *Lost in Space* fans are calling you.

*

We were celebrating Sue's fiftieth birthday when a friend told me that a missing episode had been discovered in an old man's shed. I should have jumped for joy, or at least smiled, but all I could think was: of all the episodes they had to find, why did it have to be an episode of 'Galaxy 4'? Nobody stayed awake at night worrying about what had happened to 'Galaxy 4'. Why couldn't they have found one of the good missing episodes instead?

My friend swore me to secrecy. The recovery would be officially announced at a 'Missing Believed Wiped' event at the BFI in three months' time, and he begged me to keep the news to myself until then, even though he clearly hadn't been able to do that himself, which is why I didn't feel too guilty when I betrayed his confidence a few hours later. Of course I had to tell somebody. Privileged information like that didn't come along every day, even if it was vaguely disappointing. I just had to make sure that I told somebody who wouldn't yell it from the rooftops (or worse, a *Doctor Who* forum). So, naturally, I chose Sue:

Me: You won't believe this but they've found a missing episode of *Doctor Who*.

Sue: Is it a good one?

Me: It's an episode from a William Hartnell story called

'Galaxy 4'. You didn't like it very much when we
watched the reconstruction.

Sue: Does this mean I'll have to watch it again?

Me: If they release the episode on DVD before we finish
this thing, then yes, you probably will. Sorry.

Sue: Then let's get this over with before the bastards can
find any more.

Apart from Sue, I never told another soul about 'Galaxy 4'. And then, two months later, something even more
remarkable happened . . .

> Transcript of Internet Chat with John Williams
> 2 November 2011 12.17 p.m.:
> **John**: They've found a *Doctor Who*.
> **Me**: Really? Which one?

I decided to feign ignorance so my friend could savour
this moment. Who knows, I thought, I might even be able
to fake some excitement this time, too.

> **John**: It's a Troughton.

Wait a minute. 'Galaxy 4' wasn't a Troughton . . .

> **John**: You'll laugh when I tell you which one it is.
> **Me**: Is it 'The Space Pirates'?
> **John**: Worse.
> **Me**: 'The Underwater Menace'?
> **John**: Yes. They've found part two. It could hardly be
> more disappointing.
> **Me**: Where did they find it?
> **John**: It was recovered along with 'Galaxy 4' in an
> old man's shed. He was a perverse collector of crap
> episodes it seems. This is totally hush-hush by the way.

Me: Of course.

John: We don't want to start a riot.

Me: How did you know about 'Galaxy 4'?

John: You told me.

Me: I did?

John: At Sue's party. You were very drunk at the
time. Drunk and disappointed.

*

People continued to leave comments on the blog. Most of
them were positive, some of them were troubling, and one
of them was put to music. It arrived in an email, sent in
the middle of the night, with the subject line: 'A Song for
Susan'. When I clicked the link contained inside it, and the
song began to play, I didn't know whether to laugh, cry or
call the police.

> *Neil and Sue and Doctor Who*
>
> *Are required just to get me through*
>
> *Especially Sue, with her not-we ways*
>
> *She can reverse the polarity of my neutron flow any day*
>
> *And I wish Neil would pass through a CVE*
>
> *Then it would be just sweet Susan and me*
>
> *The Wife in Space – la la la la la la (and repeat)*

If you're not a *Doctor Who* expert, a CVE is a charged
vacuum emboitment, which is just a fancy way of describing
a large hole in space. Anyway, if you were to pass through a
CVE, you'd end up in a completely different universe, and
that's where this budding singer/songwriter wanted me to
go, so he could make a move on my wife.

The song was accompanied by a video* but I hesitated before I showed it to Sue.

I wasn't sure how she'd react to a young man in his early twenties crooning his affection for her, especially when he had taken the trouble to source a photograph of her from the internet, which he was now stroking seductively during the song's middle-eight. I was probably worried that she might like it.

If that wasn't unsettling enough, a few weeks later, Sue received an email from somebody very high up in the university where we both worked. When she saw the email's subject line – 'The Wife in Space' – she thought she was in trouble for being too sweary on a blog, but it was much, much worse than that. Sue's fans were crawling out of the woodwork, and her biggest fan just happened to be related to someone who worked at the same campus as us. According to this email, our colleague's son was obsessed with Sue and he wouldn't stop talking about her. It was Sue this, Sue that, morning, noon and night. Sue thought the email was going to warn her to lock her office door for the foreseeable future, but what the father was proposing was even stranger: a meeting with him and his wife so Sue could help them arrange the perfect Christmas treat for their son.

We agreed to meet Sue's biggest fan's parents in her office one Friday afternoon in December. What else were we going to do? His dad was *very* high up in the university. However, as she shook their hands, Sue unexpectedly blurted out:

* www.youtube.com/watch?v=uM1-8LqFYzU (if he hasn't taken it down in shame yet).

Sue: You can tell your son that they've found two missing episodes of *Doctor Who*. He'll love that.

Which ones are they again, Neil?

Me: I've forgotten.

Sue: No, you haven't.

Me: They lost them again. It's very tragic.

Happily, the parents didn't seem to care. They were chatty and friendly. Would Sue mind autographing a selection of Christmas presents they had bought for their son? This bundle of delights included a T-shirt, a calendar, some DVD covers and, most bizarre of all, a handwritten invitation from Sue asking their son to join her for a coffee the next time he was in town. She signed them all.

Before the parents left, they took some photos as a memento of our meeting. Funnily enough, I don't appear in any of them.

*

Unlike the Miserable Git, the Scruffy Drunk went out in a blaze of glory. His final ten-part story, 'The War Games', scored an impressive 9 out of 10, and if you'd have told me at the start of our quest that Sue would have sat through a ten-part black-and-white story and given it a score like that, I wouldn't have believed you. Actually, *I still don't believe it.*

It took Sue nine months and three weeks to watch *Doctor Who*'s black-and-white years. We could have had a baby together in the same amount of time – William Patrick Perryman, perhaps – and I'm sure it would have been less stressful. But it was at this point in the experiment that I knew for certain that my wife would definitely make it to the end, even if I didn't. If she could sit through all the black-and-white episodes, including the ones that didn't exist any more, then the next phase of the experiment should be easy – things were about to get exciting. U.N.I.T.! Sea Devils! Drashigs! And the *real* caped crusader himself – Jon Pertwee!

Me: Are you looking forward to Jon Pertwee?
Sue: No, I'm dreading it. I have very vivid memories of him driving around in a stupid yellow sports car and I hated him. It was difficult to take him seriously.
Me: Why?
Sue: Because he looked like my mam.

Colgate

I can count the number of famous people I've met on one hand, and by famous I mean my mum has heard of them. Two of these encounters were work-related: I had to show the film producer David Puttnam and the journalist Kate Adie around the university once, while the third occurred when the Green Cross Code man came to my school in 1983 to promote road safety and *The Return of the Jedi* (and not necessarily in that order). I asked David Prowse if he really was Luke Skywalker's dad, and the barefaced liar told me that he wasn't.*

However, if there's famous, there's also *Doctor Who*-famous. Now, my mother might not recognise them but if I had to talk to, say, Paul Cornell or Graeme Harper, then I'd experience exactly the same sense of tongue-tied awkwardness I'd feel if I had to talk to George Clooney or Steven Spielberg – well, maybe not as bad as that. The point is, I would probably be able to chat to them normally as long as nobody mentioned *Doctor Who*.

If you are a *Doctor Who* fan, it is comparatively easy to meet your idols and put the fear of God into them. I once accidentally spent half an hour in the company of Wendy Padbury, who played the Second Doctor's companion, Zoe,

---

* I also went to the same school as Clive Owen, but he was three years older than me so we only ever shared assemblies and fire drills, and he wasn't exactly famous back then either, except amongst the girls in the lower sixth.

over forty years ago and still has to suffer the attentions of over-excited middle-aged men. Wendy was smoking at the time, as was I. I recognised her immediately. However, I didn't want Wendy to think that I was just another sad Whovian with only one thing on his mind so I made polite small talk about the weather and the rising costs of pet insurance instead. Wendy was delightful, and she gave me some very sage advice about fixed-rate mortgages, but by the time she finally got up to leave, I was exhausted. But I had done it. I had got through it without once mentioning the D-word.

Wendy: Goodbye. It was lovely to meet you.
Me: Bye, Zoe! Sorry, shit, I mean Wendy. Sorry!

This partly explains why I didn't go to a *Doctor Who* convention until I was well into my thirties. Also, I couldn't see the point of them. Why would I pay to listen to actors and directors telling the same stories that I'd already read in magazines and books a hundred times before? But in 2003, the year *Doctor Who* celebrated its fortieth anniversary, a convention called Panopticon announced that every surviving Doctor would be in attendance at the Metropole Hotel, London, in November to mark the special occasion. It sounded like an opportunity too good to miss.

The first thing that struck me when I walked into the lobby of the Metropole wasn't the home-made Dalek bumping into the furniture, or even Mr Bronson from *Grange Hill* posing for a photograph with the concierge. No, it was the line of beautiful women standing at the check-in desk. I'd never seen so many gorgeous women assembled in one place before. Seriously, these women were stunning.

Sue: OK. I get it. Move on.

These women were supermodels.

Sue: Yes, OK, *we get it.*

No, a supermodel convention was taking place in the same hotel, in parallel with ours. So one half of the hotel was full of beautiful women while the other half, well, wasn't. There wasn't a great deal of crossover between these two events, although this didn't stop several guests from my side of the divide from trying. If one of the supermodel panels that weekend had been a master class in how to avoid being chatted up by men who liked to punch well above their weight, then they certainly had ample opportunity to put what they learned into practice every time they went to the bar.

I can't speak for the supermodels but the convention I attended was a disaster. Three out of five surviving Doctors failed to materialise, while the absence of an event time-table meant it was practically impossible for anyone there to locate any of the panels they wished to attend and/or avoid. Couple this to the fact that it cost more money to buy a pint of lager than it did to buy a Tom Baker action figure from the dealer's room, and that the cashpoint in the lobby had been hacked so when you got home you discovered that your bank account had been emptied, and my overall impression of conventioneering was that it was an expensive, and frankly disappointing, hobby, one I had been entirely justified in avoiding for the previous thirty-odd years.

But at least I got through that weekend without having

to speak to anyone who might make me feel nauseous and inadequate, other than the supermodels. The closest I got was when I accidentally held a door open for Paul McGann. I couldn't believe it. He was tiny.

*

Although I have never spoken to a Doctor, a Doctor has spoken to me. Well, I say, spoken. Attacked is more accurate.

I blame Issue 1 (of 1) of the Tachyon TV Fanzine. It was 2006 and the website of the same name was still soldiering on, mainly thanks to my friends John Williams and Damon Querry. We had decided that it might be fun if we transformed our digital fansite into an old-fashioned printed fanzine. It would be a one-off homage to a simpler time, when expressing your love for a television programme had more to do with Letraset and glue than HTML coding and CSS style sheets. The finished fanzine was a light-hearted and affectionate celebration of *Doctor Who* and its funny little ways. It included reviews, its very own Agony Aunt, a pin-up poster of Adric and even a couple of songs. We were so proud of it, we decided we would hand out free copies at a local *Doctor Who* convention in Stockton-on-Tees. John and Damon drove to the hotel on the Friday night with hundreds of copies bundled in the boot of their car. I planned to join them in the morning and help distribute them.

John texted me just as I was climbing into bed:

> Just gave Colin Baker a copy of the fanzine.

This was unexpected. Colin Baker wasn't supposed to be at the convention. I texted back:

You gave Colin the fanzine? Are you INSANE?

John may have been too drunk to remember what was in our fanzine, but I wasn't. I knew its contents inside out, specifically the cheap joke on page 17 about Colin Baker's weight. It was a barely legible 6-point headline on the cover of an imaginary back issue, but it was there all right:

COLIN BAKER: THE TRUTH, THE WHOLE TRUTH AND A TRAY OF DOUGHNUTS

I don't know who came up with this joke. It's not remotely amusing, is it? All I know for sure is that it wasn't me. I also remember thinking at the time that no possible harm could come of it because Colin wouldn't be at the convention, and I doubted that he collected *Doctor Who* fanzines in his spare time, so the chances of him seeing the offending remark were slim.

The next morning, after a sleepless night, I arrived at the convention hotel to find John and Damon sitting in the ballroom, waiting for the first panel of the day. They looked a little the worse for wear, but that didn't stop me from chastising them for their spectacular lapse of judgement the night before.

John: Calm down. Colin won't read it. And even if
he did, he'd need an electron microscope to find
anything that might upset him. Relax. Anyway, it was
Damon's fault. He made me do it.

The first panel of the day wasn't supposed to be anything special – a couple of guest actors with small parts in the new series according to the convention timetable – so when I saw Colin Baker striding purposefully towards the stage with something rolled up under his arm, I knew that something had gone terribly wrong. And I wasn't just talking about the timetable. Colin didn't look very happy when he took his seat, and the interviewer's first question didn't improve his mood.

Interviewer: Do you like your fans, Colin?

Colin Baker: It's funny you should say that. I love the fans, and I have a great deal of time for them, as you well know. However, every once in a while, I find myself in the presence of an individual who says he's a fan, when in actual fact he's nothing more than a parasite.

When Colin spat out the word 'parasite', I could sense John's back straightening in the chair next to mine.

Colin: Take last night, for example, when some blithering idiot came up to me at the bar . . .

I glanced at John. John didn't glance back.

Colin: . . . and he gave me *this*.

Colin held up a copy of our fanzine for the crowd to inspect. It looked like it had been scrunched up and thrown across the room a few times.

Colin: This so-called *fan*-zine is a disgrace. Childish, undergraduate humour from cover to cover. Yes, 'The Twin Dilemma' isn't the best *Doctor Who* story ever made. How original! I've put on some weight. Big deal! Is that the best you can do? Look, if you don't like the programme, don't watch it. Don't spend so much time and energy slagging it off. Do something productive with your sad and pathetic lives instead.

The crowd applauded. John joined in.

John: Quite right too!

A woman sitting two rows in front of us stood up and cheered. I sank into my chair as the applause swelled. Two more fans stood up. Flaming torches were lit and smoke alarms starting going off.

I sat through the rest of Colin's panel in stunned silence and when it was finally over, I sheepishly turned to my friends to confirm that I hadn't imagined it and a bona fide Doctor had just slagged us all off. John shrugged his shoulders. Damon had obviously been crying.

*

This put me off conventions for a while, especially conventions that Colin might turn up to (and he turned up to *a lot*). We tried to make ourselves feel better by selling the last remaining copies of the fanzine online and we donated the proceeds to a charity that Colin was the patron of, but I don't think Damon ever fully recovered from the haranguing he received that morning; he *adored* Colin. I still occasionally wake in the middle of the night with the ex-Doctor's words ringing in my ears and John refuses to discuss the incident. I suspect – I hope – that Colin hasn't given it a second thought.

However, back in the present, with the experiment well under way, I began to think that it might be fun to expose Sue to the special thrills of the convention circuit. So meet me back here after the next chapter and I'll tell you about something even worse.

The Pompous Tory and the Mad One

I feared Stockholm syndrome might be setting in when Sue gave Jon Pertwee's debut story a perfect ten. Perhaps she was missing her mum.

Sue: It was four parts long and it was in colour. If all the Pertwee stories are like this, we'll be fine.

The routine we had settled into went something like this:

After confiscating Sue's mobile phone, I press the Play button on the PS3 with a cigarette in one hand and a notebook in the other. Nine times out of ten I have to pause the episode straight away to let the dog out – the theme music has an unsettling effect on Buffy – and then I'll make notes in shorthand as Sue rattles off her increasingly outrageous theories about the Time War. Every so often, I will pause or rewind the DVD to make sure that Sue hasn't missed anything important, which means, on average, that a twenty-five minute episode takes us forty-five minutes to watch. And then we do it all over again the next night. And the night after that. And the night after that . . .

I began to fantasise about watching episodes of any television programme other than *Doctor Who*: *Babylon 5*, *I, Claudius*, even *Downton Abbey*. And I was worried I was developing early onset RSI from constantly tapping out 'Is it the Master?' But Sue was indomitable.

Sue: I thought you said you liked *Doctor Who*.

Give it a rest, love, I thought.

*

'Is it the Master?'

Because Sue was an avid viewer of the new series of *Doctor Who*, she knew that the Doctor's arch-enemy was a rogue Time Lord called the Master. And because she knew that the Master had been the Doctor's arch-enemy for many years, if anyone even remotely villainous or suspicious or bearded appeared in an episode, she became convinced it was him, and was always disappointed when it wasn't. This reached its nadir during the 'The Mind Robber', because in that story the villain is called the Master – but he's just *a* Master and not *the* Master.

The definitive article finally showed up at the beginning of Jon Pertwee's second season in 'Terror of the Autons', but because he then proceeded to appear in practically every Third Doctor story thereafter, usually in disguise, the refrain 'Is it the Master?' never really went away. It was endearing at first, in a naïve sort of way, but it drove me mad towards the end. I began to suspect that Sue was doing it on purpose. She alternated between 'Is it the Master?' and 'Is it the Great Intelligence?' for the last few stories, which was even more annoying because it took longer to type.

However, Master-spotting wasn't the only thing that obsessed Sue. As the blog continued a series of recurring themes and motifs began to creep into her commentary:

- **Wood**. One of my biggest challenges in this experiment was keeping Sue's attention on the plot if a fine oak table or shabby-chic cabinet appeared in shot. No matter how lively the dialogue or convoluted the action, if Sue spotted some Shaker carpentry, everything else went out of the window. To Sue, 'The Talons of Weng-Chiang' will always be 'The one with the lovely antique furniture'.

- **Terry fucking Nation**. Terry Nation became famous for inventing the Daleks and infamous for re-writing their initial adventure 'The Daleks' over and over again in subsequent stories. Sue wasn't a fan of Terry's derivative scripts. Whenever she spotted his name in the opening credits, she would bellow 'Terry fucking Nation!' at the screen and threaten to watch the episode in complete silence. This might have saved me from an awful lot of typing but it would have resulted in some very uneventful blog updates.

- **An over-reliance on hypnotism to forward the plot**. Mesmerism was used so frequently in the programme, Sue decided to blame it on me, and it wasn't long before she was throwing cushions in my general direction whenever somebody fell under the bad guy's spell. This only stopped after I hypnotised her into forgetting that hypnotism annoyed her so much.

- **Not for kids!** When I told her that some of the most violent episodes were broadcast before 6 p.m., she opined that perhaps Mary Whitehouse had had a point. At twenty years' distance, she also thought I had a cheek for trying to ban Nicol from watching *The Breakfast Club* when, if I'd have had my way, she would have been watching brains splattering on floors, faces melting off, and hands being squashed to a bloody pulp.

- **The Time War.** Because Christopher Eccleston and David Tennant couldn't stop emoting about some terrible war that wiped out both the Daleks and the Time Lords, and because those events must have taken place *before* the new series started, Sue expected to see the conflict played out in the classic series. Poor Sue.

However, what obsessed Sue the most about the Third Doctor (aside from the fact that he was the spitting double of her late mother) was his politics.

Sue: You know what, Neil? He's such a pompous Tory. I bet this Doctor hangs around gentlemen's clubs, drinking brandy and being a twat.

Me: Unless he's acting, of course.

Sue: If this was Patrick Troughton, maybe. But look at Pertwee – he always dresses like he's on his way to a Masonic Lodge. I'm going right off him.

Some readers were annoyed by what they perceived as political bias. A few commentators suggested that Sue had a chip on her shoulder:

She goes on so often about poshness that it would be easy to wonder if she's someone in denial or for anyone to wonder if she's flaunting her politics. I don't think it's political on Sue's part but rather an outlet for her frustrated social ambitions at finding herself married to a man who spends his cash on Doctor Who *DVDs instead of silk antimacassars and mother-of-pearl bathroom fittings.*

She told me she didn't care, although whenever I published one of her reviews, she'd always ask me the following question over breakfast:

Sue: Do the fans hate me yet?

I assured her that most of them didn't and even when they did disagree with her – which happened quite a lot – most of them took it in good spirits.

Sue: That's nice. Not that I'd care if they did hate me.

One morning, however, I had to give her a slightly different answer:

Sue: Do the fans hate me yet?
Me: Most of them don't. Somebody did call you a sour-faced c**t last night though.
Sue: WHAT?

Shortly after this, Sue agreed to let me take her to the Doctor Who Experience in London, a high-tech exhibition of costumes, props and special effects from the programme. It was the closest I could get her to Longleat. While she studied the exhibits and tried to look interested in the vintage 1980s TARDIS console, I could tell her heart wasn't in it.

Sue agreed to have her photo taken in the green-screen studio. I thought that a photo of her stuck in the Pandorica would result in an amusing image for the website – I could pretend that this was how I made her watch Doctor Who *every night. So she sat in the prison and the photographer asked her to smile . . .*

Sue: I can't. I'm supposed to be bored and fed up.
Photographer: Because you've been trapped in a box for untold millennia?
Sue: No, because my husband is making me watch Jon Pertwee.

The only occasion on which Sue didn't want to watch *Doctor Who* with me was when one of our cats, Captain Jack, came down with a serious urinary tract infection and she couldn't give 'Frontier in Space' her undivided attention just in case he had a wee and killed himself. But we kept going. Sue rarely complained and never flagged. That said, all she had to do was sit in front of the television for twenty-five minutes, swearing and criticising the joinery, whereas for me the experiment was rapidly becoming a full-time job: taking notes, transcribing the notes, choosing the right images, moderating the comments, publicising the blog, getting into arguments on internet forums – it never seemed to end.

Gary agreed to return for more abuse by appearing in an audio commentary for the tenth anniversary story, 'The Three Doctors'. Nicol also joined us for this commentary. We'd come a long way since that time I tried to make her watch *Doctor Who* with me all those years ago in Christopher Street. She was still bored senseless, of course, that much hadn't changed, but because she was now a young woman with a first-class degree in mathematics, instead of sighing and yawning she took the programme to task for setting a story in an anti-matter universe, when anti-matter universes are, as everybody knows, a scientific impossibility. It was in this capacity that she became, somewhat against her will, the blog's Scientific Advisor.

Me: They tried to send three Doctors but one of them got stuck in a time eddy.
Nicol: A time eddy? A turbulent eddy?
Sue: What's a time eddy?
Nicol: It's just a timey-wimey spinney thing, Mam.
Sue: You sound like Matt Smith.
Nicol: Do they actually refer to it as an anti-matter universe?
Me: Yes.
Nicol: I'm not happy with that term. That term is *not correct*. It doesn't make any sense.
Me: What do you think, Gary?
Gary: Sorry, I was miles away.

It is official: Sue's favourite classic series Doctor is the Third. After we completed our journey, and I told Sue that the Pompous Tory had averaged the highest score of all the Doctors, she accused me of fiddling the figures like George Osborne. But the statistics speak for themselves (see the Average Score by Doctor chart in Appendix 3), and even though the science in our experiment was never meant to be taken that seriously – who was going to peer review it? – it did prove one thing: you can still enjoy *Doctor Who* even if you hate the Doctor so much you'd like to replace him with his arch-enemy.

Sue: I think I'd prefer to see the Master working with U.N.I.T. He should swap roles with the Doctor. I'm always disappointed when we cut back to Pertwee gurning in a chair.

---

*

It never really upset me that Sue thought the Third Doctor was a Pompous Tory. However, as we approached the point where Jon Pertwee would regenerate into Tom Baker, I began to grow apprehensive. What would happen if Sue hated the Fourth Doctor? What if she didn't like 'The Seeds of Doom'? If I couldn't be friends with someone who didn't like *Jaws*, how could I possibly stay married to a woman who didn't like Tom Baker?

When I watch Tom Baker's Doctor, I partly watch him from my childhood. This is why there will always be a special place in my heart for 'Revenge of the Cybermen', even though Sue is technically correct to describe it as 'a load of old rubbish'. Unlike me, Sue didn't bring any nostalgia with her to this experiment. She took each Doctor as she found him. In the case of Tom:

> **Sue:** Look at his eyes, Neil. He just looks mental. Is that what you all call him? The Mad One?

I knew my childhood hero wouldn't let me down and he didn't. Take the Mad One's second adventure 'The Ark in Space'. How could anyone not love 'The Ark in Space'?

Sue: It's bubble wrap painted green. There's no getting round that.

Me: You have to remember that bubble wrap was quite exotic in 1975. Give them a break.

Sue: You never got this defensive when I criticised the monsters in Jon Pertwee's stories.

Me: Yes, but this is an incredible performance from Kenton Moore. Look at the anguish etched into his face. It's incredible!

Sue: He looks like Rod Hull practising with Emu in his bedroom. But full marks to the actor. He managed to bang his hand on that desk without popping it.

Me: What about Tom?

Sue: Does Tom Baker ever blink? I don't think I've seen him blink. He'd be good against the Weeping Statues in the new series.

Me: Is that it?

Sue: OK, I admit it. He's brilliant.

But everything kicked off when we reached 'Terror of the Zygons'. Now Sue enjoyed 'Terror of the Zygons' and she awarded it a perfectly respectable 7, which I think is charitable for a story that features some thinly veiled racism towards the Scots and a creature which is more Loch Ness Muppet than Monster. Sadly, for some of our readers, this score wasn't nearly high enough:

No No No. Enough with the less than funny insults etc. – you need to start appreciating WHEN this was made and WHO its intended audience was for (sic)! The monster does the job, the Zygons are bordering on the BEST that WHO has come up with . . . basically this story is bordering on the best the doctor offers . . . it's a mighty 9/10 . . . aside from Pyramids, Talons, City . . . there's little else to touch it. I've followed this site for a while but going by your recent lacklustre scores for some classic episodes I'm afraid my experiment stops here!

Comments were moderated on the blog, so if anyone posted something from an IP address that I didn't trust or recognise, their message would sit in my inbox, awaiting my approval. This usually meant that I would spend my mornings wading through the reams of abuse that had been posted in the middle of the night (and it was always the middle of the night). The 'sour-faced c-word' comment wasn't the worst insult by a long chalk, and there are one or two messages that I will never let Sue read as long as I live. I wanted – and still want – to protect her. Plus I felt guilty. I was the one who had convinced her to do this insane thing in public, and while I never set out to make everybody love my wife, I didn't expect anyone to hate her either.

Sue said she didn't care, but I did, and that's why, in the wake of 'Terror of the Zygons', I put the experiment on hold for a few days. Other People were ruining it, like Other People tend to do; I was up to almost two packs of cigarettes a day. Sue told me to take the criticism on the chin. I told her that it wasn't just her scores they were criticising – they were running her down for misidentifying Land Rovers as well.

There aren't any Land Rover Defenders! The Defender title and badge was only introduced in 1991: a re-badging of the 'Land Rover Ninety' and the 'Land Rover One Ten'. The ones seen here are probably Series III Land Rovers, as they are very similar to the Ninety One/One Ten/Defender!

For the first and only time, Sue apologised.

*

Nicol baked a cake for the 100th story, 'The Stones of Blood'. Funnily enough, they were going to shoot a scene with a birthday cake back in 1978 when 'The Stones of Blood' was filmed, but the producer thought it was too self-indulgent and cut it (the scene, not the cake). I had no such qualms and encouraged Nicol to conjure up a sponge in the shape of a sacrificial stone circle, with lumps of grey icing for the stones, red icing for the blood and a crow made from marzipan. As far as themed cakes go it was a bit niche but still delicious with a cup of tea.

I photographed Nicol's cake as it took shape and I posted a step-by-step pictorial on our blog's Facebook page. I never thought for one moment that posting images of my step-daughter icing a cake would cause such a uproar, but what

I didn't realise at the time was that for some of our readers, Nicol wasn't just the blog's Scientific Advisor, she was an attractive young woman who baked *Doctor Who*-themed cakes and could discuss the second law of thermodynamics and anti-matter universes with you, i.e. total nerdbait. As a consequence of this, these photographs attracted a great deal of comment, three marriage proposals, four recipe requests and another troubling song:

> *I just want a girl who likes Who*
>
> *Who's as pretty and as smart as you*
>
> *And if I get bored I could always cheat on you with Nicol*
>
> *She's nearer my age*

It takes courage for a man to tell someone that he wants to sleep with their wife *and* stepdaughter. *But to do it in a song?* That takes balls of steel. Sue received the risqué lyrics in good humour. Nicol, on the other hand, considered taking down her Facebook profile and changing her name.

Nicol: I should change it to John Smith or something. That would put them off.
Me: It might make it worse, Nic.

One of our most loyal followers was a man called Glen Allen. Glen used to be the continuity announcer on UK Gold, and when I first visited Sue's home in Christopher Street in 1993, it was Glen's voice that I heard coming out of her television set when she snogged my face off and I missed 'The Curse of Peladon'. So when Glen began submitting wonderfully inventive audio trailers for the blog, it felt like kismet. Glen's trailers were brilliant and they quickly became an integral part of the Wife in Space project.

For his final trailer, Glen convinced Daphne Ashbrook, who portrayed the Eighth Doctor's companion, Grace Holloway, to join in. Obviously, this was a huge thrill for me. However, every so often, Glen's habit of contacting celebrities so they could discover what my wife had to say about them would backfire. Like the time he tweeted Sue's review of 'The Horns of Nimon' to one of its stars, ex-*Blue Peter* presenter Janet Ellis. In that particular blog entry I admitted that I used to have a crush on both her and her daughter, Sophie Ellis-Bextor. I almost fainted on the spot when she tweeted back that she'd read it. But the experience taught me something: perhaps I wasn't any better than that cad who had been wooing Sue and Nicol. At least he could play the guitar.

*

It took us seven months to watch all of the Mad One's stories, and Sue's opinion of the fourth incarnation of the Doctor varied wildly from week to week as, it must be said, did Tom Baker's performance. By the time we reached the end of Tom's tenure, all of us looked and felt like we needed a long lie down. When the Fourth Doctor fell from the top of a radio telescope in 'Logopolis', I asked Nicol to bake a cake in the shape of the Pharos Project. She told me it would be much too complicated to make a radio telescope out of gingerbread, and we had to settle for a bottle of champagne and a slice of multicoloured Battenberg instead.

Sue: I feel cheated.

Me: You're not sad, then? Not even a little bit?

Sue: I'm sad that Tom went out like that. He deserved better. And he didn't know any of those people who were by his side when he died. He only met one of them a couple of hours ago!

Me: But he died saving the universe . . .

Sue: Did he? I think he let go of the telescope on purpose. He's been in tighter scrapes than that. I think Peter Davison's Doctor told him that he had to kill himself or the ratings would never improve.

The Woman from Hartlepool and the Dark Dimensions

I wanted Sue to experience everything that *Doctor Who* could throw at her; the sights, the sounds, even the smells. The only way she was going to get a whiff of the latter would be if I took her to a convention. And that's how we ended up at a Holiday Inn on the outskirts of Newcastle for Dimensions 2012. I even took a microphone with me so I could document her experiences for a special podcast. What could possibly go wrong?

When we arrived at the hotel, I headed straight to the bar. Was 11.00 a.m. too early for a gin and tonic, I wondered, as Sue glanced furtively around the lobby.

Me: First impressions?

Sue: There are people dressed as characters from *Doctor Who*. There are two Peter Davisons over there – one of them could be a woman, it's hard to tell. There's a Tom Baker over there, and I think that's Jon Pertwee sitting next to him. It's very strange. I feel like I'm under-dressed.

I said nothing. Any Whovian looking at her would think she was wearing a combination of Peter Davison's plimsolls, David Tennant's glasses, Patrick Troughton's checked trousers, a jacket that Lalla Ward would have looked great in, and the inevitable scarf. I bought her a G and T.

Sue: So, when do I get to meet the real thing?

Sue was particularly looking forward to a panel discussion featuring Fifth Doctor Peter Davison – or, as she referred to him, the Fit One.

Me: Peter Davison's panel begins in less than an hour.
Sue: So, what happens at one of these panels, then? They don't re-enact scenes from the episodes on the stage, do they? That could be embarrassing.
Me: No. The guests talk about their time on the programme, and then the audience asks them questions. It's a bit like *Inside the Actor's Studio*, but with less flattering lighting.

I wanted to subject Sue to the full convention experience, and that included her asking one of the guests a question (and if I could capture this on tape for our podcast, so much the better). I decided that Peter Davison was the safest bet. He always seemed to be a thoroughly decent chap, so even if Sue did muck it up, I didn't think he would embarrass her too much. Plus, Sue had a soft spot for Peter (she loved *All Creatures Great and Small*) and I thought she might get a thrill out of it.

I had a few questions lined up for Sue to ask the actor, having solicited suggestions from the Wife in Space's Facebook community in the days leading up to the event. I'd whittled the choice down to: 'Does anyone ever ask you to sing the theme to *Button Moon*?' and 'Why do you spell your surname with only one D?' Some of the suggestions were very rude – Sue asking Peter Davison for his room number was a popular choice – but I was worried that if I suggested that one to her, she might agree to give it a go.

When she reluctantly raised her hand into the air during the panel's Q&A phase, she wasn't chosen. Instead, the first question directed to Peter was about the Jimmy Savile sex scandal, which brought the mood in the room down a notch. As the audience silently contemplated some of the atrocities committed in the bowels of BBC Television Centre, my wife leapt to her feet with her hand in the air.

> **Sue:** Hello, Peter. On a lighter note, could you tell me what your first words in the fiftieth-anniversary special are?

Peter had been looking rather glum after the Jimmy Savile question but he laughed at Sue's cheekiness. Then he denied knowing anything about the fiftieth-anniversary special and looked a little bit sad again. In the bar, Sue was triumphant.

> **Sue:** I've spoken to two Doctor Whos, now. You haven't spoken to any. How does that make you feel, Neil?

But Peter Davison was just the *Whors d'oeuvres* (see Glossary on page 259). The main dish was John Levene.

John Levene is the actor who played Sergeant Benton in *Doctor Who* between 1969 and 1976. Sue adored Benton:

- I'm warming to Benton. He's so much better than Captain Yates. ('The Mind of Evil')
- Benton isn't just a pretty face. ('The Time Monster')
- Good old Benton. You can always rely on Benton. I bloody love Benton. ('Invasion of the Dinosaurs')

- Benton and I would get on like a house on fire. Is the actor who played Benton still alive? ('Planet of the Spiders')

When I told her that the actor who played Benton was not merely alive but would be performing his cabaret act at the convention, it sealed the deal – more than the promise of a photo opportunity with Peter Davison or a pint with Terrance Dicks. She agreed to attend Dimensions 2012. That's how much Sue loved Sergeant Benton.

Not only was John Levene MC-ing the charity auction, he was going to sing a few selections from his new album, *The Ballads of Sergeant Benton* – 'If I Were A Carpenter', 'Wind Beneath My Wings' and 'Lady in Red'. Look out Bublé! As we took our seats in the hotel's ballroom, I noticed that several women in the audience were wearing red cocktail dresses. When I pointed this out to Sue, she removed her jacket to show off the red T-shirt she was wearing and perhaps catch John's eye.

John bounded onto the stage to muted applause.

John Levene: *I've got twelve suits just like this one at home. I don't like the suit that much. I just like being measured!*

After this zinger, John broke the sad news that he wouldn't be singing anything from his new album after all. He told us that the engineer who had mixed his record in LA had altered the tempo without his permission and that's why he couldn't do it. Sue wasn't convinced. She thought that John was too frightened to go through with it and she felt sorry for him. Singing or not singing, even at this stage John Levene could do no wrong.

But then the charity auction showed Sue a side of *Doctor Who* fandom that horrified her. John was auctioning some signed merchandise when a small boy, who couldn't have been more than ten, got into a vicious bidding war with a man in his late forties. When the boy reached the limits of his pocket money allowance, the man continued to steamroller him. Sue told me later that she considered out-bidding him so she could donate the item to the clearly distressed child, but there was no way she was going to pay £150 for a painting of Nicola Bryant in a bikini. Meanwhile, John Levene did nothing to prevent this injustice happening. The contrast between the actor and the heroic Sergeant Benton was stark.

When John broke for an interval, I noticed Robert Dick loitering next to the exit. Robert was working at the convention as an interviewer and a chaperone, and because he was an avid reader of our blog I stopped to say hello. Robert asked Sue what she thought of John Levene's act.

Sue: I love Benton, I really do. But this . . . I don't want to see Benton like this. It's a bit sad, really.
Deep voice: Yes, it is, rather.

This disembodied voice emanated from a face that loomed out of the shadows behind Robert's shoulder.

Sue: Oh my God . . . You're . . . You're Patrick Troughton's son. I . . . I recognise your voice.
Robert: This is Michael. I've been telling him about your website, Sue.

Michael: Yes, it sounds fascinating. What a jolly good
idea for a website. How far have you got with it?

Sue: We've just finished Peter Davison but your Dad
is my favourite Doctor so far. No one else has even
come close.

Michael: Oh, that's wonderful!

Sue and Michael were still chatting as I edged my wife
towards the exit. As we were leaving, she promised that she
would attend his panel the next morning, and I believed her.
In fact she was still buzzing when we reached the hotel car
park for a much-needed cigarette a few minutes later.

Sue: That was Michael Troughton! That was Patrick
Troughton's son!

Me: Yes, I know who he was.

Sue: What a lovely man. I'm a bit starstruck, actually,
and he's only a Doctor's son. Isn't that funny?

Me: I know, why don't you go back in there with the
microphone and ask him to record a sting for the
podcast. You know, something simple like: 'I'm
Michael Troughton and you are listening to the Wife
in Space'. I'll wait here for you.

I smoked a cigarette and waited. And then I smoked
another cigarette and waited some more. I glanced at my
watch. What was taking her so long? She was supposed
to record a ten-second sting for a podcast, not Michael
Troughton's life story.

I was about to light a fourth cigarette when I noticed Sue
through the glass doors of the hotel lobby. It was her scarf

that gave her away. And then my heart skipped a beat. She wasn't alone. Sue was talking to John Levene. Worse than that, she was waving a microphone in John Levene's face. I couldn't bear to watch, so walked round the block. When I returned five minutes later, Sue was running out of the lobby. She looked like she had seen a ghost.

Sue: You won't believe what's just happened!

My first thought: John is a big fan of the blog and he asked Sue to come back to his room.

Sue: I've upset John Levene.

My second thought: John is a big fan of the blog and he asked Sue to come back to his room and she turned him down.

Sue: He's really angry with me. He's threatening to walk out of his own gig.
Me: Are you serious? What did you do to him?
Sue: I accidentally bumped into him and he spilt some drink on his suit. And then he went mental! I've got it all on tape. Here, listen . . .

Transcript of Sue meets Benton

Sue: Can I ask you to do something for me?
John Levene: Yes, you can.
Sue: Could you say, I'm John Levene and you're listening to the Wife in Space?
John Levene: You want me to say a bit more than that, though?

Sue: Well, it's just for a podcast . . .

John Levene: Oh. OK.

Sue: Would you mind?

John Levene: Hang on . . . So, it's – I am John Levene . . .

Sue: And you are listening to the Wife in Space.

John Levene: The Wife?

Pertwee lookalike: Wife. Wife. WIFE!

Sue: Yes, the Wife in Space.

John Levene: Wife as in wife?

Sue: Yes.

Pertwee lookalike: WIFE!

John Levene: OK, OK. I am John Levene and I am listening to the Wife in Space.

Sue: Well thank you for listening to the Wife in Space, but could you say, I am John Levene and you are listening to . . .

John Levene or Pertwee lookalike (*it's not entirely clear*): WHOAH!

Sue: Sorry, John. Sorry, John. Sorry, sorry, sorry.

John Levene: Let go. Let go!

Sue: Sorry. Let me get you another one . . .

John Levene: It's not the drink – it's the f**king suit.

Sue: Sorry, chuck. Sorry.

John Levene: Ah, shit.

Sue: Let me get you something . . .

John Levene: Leave it for now. You've killed it dead now.

Sue: Let me get you something. Would you like me to get you a cloth?

John Levene: I'm in the toilet. Now leave the f**king mic alone.

I listened to all this with a mixture of glee and growing dismay.

Sue: He's so angry with me, Neil, he'll probably get us thrown out of the hotel. I'm not going back inside there. No way.

Me: But we have a hotel room booked. We have to go back inside.

Sue: Sod that. I've had enough. I want to go home.

I gave our room to a friend and then I gathered our things together while Sue hid in the Little Chef next door. She was still fuming about it when we arrived home an hour later. She blamed the Jon Pertwee lookalike who had put John Levene off by repeatedly shouting the word 'Wife!' at him, like he was deaf or something.

Sue: Michael Troughton was lovely. I really wanted to go to his panel in the morning. But there's no way in hell I'm going back to that hotel. John Levene has killed it.

When I uploaded the podcast to the blog (Michael Troughton's introductory sting was perfect), there were listeners who believed that Sue must have been drunk that night because her voice sounded 'a bit weird'. But Sue *always sounds like that*. Even I can't understand her sometimes. No, she was sober; what you can hear in her voice is probably heartbreak. If you meet Sue at a convention after this book comes out, just a word of warning: don't mention John Levene or Sergeant Benton. You'll kill it. And then she'll kill you.

The Fit One and the Court Jester

Sue threw more than thirty cushions at me over the course of the experiment – or one cushion more than thirty times – although only one projectile ever caused me any serious harm (I was drinking hot tea at the time). Reasons for a cushion in the face were many and varied. Maybe I'd been too complimentary about the attractiveness of a female guest star. Maybe I'd misled Sue about the number of episodes she was about to sit through. Maybe I'd accidentally on purpose led her to believe that the Doctor was about to regenerate when he quite clearly wasn't. What can I say? It kept me amused.

Sue could have shut this down any time she liked. A quick visit to Wikipedia could have told her that the next story featured the Daleks. There was nothing preventing her from reaching over and reading the back of the DVD cover either. The comments section of the blog was riddled with spoilers, too, because some of our readers just couldn't help themselves:

I wonder what Sue will think of the next one when the Master turns up again for the first time in five years?

The idiots.

Me: I'm sorry, but I need you to close your eyes during this title sequence.

Sue: Why?

Me: Because the title of this story is a massive spoiler.

Sue: Is it 'The Return of the Master'?

Me: No.

Sue: Is it 'The Return of the Cybermen'?

Me: Look . . .

Sue: Is it 'The Return of the Daleks'?

Me: Stop it!

One title that I didn't need to hide from Sue was 'Earthshock'. This was the story that had made me fall out of my chair when I was a teenager back in 1982, and I couldn't wait to see if the Cybermen turning up at the end of part 1 would have the same effect on Sue. When it came down to it, she didn't fall out of her chair, but she did lean forwards a teeny bit, which was almost as satisfying.

Sue gave 'Earthshock' 9 out of 10 and the blog's readers were thrilled, although somebody did accuse my wife of letting the side down because she didn't approach the story with the mindset of a twelve-year-old amnesiac.

Sue's reaction to the episode one cliffhanger is just plain wrong, because she already knows about Cybermen. Most of us watching at the time didn't. We'd never heard of them. We just thought 'OK, so the androids are being controlled by some other androids. Big deal. What a boring shitty cliffhanger.' By putting Sue's reaction on the blog like that, you're playing right into the hands of all the shit-for-brains sheep who infect fandom with their endlessly repeated crap about how brilliant the reveal of the Cybermen was.

But there was more to 'Earthshock' than just its brilliant reveal of the Cybermen. There was also Adric's unexpected death to cope with.

Sue liked Adric at first ('He's adorable') but her affections soon turned to loathing ('He's a thick, whining brat'). In fact, one of the most entertaining things for me was watching Sue slowly fall out of love with the Alzarian pup. One minute she wanted to mother him, the next minute she wanted to smother him ('He can't act – and it doesn't take a boy genius to work that out'), and when Adric was finally blown to bits, she definitely wasn't moved to tears.

Sue: Oh, there's no theme music.
Me: Yeah, what do you think about that?
Sue: It might have worked if a better character had died. It's making me feel uncomfortable. Maybe they should have used a sad version of the theme music instead, you know, like they do in *EastEnders*. Do they have a tinkly piano version of the theme tune?
Me: No.

On the blog, several people suggested that one possible explanation for my wife's reaction to 'Earthshock' is that the experiment was a complete success and I'd turned Sue into a *Doctor Who* fan. More *prima facie* evidence for her transformation into a fangirl could supposedly be found in her commentary for the twentieth-anniversary celebratory romp, 'The Five Doctors'.

Me: Are there any old monsters you'd like to see?
Sue: The Yeti, obviously. Autons would be nice, too. Oh, and some Ice Warriors. And maybe a giant snake . . .

Someone on Gallifrey is misusing the Death Zone . . .

Sue: It could be the Black Guardian. I don't think it will be Omega again, because it's far too soon to have him back. Or maybe it's the Toymaker. He is making toys after all. Or it could be the Monk . . .

But people needed to read on a little further to see Sue wasn't about to turn into a fully fledged Whovian.

Me: Are you saying the Monk and the Master are one and the same person? Shall we pause the DVD and chat about that possibility for a couple of hours?
Sue: No thanks.

I believe that there's a simpler explanation for my wife's ebullience during this phase of the experiment: she fancied Peter Davison, aka the Fit One. She wasn't keen on some of the Fifth Doctor's stories ('"Time-Flight"? They should have called it "Time-Shite"!'), but when she noticed that he was sporting black underpants under his cricket whites in 'Castrovalva', it was clear to everyone that she was smitten.

In fact the only time my wife wasn't ogling the Fit One was when she was drooling over Adric's replacement, Turlough, aka actor Mark Strickson, aka the Ginger One. As far as Sue was concerned, this was an era in *Doctor Who*'s history when it had 'something for the mums' for a change.

Peter Davison has been quite open in dismissing most of his stories as 'crap'. And with some justification. He had to put up with not just the Myrka but also pink inflatable snakes, homicidal woodlice and an increasingly tedious and inept Master. Sue was mostly in agreement but she still seemed to be enjoying the adventures of the Fit One. If some of his stories had starred anyone other than Peter Davison – with the possible exception of David Tennant – she might have been less forgiving. When the Fifth Doctor bravely sacrificed himself to save the life of his companion in 'The Caves of Androzani', I noticed that my wife's bottom lip was wobbling.

The Fifth Doctor's final words . . .

The Doctor: Adric?
Sue: He still feels bad about it, doesn't he? If I had to sum up this regeneration in one word it would have to be 'tragic'. But in a good way.

The Doctor regenerates . . .

Peri: Doctor?
The Sixth Doctor: You were expecting someone else?
Sue: Well I certainly wasn't expecting Art Garfunkel!

---

*

Sue didn't have any preconceptions about Colin Baker when we started this. All she knew about him was that (a) he didn't play the Doctor for very long and (b) he once shouted at me at a convention. However, by a strange quirk of fate, just as we were preparing to engage with the Sixth Doctor, Colin appeared as a contestant on the reality TV show *I'm a Celebrity . . . Get Me Out of Here!*

Sue: Colin's lovely. He's my tip to win. Colin doesn't have a bad word to say about anyone. He's the perfect gentleman, always comforting everyone around him. He's really, really nice. I want to give him a big cuddle. Shame on you and John for upsetting him.

I was concerned that Sue's newfound love for Colin Baker would skew her opinions of his Doctor. But within minutes of starting the Sixth Doctor's first story 'The Twin Dilemma', it was clear that normal service had been resumed.

Sue: That was rubbish. I liked the first episode but it went downhill rapidly. Crack was very big in the 1980s, wasn't it?
Me: What about Colin?
Sue: It's too early to tell. He's very loud, though. And I'm not just talking about his coat.
Me: Do you like it?
Sue: It clashes a bit.
Me: *A BIT?*

A brooch completes the Sixth Doctor's new look.

Sue: At least this Doctor likes cats. He's OK in my book if he likes cats. It's just a shame that he's stuck in that bloody costume. He looks like a court jester.

Around this time, we took a break from the blog and spent a few days in London. After a quick pint at the Tavern in Fitzrovia (we were quite safe, it was the wrong Thursday), we decided that it would be a good idea to get hold of tickets to the mentalist* Derren Brown's live theatre show. During the interval, Sue's mobile phone lit up with a text from an unrecognised number:

I can see you

We scanned the auditorium for a familiar face but couldn't spot anyone we recognised. I was convinced the text must be part of Derren Brown's act so I found it hard to relax and enjoy the second half; I kept thinking Derren was about to ambush us. When the curtain eventually came down, there was another text waiting:

It's Nev and Nicola

Phew. Nev was Nev Fountain, the comedy writer best known for his work on the satirical impressionist show *Dead Ringers* and *Private Eye* magazine, as well as various plays for Big Finish and comic strips for *Doctor Who Magazine*.†

---

*In a good way.

† Nev sent the text to Sue because when I arranged to meet him at the Tavern in 2001, I didn't own a mobile phone and I ended up borrowing hers. I gave Nev Sue's number and he must have kept it.

Nicola, meanwhile, was Nev's girlfriend. But this wasn't any old Nicola. This was Nicola Bryant, the actress who played the Sixth Doctor's companion, the American biology student Perpugilliam Brown – or Peri for short. We arranged to meet up after the show, even though I wasn't too keen; I was terrified of accidentally calling Nicola Peri. But it was OK, I didn't disgrace myself and nor did Sue – and nor, for that matter, did Nicola.

When we got home, I cued up the 1984 story 'Planet of Fire'.

Meanwhile, on Lanzarote . . .

Sue: It's . . . it's . . . it's . . .

Sue is pointing excitedly at Nicola Bryant.

Sue: It's Nev Fountain's girlfriend!
Me: Yes, it's Nicola Bryant.
Sue: I'm not going to say anything about her American accent because I know it's not real. I know this because I've met her. She was lovely.

As we progressed through the Court Jester's time – which took little more than a month; Colin Baker had been the Doctor when the show went on hiatus – Sue began to wonder whether his whole run was a prank as ill-judged as his costume.

> **Sue**: It seems mean to say it, but he did put on a lot
> of weight, didn't he? His perm is a disaster and he's

got Bonnie Langford as a companion. He must have done something really bad in a previous life. Maybe that's why he's such a nice man now. He wasn't given a chance to be a proper Doctor. The scripts weren't good enough. He didn't stand a chance.

When the time came for the Court Jester to regenerate, Sue was understandably confused.

Sue: Right, so what the f**k just happened?
Me: The Sixth Doctor fell off his exercise bike and regenerated. What's not to get?
Sue: F**k off. Come on, what really happened?
Me: Colin Baker was understandably upset when the BBC fired him and he refused to take part in the regeneration. Either that or he was double-booked on *Crosswits*. Anyway, this was the best they could come up with at such short notice.
Sue: Right, so that wasn't Colin Baker lying on the floor just then?
Me: No, that was Sylvester McCoy in a wig.
Sue: It's not a great start, is it?

Six Things We Might Do Next

As the experiment neared its conclusion, our thoughts turned to what we might do together once it was over.

1. Become Olympic archers

Like so many others who watched the London Olympics, Sue has been inspired to become an Olympian herself. She says it would be something we could tell our grandchildren when we're older, as if sitting through every episode of *Doctor Who* in public wouldn't be worth bragging about. Sue's first choice of sport – tennis – was ruled out because we are much too old, while mine – walking – was vetoed on account of it looking too silly. Then Sue had a brainwave. How about archery? She played darts for the county and appeared on *Bullseye* in 1989, and as darts had yet to be recognised as an Olympic sport, archery was the next best thing. Archery is not usually thought of as the poor relation of darts and I had to explain to Sue that you don't go for a double top in archery. But she seems adamant. Don't rule us out for 2016.

2. Go off the grid for a year

We are both hopelessly addicted to the internet, and the last two and a half years haven't exactly helped. Having said that, the only time Sue wasn't checking her phone for incoming messages, or browsing the web for 'doer-uppers in France', was when we sat down to watch *Doctor Who* together. When this is all over, I will probably never talk to my wife again, not unless she goes cold turkey and logs off for a while. No phone. No email. No Facebook. No French *immobilier* websites. Sue will have to quit her job if we go through with this, but that's OK because it's her turn, and she won't be able to read any online reviews of this book either, which is also a definite plus.

3. Sell a game show format and retire off the proceeds

Sue is vigorously pursuing this dream right now, and to be fair she does have some form when it comes to developing television formats. In the early 1990s she came up with an idea for a programme where a panel of venture capitalists would give their money away for a share in someone's business. She called the show *The Entrepreneurs* and I didn't waste any time in telling her that it was the worst idea I had ever heard. No one would be interested in watching smug millionaires doling out cash to hapless inventors and failed businessmen, I told her. Unfortunately, for once she listened to me. Sue likes to bring this up quite a lot.

At present Sue is developing a Top Secret idea about which she is understandably cagey. All she will tell me is that it involves John Barrowman, a coachload of people and a trip to the Australian Outback. It doesn't sound very promising to me, but don't be surprised if a programme called *Barrowman's Big Boomerang Charabanc* appears on BBC Three next year.

4. Follow Michael Bublé on every date of his 2013
European tour

I am more than willing to accompany Sue on this jaunt, as long as she understands that its purpose is the decommissioning or 'retirement' of Michael Bublé, with a well-aimed poison dart if necessary.

5. Get a divorce

Sue refuses to see the funny side of assassinating Michael Bublé.

6. Watch another TV series together and blog about it

I would quite like to do this and have considered several possible candidates – *Blake's 7*, *Star Trek*, even *All Creatures Great and Small*. The only exception is *Doctor Who* since its comeback. I wouldn't want to commit myself to a blog that theoretically might never end and would probably result in something that looked like this:

Sue: David Tennant is very easy on the eye. I would definitely run away in the TARDIS with this Doctor.
Me: That puts the website's 'I fancy David Tennant' counter at 583. And we're only on his fourth story.

And yet, for more than two years, visitors to the blog kept begging us to extend the experiment and do the new series as well. For all those people, and for anyone interested in Sue's theory about the Doctor's real name, I have included a very special treat in the epilogue to this book. The only possible thing that could persuade us to tackle Eccleston, Tennant and Smith in full – or as Sue calls them the Hard Guy, My Third Husband and the Pipsqueak – is a series of record-breaking pledges on Kickstarter. Actually, that's not a bad idea . . .

The Crafty Sod and the One-Night Stand

'I thought you said you liked *Doctor Who*.'

Sue had stopped asking me this some time ago. However, it was something I now thought about every day. Even though the end was in sight, I found the last few months of the experiment the hardest of all. I even contemplated including one final list of six things as a very brief chapter in this book: Six Things I Hate About *Doctor Who*

1. The theme music
2. The scripts
3. The actors
4. The camera work
5. The fans
6. Myself

We were halfway through Sylvester McCoy's first story when Al Jazeera invited me to appear on a programme called *The Stream* to talk about *Doctor Who*. All publicity is good publicity, said Sue. So I caved in and accepted the invitation. It was only when I logged on to Skype a few minutes ahead of my scheduled appearance that I was told that I hadn't been booked to talk about the pros and cons of subjecting your partner to your favourite television programme, and I was there to take part in a debate about the ways in which online fandom can drive civic participation.

I'm sorry . . . *what?*

Put bluntly, Al Jazeera wasn't interested in my wife's battle with *Doctor Who* – they just wanted me to tell them how I was changing the world and promoting social harmony through my website. But I wasn't promoting social harmony; if anything, Sue and I were winding people up. My fellow guests in the symposium were to be a *My Little Pony* aficionado (for some inexplicable reason, they like to call themselves Bronies), a cosplayer (which is a fancy word for someone obsessed with fancy dress), a hyperactive academic from the University of Pennsylvania and somebody high up in The Harry Potter Alliance. And, although I was not one, I was there to speak for the Whovians.

Should I have pretended that *Doctor Who* fans are trying to make the world a better place? I knew perfectly well that most of them were only interested in making *Doctor Who* a better television programme. The best I could hope to do was muddy the waters by suggesting that the *Doctor Who* franchise was currently run by the fans themselves – the writers, directors, producers, even the actors, many of whom had grown up with the programme. The presenter didn't believe me. In fact she obviously thought I was an unsafe interviewee and so cut me off in mid-sentence to get a more sensible point of view from the Bronie. Millions of viewers must have been left with the overwhelming impression that Whovians are selfish, uncaring fantasists. Watching myself back, I was half-inclined to agree.

*

The Seventh Doctor didn't get off to the best of starts and his debut story, 'Time and the Rani', was awarded the only minus score of the whole experiment; Sue described it as the worst *Doctor Who* story she had ever seen. But when McCoy found his feet, and his companion, Ace, started to blow stuff up, Sue warmed to him. She didn't even seem to mind that the Doctor was now a manipulative schemer who didn't have any qualms about committing genocide on a regular basis.

The Doctor tricks Davros into using the Hand of Omega. It destroys Skaro.

Sue: Shit. Did that just happen?
Me: Yes, the Doctor just committed genocide.
Sue: F**k off! He can't do that.

The feedback from the supernova heads towards the Dalek ship . . .

Sue: Has the Doctor just started the Time War?
Me: Yes. Yes he has.
Sue: The crafty sod.

Ace isn't convinced that blowing up a planet was the right thing to do.

Ace: We did good, didn't we?
Sue: Ace doesn't trust the Doctor. That's very interesting. I don't blame her, though. He's a mass murderer!

---

*

Sue watched 'Ghost Light', didn't understand it, but enjoyed it anyway. She thought 'Remembrance of the Daleks' was 'bloody brilliant', and she felt sorry for the dead dog in 'The Happiness Patrol'. And then, as we watched the Crafty Sod's penultimate story, 'The Curse of Fenric', my wife stunned me with a confession:

Sue: I'll miss this when it's all over.
Me: I beg your pardon?
Sue: This. I'll miss it when it's over.
Me: What? 'The Curse of Fenric'?
Sue: No, *this*. Watching *Doctor Who* with you.

*

When the Seventh Doctor and Ace walked off into the sunset at the end of 'Survival' we felt euphoric, although the two bottles of champagne we consumed during part 3 probably helped. We had done it. Twenty-six consecutive years of *Doctor Who*. Over. Finished. Complete.

Except it wasn't quite over yet. We watched 'Shada' (an official recon of an unfinished Tom Baker story), the 3D *EastEnders* charity crossover 'Dimensions in Time', the 'Thirty Years in the TARDIS' documentary,* and the fan film 'Downtime' (6 out of 10 – higher than 'The Robots of Death'). I kidded myself that I was prolonging Sue's torment so I could replicate the feelings of despair I'd had during those years when *Doctor Who* was off the air. The truth was, now the experiment was almost finished, I didn't want it to end.

I always assumed that I'd be overcome with feelings of

---

* Later, the documentary's director, Kevin Jon Davies, recorded a podcast where he turned the tables on Sue by commenting on everything she said instead. Sue was flattered and frightened in equal measure.

relief and joy when we finally crossed the finishing line but, over time, the journey for me became less about *Doctor Who* and more about my relationship with Sue. It was the fact that we were doing something *together* that was the important thing. I climbed Mount Kilimanjaro without her; Sue built five houses with next to no help from me; I wasn't there when Nicol was born. When we did do anything together it was always to do with work: in-joke in the middle of a departmental meeting or a rant about a new module in the car on our way home. But this had been different. We had been on the mission *together*. We were a team.

I'm not suggesting that watching *Doctor Who* all the way through saved our marriage, or anything like that, but I had, accidentally, been correct when I predicted that it might bring us closer together, because it did. The adventure we had embarked upon not only provided a fresh insight into *Doctor Who*, for me and thousands of people like me, it also reminded me that if I had to choose between the programme I love and the woman I love, I would choose Sue. Every time. The really brilliant thing was, I didn't have to choose.

I thought about revisiting 'Marco Polo'. A handful of readers hadn't forgiven us for watching the condensed thirty-minute recon of this Miserable Git's historical; and they were clamouring for us to remedy our oversight before we finished the blog. However, in the end I couldn't go through with it. The thought of going backwards for the sake of completism seemed absurd to me. Besides, subjecting Sue to seven more black-and-white recons at this late stage would arguably have crossed the line into spousal abuse.

Sue: So you've given up?

Me: I admit it. I can't do it any more.

Sue: We should watch it.

Me: Do you want to watch it?

Sue: No, of course not. I'd rather watch *All Creatures Great and Small*.

Me: Then we're not watching it, and that's final.

Sue: Won't people be upset?

Me: Sod the completists. You've seen more episodes than most of them, anyway. Enough is enough.

Sue: I thought you liked *Doctor Who*.

Me: I do. That's why we should stop.

In a bout of cutting-edge 'cosplay' – thank you, Al Jazeera – we dressed up as the actors from 'Marco Polo' and restaged a selection of telesnaps in our living room instead. Sue's impression of Tutte Lemkow, complete with eyepatch and stuffed monkey on her shoulder, was uncanny. Gary and Nicol joined in too, although Nicol was much too busy baking a celebratory Dalek cake to give our re-enactment her undivided attention. In the end, it would have taken us less time to watch the recon.

I also had an ace up my sleeve: 'The Underwater Menace', part 2. The recovered episode hadn't been released on DVD yet, but, thanks to an anonymous benefactor, we had been sent an advance copy. 'The Underwater Menace' part 2 would have been the *coup de grâce*. My wife could have finished the blog knowing that she'd seen more episodes than most of the people who read it. That would have driven a small fraction of our readership insane (the 9s and 10s who were up in the middle of the night) but, once again, I couldn't go through with it.

Sue: But I like Patrick Troughton. I wouldn't have minded watching that one.
Me: Do you want to watch a recovered Patrick Troughton episode completely out of context, just so I can parade you around on the internet like a freak?
Sue: It's a bit late to start worrying about that now, Neil.

---

*

I always intended to end the experiment with the first new episode of *Doctor Who* that Sue and I ever watched together, all those years ago in Christopher Street, when we were young and foolish and only weird people did things together on the internet.

Unfortunately, thanks to Russell Toughnut Davies, Sue was convinced that Paul McGann's Doctor didn't count. It wasn't that the Time War had erased all traces of the Eighth Doctor from the timeline. No, a conversation between two characters in his Channel 4 drama series *Queer as Folk* had lodged itself in her brain and wouldn't budge. It's understandable, I suppose. There are plenty of fans, just like the one portrayed in *Queer as Folk*, who like to believe that *The TV Movie* never happened, mainly because they don't like it when the Doctor admits that he's half-human on his mother's side. And by 'they' I mean 'me'.

Sue: He's like Spock. Maybe that's why he left Gallifrey. Maybe all his friends were picking on him for being half-human and he got fed up with it and buggered off?

And then Sue said this:

Sue: The non-fans wouldn't have enjoyed this. It's too wrapped up in its past to appeal to a new audience. I bet the fans loved it, though.
Me: Do you like it?
Sue: Yes. It's great.

I'm saying nothing.

Sue's final commentary for *The TV Movie* is probably my favourite. For me, it's a wonderful amalgamation of everything that made the experiment work. Sue misidentifies the Master, she becomes fixated on Grace Holloway's wooden chairs, she doesn't care if the Doctor is half-human, or even if he snogs a human lady. She even explained to me what a temporal orbit is, something I have been struggling to get my head around since 1996. For that, and everything else, I will always be grateful.

Sue: Did Paul McGann make any more episodes?
Me: Not on telly.
Sue: Well, I've had worse one-night stands.

Sue gave the one-night stand a 9 out of 10 and lots of people cheered, including some people who hated *The TV Movie*. Yes, even me.

Me: Come here and give us a kiss.

I switch off the TV.

Me: It's over. We're free.
Sue: Are we?
Me: Yes.
Sue: What shall we do?
Me: Dunno. Kill Michael Bublé?
Sue: Don't push it, Neil.

The Experiment Ends: Assessing the Results

Over the two and a half years it took the experiment to run, Sue viewed over 350 hours of classic *Doctor Who*. Her highest rated Doctor was the Third; her lowest rated Doctor was the First. She loved season 24 (Sylvester McCoy) and she didn't care very much for season 15 (Tom Baker). She didn't cry when Adric died; she fell in love with Sergeant Benton and out of love with John Levene; she felt sorry for Colin Baker; she grew fed up of the Daleks; and her soft spot for Peter Davison remained soft. Her average score for the classic series is 5.77 out of 10.

Sue: It was all right, I suppose.

I am satisfied with this result. A slightly above average 5.77 sounds pretty good to me. If anything, it's a relief. If Sue's score had been any higher, I would have been concerned. I don't want to be married to me; I want to be married to her.

Yes, it's sad that she'll never experience the joy one gets from knowing that the production code for 'Planet of the Spiders' is ZZZ, and it's a shame that she'll never bid for any Weetabix cards on eBay (I'm still missing Davros), let alone a painting of Nicola Bryant in a bikini. But I'm fine with that. I never set out to turn my wife into a fan, which is just as well really, because if I had, the last two and half years would have been a complete waste of time.

Sue: I can't remember half of them. I can't see myself watching any of them again, I'll never read the magazine, or the books, and I'll never go to another *Doctor Who* convention as long as I live.

Me: Can you name any of the stories you gave 10 out 10 to?

Sue: Yes, don't tell me . . . 'The Seeds of Death'?

Having said that, Sue's sustained exposure to classic episodes of *Doctor Who* has had an unexpected side effect:

Sue: I appreciate the new series a lot more now. When the Great Intelligence turns up in a Steven Moffat story, *I actually get it.* I'm excited when I see Ice Warriors and Sontarans, when I didn't care before, and I understand some of the jokes that I never used to get. If anything, the old series has made me a fan of the new series. I bloody love it. But at the same time, I don't need to wallow in the past. Yes, it's nice to have it there to refer to, but you have to keep moving forward. You know, like a shark.

And what about me? What did the experiment reveal about me?

If I'm honest, there were times when I hated it; I often wished we'd never started. Sometimes I would blame the programme; sometimes it was the anonymous insults on the blog in the middle of the night; sometimes real life got in the way – we came close to throwing in the towel halfway through 'The Moonbase' because we had had a row over some washing-up liquid but, five minutes later, still had to

go through with the blog; and sometimes it was my ego that
got the better of me. Never mind Sue, never mind someone
calling themselves CloisterBalls, why wasn't anyone interested in what *I* thought about *Doctor Who*? I'd studied for
a PhD in the subject; no one cared about that. Whereas
my wife couldn't tell the difference between a Quark and a
Chumbley and she had her own fanbase. *How the hell did
that happen?* If only there was somewhere I could leave an
anonymous insult in the middle of the night. But that outlet
was not available to me.

There were even times when I imagined the blog finishing with a YouTube video which would feature me throwing
my collection of *Doctor Who* DVDs onto a huge bonfire
(in strict chronological order, of course) because that's what
happens when you turn something you love into an endur-
ance test – it's what happens to some marriages. But a week
after I published Sue's review of *The TV Movie*, I woke in the
middle of the night and felt compelled to sneak downstairs
to watch 'Horror of Fang Rock'. On my own. And for the
first time in almost two and a half years, I enjoyed a *Doctor
Who* story for what it was: a thrilling, slightly scary, slightly
ridiculous adventure in time and space – well, a lighthouse,
but you get the idea. Only this time, when I watched 'Horror of Fang Rock', I wasn't only reminded of what it felt like
to be a frightened seven-year-old boy in Lavender Avenue, I
was also reminded of what it felt like to watch it with Sue.
She's quite right, you know: the Rutan does look like a giant
zit and the Doctor definitely should have stepped on it.

I would never have held it against Sue if she had given up
before the end; but I also knew that would never happen.

She is special and funny and ever so slightly mad, you see, and I also knew that it didn't matter to her if we did this thing in public or not – that was a trap I set for myself. Sue just wanted to make me happy. She must be indomitable; after all, we are still married.

Me: Would you ever do anything like this again?
Sue: I thought you'd never ask.
Me: Are you joking?
Sue: I miss it. I never thought I would, but I do.
Me: Maybe I was wrong. Maybe the specialists are right, maybe I have turned you into a fan after all.
Sue: It's not fucking *Doctor Who*. I miss sitting down with you every night and the two of us having a laugh together. It doesn't matter what we watch – it could be *Downton Abbey* for all I care. Just so long as we do it together.

And for me, this is the only result that matters. The experiment is over.

Sue: Saying that, it's my turn next. I've found a nice place in France that needs doing up, which means you'll have to live in a caravan again, but we could do it in public this time, which means you'll have to take an active interest in the design, the plans, and all the building work. Hey, you never know, you might enjoy it.

Epilogue

It's Sunday 12 May 2013 and *Doctor Who* has leaked all over the internet. Again.

The last time this happened it was 2005 and a friend had to send the episode to me in a taxi. This time, I live in a real house, with real broadband, and that means nothing will stop me from capitalising on the fact that the season 7 Blu Ray box set has been sent to a handful of lucky Americans by mistake – a whole week before the season finale is supposed to be broadcast on British television.

It's now Friday 17 May 2013 and the episode still hasn't surfaced on the internet. Either the Americans didn't get their hands on a copy and the leak was just an elaborate hoax, or the Americans don't know how to torrent Blu Rays. This never would have happened if the box set had been sent to Canada.

In the end, we had to wait until Saturday, just like everybody else.

'The Name of the Doctor' begins on Gallifrey, a very long time ago . . .

Sue: Are they finally going to blow it up? I wonder which Doctor will be responsible for pushing the button. Because I'm still not sure, you know.

A white-haired old man in a frock coat is seen getting into a faulty TARDIS with a teenage girl . . .

Sue: Is that who I think it is?
Me: Richard Hurndall?
Sue: It's the First Doctor! In colour! How exciting is that?
Me: I've seen better-executed mash-ups on YouTube, but yes, it's very exciting.

Clara bumps into several incarnations of the Doctor, but none of them notices her.

Sue: Oh look, she was almost run over by Bessie. I bet Jon Pertwee wouldn't have stopped if he'd hit her. He was probably late for his monthly Masons meeting.

Clara is now in Los Angeles, where she bumps into two more Doctors . . .

Sue: I find it hard to believe that the Second Doctor would go to Venice Beach. Especially in a big fur coat. He was daft, but he was never *that* daft.
Me: It's probably because Los Angeles is where they hold the biggest *Doctor Who* convention in America. In fact, that's probably not even the Doctor. It's probably a fan running late for a fancy dress competition.
Sue: So where's Paul McGann?
Me: We just saw his elbow.
Sue: Why doesn't Paul McGann come back? He can't have changed that much over the last how-ever-many-years it's been. Just stick a wig on him. No one would mind.
Me: Paul McGann would mind. He hated that wig.

Cue titles: The Name of the Doctor by Steven Moffat.

Sue: Exciting, isn't it? I can't wait to find out what his real name is.

Me: Just so long as it isn't Bob. It's a shame that Nicol isn't here. She wanted to know what the Doctor's name was when she was four, although she probably hasn't given it much thought since then, which is just as well because we won't find out anyway. It's just a big tease.

Sue: What do you think the Doctor's name is?

Me: I don't even know what my *real* doctor's name is. It's not important.

Sue: I think his name is John Smith. You know, because he's half-human.

Me: He's *not* half-human. That never happened.

Sue: Give your head a shake, Neil. You sound like Russell T. Davies.

In a prison cell in 1893, the Silurian detective Madame Vastra is questioning a serial killer. The killer tells her that the Doctor's greatest secret has been discovered . . .

Sue: He is human on his mother's side and his mother's name was Mary. Joseph was not amused. Is his real name . . . ?

Me: Please, don't say it. I mean it.

Madame Vastra contacts Strax the Sontaran, who is holidaying in Glasgow . . .

Sue: I love the comedy Sontaran. That's what the classic series needed – more comedy Sontarans.

Me: Then you've forgotten 'The Invasion of Time', which is unforgivable, frankly, because they just Photoshopped Clara into it.

Meanwhile, on contemporary Earth, Clara is babysitting the children who were violently assaulted by Cybermen a week ago . . .

Sue: I hope Clara leaves those bloody kids at home this time. Children shouldn't be allowed in the TARDIS, not unless they're visiting The Doctor Who Experience with a responsible adult.

Clara is 'the impossible girl' . . .

Me: I think Clara might be the TARDIS in disguise.
Sue: But how would you get in and out?
Me: I'm not going to answer that.
Sue: I think Clara is either a Time Lady, like Romana, or she's a Doctor from the future.
Me: If Clara is a Doctor from the future, I will write a strongly worded letter to the BBC.
Sue: I thought you were supposed to be a feminist? Why can't you have a female Doctor?
Me: Because we don't need one. We've already got *her*.

I'm pointing at Professor River Song . . .

Sue: I love River Song. She's a strong woman in her early fifties who doesn't mess about and gets her own way. What's not to like?

Madame Vastra has gathered all the Doctor's friends together to discuss his greatest secret.

Vastra: What is his name?

Sue: It must be something really silly otherwise he wouldn't try to hide it. Eugene, maybe? Or Horace? Something really embarrassing like that.

The evil Whispermen murder Jenny in her sleep . . .

Sue: That was very clever. Horrible, but clever.

When the Doctor contemplates his greatest secret, he is moved to tears.

Me: You never saw Tom Baker blubbing his eyes out like that. Even when he knew he was going to die he didn't shed a single tear. These modern Doctors shouldn't carry a sonic screwdriver around with them – they should carry a box of tissues.

Sue didn't respond to my jibe. She probably couldn't hear me over the blaring, intrusive music, so I said it again. Still nothing . . .

Me: Are you crying?

Sue: Shut up.

The Doctor: When you are a time traveller, there is one place you must never go.

Sue: Benidorm. It doesn't matter when you visit – it's always a dump.

The Doctor decides to break into his own tomb . . .

Sue: Ooh, I can hear the TARDIS cloister bell. That can't be good. That reminds me, can I programme my phone so it plays that sound effect when you call me at work?

The TARDIS arrives on Trenzalore with such a bump, the windows break . . .

Sue: Is that the crack from Amy Pond's bedroom? Is that important, do you think?
Me: I don't know. Why don't you ask Steven Moffat the next time you see him. Actually, I've got a list of questions you could ask him. Like, why did the TARDIS explode in series 6? That's a good one for a start.
Sue: You are so impatient.

River is speaking to Clara from beyond the grave . . .

Sue: I never really know where I am with River Song. Is this River Song from the future or River Song from the past?
Me: I used to keep a flowchart, but then I ran out of colours and it got a little messy.

The Great Intelligence confronts Jenny and Vastra.

Sue: Richard E. Grant is very good. Do you think he'd have been a good Doctor?
Me: He was the Doctor, once. In 2003. In a cartoon.
Sue: Why haven't we watched that one?
Me: The same reason I didn't make you read all the old *TV Comic* strips, I suppose. You should count yourself lucky.

The Great Intelligence claims that the Doctor is 'blood-soaked' . . .

Sue: He does have a point. The Doctor can be a bit of a git when he wants to be. He even killed a dog once. I've never completely forgiven him for that.

The Great Intelligence attempts to enter the Doctor's tomb, but to do that he needs the Doctor's name.

The Great Intelligence: Doctor who?
Sue: If the Doctor tells us his name, Steven Moffat will never be able to use that joke ever again.
Me: That's why it will never happen.
The Great Intelligence: Doctor *who?*

River says the Doctor's name (off-screen) and the door to the Doctor's tomb opens.

Me: Told you. The Moff is such a tease.
Sue: You fans are never happy. If he says his name, it's rubbish, and if he doesn't say his name, it's still rubbish. You can't win.
Me: But I wasn't the one who brought it up in the first place, I never wanted to –
Sue: Moan, moan, moan. You're never satisfied.

We find ourselves in the ruins of a TARDIS console room where the voices of all the old Doctors can be heard.

Sue: The TARDIS is playing recons on a loop.

The Great Intelligence inserts himself into the Doctor's time stream, with catastrophic results.

Sue: I don't see how almost getting run over by Bessie is going to help the Great Intelligence.

But when the Doctor's incarnations begin dying simultaneously, Clara realises that she has to enter the Doctor's time stream to put things straight.

Me: We should watch all the episodes again, only this time you could ask 'Is it Clara?' every five seconds.
Sue: Be quiet. This is really emotional.

The Doctor promises to save Clara, but before he bids farewell to River Song, he snogs her face off.

Me: Oh my giddy aunt.
Sue: I love it. And to think there was a time when I thought she was his mum.

Clara finds herself in the Doctor's time stream . . .

Me: Do you understand what's going on here?
Sue: Yes.
Me: Could you explain it to me, please?
Sue: Clara is floating around the Doctor's past, so she can see echoes of the old Doctors. Look, there's Tom Baker. You can tell that it's Tom Baker because of the scarf.
Me: I know who he is! I just don't understand how this is supposed to work.

Sue paused the live transmission to explain it to me. Her explanation didn't make any sense, and my phone was buzzing with incoming messages from my friends who hadn't paused it and had seen the end, which meant something momentous was about to happen . . .

Sue: And that's why Clara is the impossible girl. There's just one thing I don't get and that's why haven't we seen David Tennant? He wouldn't need a wig to come back.

The episode concludes with a stunning twist. Another Doctor is lurking in the time stream. A Doctor we don't recognise . . .

The Doctor: He is my secret.

When the mysterious Time Lord turns to face the viewer, a caption appears: Introducing John Hurt as the Doctor.

Sue: That will confuse the children.

Me: The children? I'm the one who's confused!

Sue: The kids will think the Doctor's real name is John Hurt. He's John Smith when he's nice and he's John Hurt when he's nasty.

Me: According to *The Sun*, John Hurt plays a Doctor who has been forgotten.

Sue: Oh, I thought Colin Baker had already done that.

Me: It's rumoured that John Hurt is playing a Doctor between Paul McGann and Christopher Eccleston.

Sue: Does that mean Matt Smith isn't the Eleventh Doctor any more?

Me: That's right. If the rumour turns out to be true, Matt Smith is the Twelfth Doctor. God knows where that puts Richard E. Grant's cartoon in the grand scheme of things. It's too complicated to think about.

Sue: Does that mean your toys, books and DVDs are labelled incorrectly, now?

Me: I don't want to talk about it.

Sue's Final Score:

Sue: That was fantastic. It was a bit timey-wimey, but I really like that about modern *Doctor Who* – it means you can get away with anything. I can't wait for November, can you?

Me: That's the month that this book comes out, so no. I'm dreading it.

Sue: I bet it will be great. The anniversary special, I mean.

10/10

Sue: What did you think?

Me: It was all right, I suppose.

Sue: It was better than all right. It was fantastic.

And that's when my trousers buzzed again . . .

Me: It's a text message from Nicol.

Sue: What does it say?

Me: She wants to know: 'Is the Doctor's real name John Hurt?'

Appendices

Appendix 1: Glossary

Whovian: A *Doctor Who* enthusiast

Whoniverse: The place where all the Whovians live

Whotoxetter: Centre of the Whoniverse

Whoniversal Studios: The place where *Doctor Who* is made

Whoniform: Clothes worn by Whovians (scarves, fezzes, celery, etc.)

Whoniversity: The place where Whovians go to learn about *Doctor Who*

Whomanities: Subject studied by Whovians at Whoniversity

WHONICEF: Whovians' charity of choice

Whomus: Whovians' favourite chickpea-based dip

Whola-hoops: Whovians' favourite starch-based snack

Whors d'oeuvres: Warm-up act for John Levene

Whooping cough: Crippling affliction suffered by Whovians just as they're about to ask their favourite Doctor a probing question at a convention

Whonicycle: When you can't afford a Whomobile

Whomour: Cognitive experience which provokes laughter, sense of which is sorely lacking in most Whovians

Whonanimous: When two or more Whovians agree (very rare)

Whotenanny: 1. Party thrown by Whovians every 23 November. 2. (*slang usage*) Whovian's childminder

WhoTube: A place where Whovians flirt with copyright law

Whooters: The place where Whovians go to get drunk

Whomiliation: Season 24

Whoniqueness: The dissimilarity of *Doctor Who* to any other television programme (as in 'the whonique appeal of *Doctor Who*').

Pet Shop Boys: Whovians' favourite pop group

Whotopia: A mythical place where brand-new episodes of *Doctor Who* are endlessly and continuously broadcast

Whomanoid: Someone resembling a Whovian (but you're not quite sure)

Whogenot: Sixteenth-century French Protestant Whovian

Who and cry: Historically, what Whovians raised when pursuing a thief

Whoer: A Whovian prostitute; *see also* Whonisex, Whorinary infection

Appendix 2: Sue's Scores

The First Doctor, William Hartnell

'An Unearthly Child': *The Doctor doesn't get a look in. He's horrible.* 7/10

'10,000 BC': *Stone Age nonsense.* 4/10

'The Daleks': *They should have called the show* Ian. 3/10

'The Edge of Destruction': *It wasn't boring.* 2/10

'Marco Polo': *It's a shame it's missing.* 6/10

'The Keys of Marinus': *The acting was dreadful.* 4/10

'The Aztecs': *Pretty good.* 7/10

'The Sensorites': *If that's the worst you can throw at me we'll be fine.* 5/10

'The Reign of Terror': *If I want to see a revolution, I can turn on the news.* 4/10

'Planet of Giants': *I like it when the story is self-contained.* 7/10

'The Dalek Invasion of Earth': *I'm really torn over this one.* 7/10

'The Rescue': *The plot was practically non-existent.* 3/10

'The Romans': *Definitely the best one so far.* 8/10

'The Web Planet': *I would have given it a 0 if it weren't for the Spanish episode.* 1/10

'The Crusade': *It was very well made and it didn't outstay its welcome.* 7/10

'The Space Museum': *It was too ahead of its time.* 6/10

'The Chase': *I'm getting a bit bored of the Daleks.* 5/10

'The Time Meddler': *It's the most enjoyable story so far.* 9/10

'Galaxy 4': *Not very good.* 2/10

'Mission to the Unknown': *It reminded me of* Babylon 5. 6/10

'The Myth Makers': *The fans should spend more time looking for this one.* 8/10

'The Daleks' Master Plan': *Some of it was rubbish and some of it was good.* 5/10

'The Massacre': *A confusing story with a really stupid twist.* 2/10

'The Ark': *The Monoids let it down; they were too silly for words.* 5/10

'The Celestial Toymaker': *Complete shite.* 0/10

'The Gunfighters': *We could watch it again!* 8/10

'The Savages': *For a recon, it was surprisingly engaging.* 7/10

'The War Machines': *It didn't really feel like* Doctor Who. 6/10

'The Smugglers': *I'll have forgotten it by next week.* 5/10

'The Tenth Planet': *Is that it?* 3/10

The Second Doctor, Patrick Troughton

'The Power of the Daleks': *Definitely the best Dalek story so far.* 8/10

'The Highlanders': *I've seen a lot worse.* 5/10

'The Underwater Menace': *That was bonkers.* 2/10

'The Moonbase': *The Doctor needs to buck his ideas up.* 6/10

'The Macra Terror': *I'm not convinced it would be better if it existed.* 7/10

'The Faceless Ones': *I finally feel like I'm watching* Doctor Who. 9/10

'The Evil of the Daleks': *A game of two halves.* 6/10

'The Tomb of the Cybermen': *A bit racist.* 4/10

'The Abominable Snowmen': *I feel sorry for the Yeti.* 7/10

'The Ice Warriors': *Enjoyable.* 7/10

'The Enemy of the World': *A bit silly.* 6/10

'The Web of Fear': *Pretty scary.* 8/10

'Fury from the Deep': *Good script, good performances, and scary monsters.* 8/10

'The Wheel in Space': *Flabby, drawn-out rubbish.* 2/10

'The Dominators': *Dreadful.* 1/10

'The Mind Robber': *It's the dog off* The Thing! 7/10

'The Invasion': *Probably the most enjoyable story so far.* 9/10

'The Krotons': *It was only four episodes and it moved.* 6/10

'The Seeds of Death': *They've got this 'base under siege' thing down pat, now.* 7/10

'The Space Pirates': *Well, that was shit.* 1/10

'The War Games': *Epic.* 9/10

The Third Doctor, Jon Pertwee

'Spearhead from Space': *Wonderful.* 10/10

'Doctor Who and the Silurians': *Excellent.* 9/10

'The Ambassadors of Death': *Too long!* 6/10

'Inferno': *The alternative reality was fascinating.* 8/10

'Terror of the Autons': *Short. Colour. Nice.* 8/10

'The Mind of Evil': *The Master is rubbish.* 5/10

'The Claws of Axos': *This would definitely work today.* 7/10

'Colony in Space': *It went a bit mad towards the end.* 6/10

'The Daemons': *It didn't know what it wanted to be.* 4/10

'Day of the Daleks': *What's not to like?* 9/10

'The Curse of Peladon': *Peladon is a shit-hole.* 4/10

'The Sea Devils': *One of the better Pertwees.* 7/10

'The Mutants': *I enjoyed that.* 7/10

'The Time Monster': *A good end to the season.* 8/10

'The Three Doctors': *I need to watch it again.* 5/10

'Carnival of Monsters': *Very good indeed.* 9/10

'Frontier in Space': *I can't believe it isn't over yet.* 6/10

'Planet of the Daleks': *Average.* 5/10

'The Green Death': *Very adult in places.* 9/10

'The Time Warrior': *Just stick your finger in his vent!* 7/10

'Invasion of the Dinosaurs': *Quite edgy.* 8/10

'Death to the Daleks': *The music killed it.* 5/10

'The Monster of Peladon': *Tedious.* 2/10

'Planet of the Spiders': *I won't be disappointed to see him go.* 7/10

The Fourth Doctor, Tom Baker

'Robot': *The story was pants.* 5/10

'The Ark in Space': *Tom Baker was brilliant.* 7/10

'The Sontaran Experiment': *Too short.* 5/10

'Genesis of the Daleks': *Excellent.* 9/10

'Revenge of the Cybermen': *A load of old rubbish.* 3/10

'Terror of the Zygons': *It had a lot going for it.* 7/10

'Planet of Evil': *The guy who played the commander was hopeless.* 5/10

'Pyramids of Mars': *I'd like less gobbledegook and more drama.* 7/10

'The Android Invasion': *It fell apart at the end.* 5/10

'The Brain of Morbius': *Some of the dialogue was priceless.* 8/10

'The Seeds of Doom': *It can't get any better than that.* 10/10

'The Masque of Mandragora': *Very accessible.* 9/10

'The Hand of Fear': *Good, very good, good, shit, really shit, then excellent.* 6/10

'The Deadly Assassin': *The first three episodes were perfect.* 8/10

'The Face of Evil': *Something was missing . . .* 4/10

'The Robots of Death': *It didn't make any sense.* 5/10

'The Talons of Weng-Chiang': *I'll knock some marks off for the casual racism.* 8/10

'Horror of Fang Rock': *I really enjoyed that.* 9/10

'The Invisible Enemy': *A terrible mess.* 4/10

'Image of the Fendahl': *I've forgotten it already.* 2/10

'The Sun Makers': *The script was very witty.* 6/10

'Underworld': *Am I allowed to give negative scores?* 1/10

'The Invasion of Time': *Oh dear.* 0/10

'The Ribos Operation': *It's not perfect, but it's pretty close.* 9/10

'The Pirate Planet': *An imaginative mess.* 6/10

'The Stones of Blood': *I really enjoyed that.* 8/10

'The Androids of Tara': *I don't think there was a bad performance.* 9/10

'The Power of Kroll': *If K9 had been in it I might have given it an eight.* 7/10

'The Armageddon Factor': *They had months to get that right . . .*
  4/10
'Destiny of the Daleks': *I hated that.* 2/10
'City of Death': *That was faultless.* 10/10
'The Creature from the Pit': *Killed by a giant cock and balls . . .*
  2/10
'Nightmare of Eden': *The premise was great and it kept me guessing.*
  7/10
'The Horns of Nimon': *I think they all need a good lie down.* 5/10
'The Leisure Hive': *Too much style and not enough substance.* 6/10
'Meglos': *Well, that was shit.* 2/10
'Full Circle': *I like Adric. So there.* 7/10
'State of Decay': *I loved the set design.* 7/10
'Warriors Gate': *I didn't understand it, but I don't care.* 8/10
'The Keeper of Traken': *Tedious.* 3/10
'Logopolis': *Disappointing.* 4/10

The Fifth Doctor, Peter Davison

'Castrovalva': *Quite profound in places.* 8/10
'Four to Doomsday': *Tedious bollocks.* 1/10
'Kinda': *I liked it but I didn't understand it.* 7/10
'The Visitation': *That was crap.* 3/10
'Black Orchid': *Rubbish.* 2/10
'Earthshock': *Excellent.* 9/10
'Time-Flight': *I'd like to give the captain one.* 1/10
'Arc of Infinity': *I can't forgive the chicken but I've seen worse.* 7/10
'Snakedance': *Nothing special.* 5/10
'Mawdryn Undead': *Very, very good.* 9/10
'Terminus': *A shambles.* 3/10
'Enlightenment': *Hire more women.* 9/10
'The King's Demons': *Rushed.* 5/10
'The Five Doctors': *That was fun.* 7/10
'Warriors of the Deep': *It pulled itself together at the end.* 4/10

'The Awakening': *The plot wasn't good enough.* 3/10

'Frontios': *They were trying to do something different.* 7/10

'Resurrection of the Daleks': *Needlessly complex but fun.* 8/10

'Planet of Fire': *One of the better Master stories.* 7/10

'The Caves of Androzani': *Fabulous.* 9/10

The Sixth Doctor, Colin Baker

'The Twin Dilemma': *What were they thinking?* 1/10

'Attack of the Cybermen': *All over the place.* 6/10

'Vengeance on Varos': *A nice change of pace.* 8/10

'Mark of the Rani': *A boring mess.* 3/10

'The Two Doctors': *Very funny.* 7/10

'Timelash': *Horrendous.* 2/10

'Revelation of the Daleks': *The Doctor did bugger all.* 4/10

'Trial of a Time Lord – The Mysterious Planet': *I've seen it all before.* 6/10

'Trial of a Time Lord – Mindwarp': *Shocking.* 8/10

'Trial of a Time Lord – Terror of the Vervoids': *Mel was great.* 7/10

'Trial of a Time Lord – The Ultimate Foe': *I don't get it.* 5/10

The Seventh Doctor, Sylvester McCoy

'Time and the Rani': *Irredeemable.* –1/10

'Paradise Towers': *The concept was better than the execution.* 6/10

'Delta and the Bannermen': *It got on my tits.* 2/10

'Dragonfire': *Cheap.* 3/10

'Remembrance of the Daleks': *I'd happily watch that again.* 9/10

'The Happiness Patrol': *That was very profound.* 7/10

'Silver Nemesis': *Worse than dreadful.* 0/10

'The Greatest Show in the Galaxy': *I can see what they were trying to do.* 8/10

'Battlefield': *Shame.* 4/10

'Ghost Light': *Very clever.* 8/10
'The Curse of Fenric': *Exciting.* 8/10
'Survival': *Almost perfect.* 9/10

The Eighth Doctor, Paul McGann

The TV Movie: *Brilliant.* 9/10

Appendix 3: Statistics

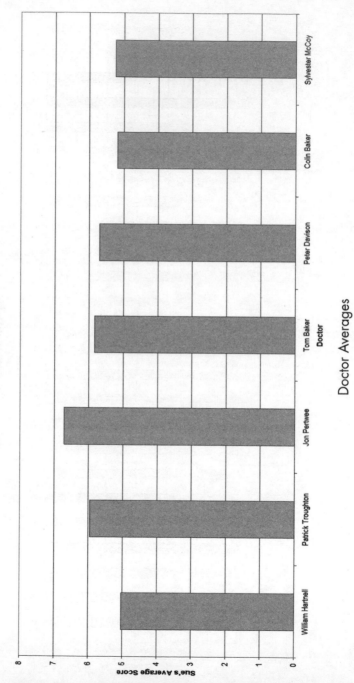

Average Score by Doctor

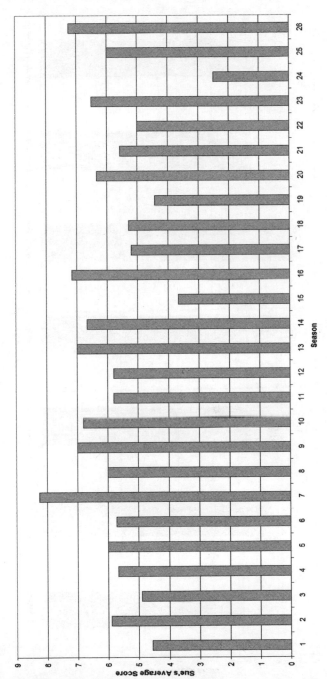

Average Score by Season

Season Averages

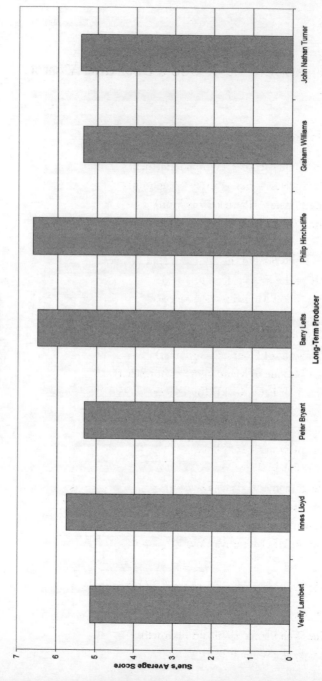

Average Score by Producer

Appendix 4: Sue's Best and Worst

The following stories all scored at least 9/10:

'The Time Meddler' (William Hartnell)
'The Faceless Ones' (Patrick Troughton)
'The Invasion' (Patrick Troughton)
'The War Games' (Patrick Troughton)
'Spearhead from Space' (Jon Pertwee)
'Doctor Who and the Silurians' (Jon Pertwee)
'Day of the Daleks' (Jon Pertwee)
'Carnival of Monsters' (Jon Pertwee)
'The Green Death' (Jon Pertwee)
'Genesis of the Daleks' (Tom Baker)
'The Seeds of Doom' (Tom Baker)
'The Masque of Mandragora' (Tom Baker)
'Horror of Fang Rock' (Tom Baker)
'The Ribos Operation' (Tom Baker)
'The Androids of Tara' (Tom Baker)
'City of Death' (Tom Baker)
'Earthshock' (Peter Davison)
'Enlightenment' (Peter Davison)
'The Caves of Androzani' (Peter Davison)
'Remembrance of the Daleks' (Sylvester McCoy)
'Survival' (Sylvester McCoy)

The following stories all scored 2/10 or less:

'The Edge of Destruction' (William Hartnell)
'The Web Planet' (William Hartnell)
'Galaxy 4' (William Hartnell)

'The Massacre' (William Hartnell)

'The Celestial Toymaker' (William Hartnell)

'The Underwater Menace' (Patrick Troughton)

'The Dominators' (Patrick Troughton)

'The Wheel in Space' (Patrick Troughton)

'The Space Pirates' (Patrick Troughton)

'The Monster of Peladon' (Jon Pertwee)

'Image of the Fendahl' (Tom Baker)

'Underworld' (Tom Baker)

'The Invasion of Time' (Tom Baker)

'Destiny of the Daleks' (Tom Baker)

'The Creature from the Pit' (Tom Baker)

'Meglos' (Tom Baker)

'Four to Doomsday' (Peter Davison)

'Black Orchid' (Peter Davison)

'Time-Flight' (Peter Davison)

'The Twin Dilemma' (Colin Baker)

'Timelash' (Colin Baker)

'Time and the Rani' (Sylvester McCoy)

'Delta and the Bannermen' (Sylvester McCoy)

'Silver Nemesis' (Sylvester McCoy)

Acknowledgements

Thanks to my editor, confidant and mentor, the incredible Mr Andy Miller. Not only did he get this book off the ground, he safely landed it again after I plunged it into a nosedive. His skill, generosity, wit and friendship are the only reasons it didn't explode in mid-air, killing everyone instantly. For that, and for everything else he did for me on this unforgettable journey, I am deeply grateful.

Thanks to Hannah Griffiths, Julian Loose, John Grindrod, Kate Burton, Anne Owen, James Rose, Trevor Horwood and everyone at Faber and Faber for believing in this book, and for being patient with me when the deadline went a bit timey-wimey.

Special thanks to 'The Three Johns': John Williams, Jonathan Grove and John Paul Green. Splendid chaps. All of them.

Thanks to Toby Hadoke and Rob Shearman for inspiring me to watch *Doctor Who* from the very beginning, and to Steven Schapansky for showing me when to stop.

Thanks to Glen Allen for his brilliant trailers; Ian Berriman for his tireless tweets; Simon Harries for his acts of kindness; Bob Fischer for his Frazer Hines B-sides; Gary Thompson for being such a good sport; Michael Ferrier for his bar graphs; and John Callaghan, Alison Eales, Alexander Kershaw, Peter Lack, Dave Sanders, Ben Swithen and Andrew Torrance for their songs.

I would also like to thank the following people for their support and encouragement: George Alabaster, Mark Ayres, Louis Barfe, Matthew Bartley, Daniel Blythe, Joe Carter, Lewis Christian, Joanne Clayton, Jenny Colgan, Frank Collins, Nathan Cooke, Paul Cornell, Paul Darrow, Kevin Jon Davies, Robert Dick, Nev Fountain, Siobhan Gallichan, Richard Garlick, Gary Gillatt, Ian Greaves, Derek Handley (both of them), Lynne Hardy, Andrew Harrison, Iain Hepburn, Matt Hills, Paul Jones, A. L. Kennedy, Graham Kibble-White, Paul Kirkley, Stephen La Rivière, Joe Lidster, Steven Moffat, Angela Morris, Jonathan Morris, my mum, Steve O'Brien, Andrew Orton, Dave Owen, Damon Querry, Radio Free Skaro, Rob Ritchie, Gareth Roberts, Steve Roberts, Royston Robertson, Dave Rolinson, Philip Sandifer, Jim Sangster, Matthew Sawyer, Paul Scoones, Andrew T. Smith, Matthew Sweet, Shirley Tindle, Mr Treacle, Phil Ware, Matt West, Auntie Celia Weston, Alex Wilcock, Roobarb's forum, and everyone who has contributed to the Wife in Space blog. Yes, even perfidious Steve (real name: Graham).

And last, but definitely not least, I dedicate this book to Sue and Nicol. You were both fantastic. Absolutely fantastic. And do you know what? So were the cats.